Dear Reader,

Welcome to the first m[...] from Silhouette Books! [...] we've invited bestselling [...] Merline Lovelace and Lin[...] [...]na to contribute three brand-new [...]es featuring the brave men and women of the United States armed forces.

In "The Dream Marine," Rachel Lee takes us back to her beloved Conard County for the emotional story of a hero's homecoming—and the spirited and beautiful marine who shows him his heart once more.

You'll be taking flight with a sexy daredevil pilot and a willful and womanly air force officer as they embark on a dangerous rescue mission—and discover soul-shattering passion—in Merline Lovelace's "Undercover Operations."

Lindsay McKenna brings you another action-packed story in the MORGAN'S MERCENARIES saga as two Coast Guard officers who were once husband and wife get a second chance at life and love when a hurricane has them battling the elements together, in "To Love and Protect."

We hope you enjoy these powerful romances!

Sincerely,

The Editors
Silhouette Books

RACHEL LEE

"A storyteller of incandescent brilliance, Rachel Lee makes each
and every love story a shattering emotional experience."
—*Romantic Times*

Rachel Lee wrote her first play in the third grade for a school
assembly, and by the age of twelve she was hooked on writing.
She's lived all over the United States and now resides in
Florida. Having held jobs as a security officer, real estate agent
and optician, she uses these, as well as her natural flair for
creativity, to write stories that are undeniably romantic. "After
all, life is the biggest romantic adventure of all—and if you're
open and aware, the most marvelous things are just waiting to
be discovered."

MERLINE LOVELACE

"Lovelace has made a name for herself."
—*Romantic Times*

Merline Lovelace spent twenty-three years in the air force,
pulling tours all over the world. When she hung up her
uniform, she decided to try her hand at writing. She's since
had over forty novels published, with more than five million
copies in print. She and her own handsome hero of thirty-plus
years live in Oklahoma. They enjoy golf, traveling and long,
lazy dinners with friends and family. Watch for Merline's
sizzling novel about Teddy Roosevelt's Rough Riders,
The Captain's Woman, available in January 2003 from
MIRA® Books.

LINDSAY McKENNA

"When it comes to action and romance,
nobody does it better than Ms. McKenna."
—*Romantic Times*

A homeopathic educator, Lindsay teaches at the Desert
Institute of Classical Homeopathy in Phoenix, Arizona. She
feels love is the single greatest healer in the world and hopes
that her books touch her readers' hearts. Coming from an
eastern Cherokee medicine family, Lindsay was taught
ceremony and healing ways from the time she was nine years
old. She creates flower and gem essences in accordance with
nature, and remains closely in touch with her Native American
roots and upbringing.

RACHEL LEE
MERLINE LOVELACE
LINDSAY McKENNA

THE
HEART'S
COMMAND

Barbara Lee Kozak

Silhouette Books

Published by Silhouette Books
America's Publisher of Contemporary Romance

SILHOUETTE BOOKS

ISBN 0-373-48466-6

THE HEART'S COMMAND

Copyright © 2002 by Harlequin Books S.A.

The publisher acknowledges the copyright holders
of the individual works as follows:

THE DREAM MARINE
Copyright © 2002 by Susan Civil-Brown

UNDERCOVER OPERATIONS
Copyright © 2002 by Merline Lovelace

TO LOVE AND PROTECT
Copyright © 2002 by Lindsay McKenna

Visit Silhouette at www.eHarlequin.com

Printed in U.S.A.

CONTENTS

THE DREAM MARINE
Rachel Lee

* * *

To the marines in my life
who have taught me what it means.

Dear Reader,

"The Dream Marine" turned out to be a long journey of sorts. When I initially agreed to write it, I thought, "Wonderful, a chance to write another Conard County story." And when I wrote the proposal, I had a somewhat different story in mind than the one you'll find here.

Because that was before 9/11.

On September 11, 2001, our world changed forever. Certainly mine did. And when I started to write this story, directly after that horrible day, I found that it was the last place I wanted to go.

My mind shied away from thoughts of war, from thoughts of the men and women who were going forth to battle. I was having enough difficulty coming to grips with the terrible events in New York and Washington, D.C. I couldn't bear to think of all the terrible things that might be about to occur in Afghanistan.

This became a story drawn from the pain and fear in my own heart, and built on my belief in the supreme importance of love.

In the end, only love matters. As Sister Joan Chittister has so beautifully said, "Love is not for our own sakes. Love frees us to see others as God sees them."

Sincerely yours,

Rachel Lee

Chapter 1

Joe Yates came home to Conard County, Wyoming, a changed man. Sitting in Mahoney's Bar with his green marine tunic and the top buttons of his shirt undone, and his tie hanging loose, he sipped a whiskey and told himself he wasn't going to do anything as clichéd as turn into a drunk over this.

But he still felt a huge hole at the very center of himself, and he couldn't figure out how to fill it. Or if he even wanted to. At the moment he didn't even want to go out to the ranch and see his sister and her family. He didn't want to see anyone who might touch that gaping hole and make it hurt.

He sipped more whiskey, and told himself not to be an ass. The words didn't help. Kara was gone and it was all his fault, and to hell with the USMC anyway.

Joe was a young man, only in his middle twenties, but he looked a lot older. Wind and weather had aged him, but so had events of the last months, especially the last week. The lines were cut deeply in his lean face now, a face that was ever so slightly exotic, hinting of his Shoshone ancestry.

After a troubled youth, he'd left Conard County nine years ago, an eighteen-year-old boy proud that he'd been accepted by the Marine Corps, and looking forward to a life of adventure. He'd come home now sickened by it all.

Any innocence he had once possessed was gone, left in the dusty, rugged mountains north of a country he wasn't allowed to name. Home didn't even feel familiar anymore. It felt as if he'd stepped out of reality into the pages of a fantasy. Nothing real could be as peaceful as Mahoney's Bar on a Wednesday night.

It offended him.

But Kara's death had been the last straw. Especially since she was there only by accident. She was a United Nations health worker from Amsterdam who'd been sentenced to die by the repressive regime for the crime of wearing a cross around her neck. She'd escaped and had been taken in by insurgents.

Joe and his unit had found her hiding in a cave with some friendlies. They'd planned to take her out after they finished their operation, but instead they had carried out her body. And Joe, recuperating from a wound of his own, had accompanied her remains home to Amsterdam.

It was enough. It was more than enough. He was done, finished, fed up, worn-out, and dead inside. It was one thing when he and his buddies risked their necks; hell, they'd volunteered for the job. It was another when innocent civilians died. He'd seen too much of that, and Kara, lovely sweet Kara who had glowed with life even in a cave where she had almost nothing to eat, was the final straw.

He looked down at the whiskey glass between his hands and almost sneered. It was a picture out of a bad movie, he thought: marine in rumpled uniform drowning his sorrows in a dark bar. The amber liquid at the bottom of the glass didn't hold any answers, and as an anesthetic it didn't come close to silencing the empty gnawing inside him. All it did was sting on the way down and remind him that he was still alive.

He didn't think he wanted to be dead. He just didn't know how to get through this. How to handle this. That was something they hadn't covered in training. Paris Island didn't prepare anybody for this.

He looked at his hands, splaying his fingers, wondering why they looked like ordinary human hands. These were killer's hands. They looked strange, though, because for the first time in months they were free of grime. He wished the memory of that place would wash away as easily.

He wished he didn't have to go back.

"You're out of uniform, Marine."

The female voice was smoky, something out of a man's most wistful dreams. It didn't seem to go with the words it spoke, though. Unfortunately, Joe wasn't drunk enough to ignore them. A spike of anger jabbed him. "Get lost."

"Look at me, Marine."

So he looked. It was probably a measure of the amount of alcohol he'd consumed that he noticed first that she was beautiful. Beautiful in a quiet way, with short dark hair, a neat figure and the tiniest waist. Legs... He wished he could see them better.

But then he registered her uniform and her rank. And the name on the badge over her breast. Gunnery Sergeant Mathison. Well, hell, wasn't it just his luck to run into another marine a thousand miles from the nearest water? And a nipped-and-tucked one, too. She couldn't have been any neater if she'd stepped off a recruiting poster.

"Go away," he said, even though she outranked him. Hell, she wasn't in his chain of command, anyway.

"No. I won't have you embarrassing the Corps in public like this."

He pushed back his stool and stood, facing off with her. "You wanna fight, Gunny? 'Cause I'm a damn good fighter. Had plenty of practice the last few months."

Her eyes narrowed, and he found himself wishing, oddly enough, that he could tell what color they were.

But the bar was too dimly lit. At least they weren't blue like Kara's.

"Hey," said Mahoney, coming up behind him. "Joey, cool it. I don't want a couple of jarheads tearing up my place. Take it outside if you wanna fight."

The gunny spoke. "I don't fight with drunks, Mr. Mahoney. It's too easy."

Oh, a spitfire. Joe had no doubt he could show her a thing or two. Or three, but he wasn't going to do it here. And come to think of it, he wasn't going to fight, either. Certainly not with a woman. Anyway, he was sick of fighting. Turning, he tossed some bills on the bar to cover his tab. "I'm outta here."

He should have guessed she would follow him. He should have known she wasn't going to have the sense to let it lie. Hell, no, she was a marine, and a marine never backed down. Except that he had, in a way, so why the hell didn't she get the message?

Out on the street, he saw the night was cool and a bit misty, unusual for an ordinarily dry climate. Fog seemed to swirl around the streetlights, creating a fuzziness that added to Joe's sense of unreality. He turned, prepared to ignore the woman who was on his heels, and walk back to the Lazy Rest Motel, where he seemed to recall having booked a room by phone before leaving the airport and catching the bus down here.

But Her Mightiness, guardian of the Corps' proper public appearance, wasn't prepared to let him go.

"You know," she said, catching up with him, "if you want to slop around, you could wear civvies."

"True," he agreed, wishing he could just bat her away like an irritating fly.

"In the meantime," she said sharply, "straighten yourself up, Marine."

That was one time too many. The volcano that had apparently been building in the vicinity of the empty hole inside him suddenly erupted.

"Look," he said, rounding on her, "I don't give a damn who you are or what your beef is. If you want to worry about creases and starch, pay attention to your own. But get the hell off my case!"

Even in the dim, fog-dampened light from the streetlamps, he could see the fire in her eyes. Well, of course, she was a marine.

"The way you wear your uniform represents *me*," she said.

Amazingly, she didn't say it hotly, as he anticipated, but rather calmly, almost as if commenting on the weather. The change in tack surprised him, and he found himself looking even more closely at her. "Who are you?" he asked.

"Gunnery Sergeant Bethany Mathison," she answered. "I'm the recruiter here."

The light went on. A drunken marine, in rumpled uniform, wasn't exactly an invitation to join the Corps. Although, at the moment, he'd have told anyone who was even considering the idea of enlisting to run, not walk, in the other direction as fast as their legs could carry them.

But he figured if he said so, she'd either try to knock his block off, or she'd write him up. He didn't feel like fighting with anyone anymore, and as for getting written up—well, it didn't scare him, but who needed the hassle?

And finally he realized that he wasn't making sense, even to himself. His thoughts were all over the place, as were such feelings as he was capable of having. It was as if he were casting around for something he could fixate on so he could ignore the emptiness inside. As if his thoughts were splintered and he couldn't gather them together.

Facing his own irrationality was uncomfortable. With a muffled oath, he started buttoning his shirt, straightening his tie and buttoning his coat. It wasn't as if anyone was likely to see him at this hour, in the dark, but what the hell. Why make this woman miserable just because he was?

"Thank you," she said.

"You're welcome, Gunny." He couldn't quite keep the sarcasm out of his voice. Then, with a smart click of his polished heels, he turned away, heading toward the motel.

"Where are you going, Sergeant?" she called after him.

"To the motel."

"Wait. I'll drive you."

The urge to tell her which plank to walk off grew

in him again, but he battled it down. What was with this woman? Why couldn't she just leave him alone? All he wanted was to be left alone.

"Thanks," he managed to say shortly, "but I can walk."

"I'm sure you can," she answered. "But you don't have to."

"What's with you?" he demanded, turning to her again. "Just get out of my face."

She didn't even flinch, just looked him straight in the eye. A good marine, he found himself thinking irrelevantly. She wasn't at all bothered by the fact that he was eight inches taller and eighty pounds heavier.

Then she utterly astonished him. "I'm being a good buddy," she said. "A good buddy gives a fellow marine a ride home."

"The walk will clear my head," he grumped, although a clear head was the last thing he wanted.

"Fine. I'll walk with you."

He didn't have an idea in hell what this woman was doing wandering the streets of Conard City at eleven at night in full uniform when she should have been home watching TV or something. Or why she seemed to have walked in on him at Mahoney's as if she were on a mission.

Nor did he care. But even in his whiskey-fogged state, he knew that if she walked with him to the motel, she was going to have to walk back alone, past the railroad tracks and stockyard, through the worst part of town.

The fact that she was probably as capable of defending herself as any other marine didn't make any difference. He couldn't allow that.

"Where the hell is your car?" he growled.

She cocked her head to the right. "Just over there."

He followed her, telling himself that this was the easiest and quickest way to get rid of her. She'd dump him at the motel, and that would be that. And man, didn't those hips of hers have a nice bit of sway to them?

He yanked his eyes away from her nether regions and forced himself to focus on the back of her head. In his present state, he wasn't sure he could trust himself.

In fact, he knew damn well he couldn't. He'd been living a barbarian existence for too long to slip easily back into the constraints of civilization.

She drove a small, economical car, and he had to squeeze his large frame into the passenger seat. In the confined space, he could suddenly smell the alcohol on his breath. He reeked. And he wasn't proud of it.

She started the car and pulled away from the curb. "You're staying at the Lazy Rest?"

As if there was another motel in this two-bit, godforsaken ink spot on the map. "Yeah." He felt her glance at him, but he refused to look back. He didn't want to think about anything except the way the beams of the headlights looked on the road. Or the way the stockyards looked ghostly and dark, a frozen tableau.

Anything but faces. He didn't want to see faces anymore. Seeing faces meant you got to know people. And then you got to see their faces when they died.

It was a relief when she pulled up in front of the motel at last. Saying nothing except thanks, he climbed out and headed for his room.

And never once did he look at her face again.

Gunnery Sergeant Bethany Mathison drove away from the Lazy Rest Motel torn between conflicting feelings. On the one hand, she'd felt bound to step in because the Yates guy had been creating a bad impression for the Corps, and given that there weren't a whole lot of examples to be had in this small town, she felt she had an obligation to uphold the best image of the marines.

On the other hand, what she had seen in the guy's eyes had spoken volumes to her. It had touched a carefully buried place deep within herself. It had reminded her of things better forgotten.

And she didn't like that.

She probably shouldn't have intervened at all. It had been unfortunate that she'd missed dinner getting ready for her evening presentation at the high school, and even more unfortunate that it had run on so late because students had wanted to talk to her afterward. She had decided to stop by Mahoney's and get a sandwich to take home with her after the last, lingering student—a young woman who saw becoming a marine as a gateway to adventures she would never find in this ranching community—had departed.

It had been unfortunate that she had run into Sergeant Yates. Another time she might just have ignored him. But after spending five hours talking proudly about the Corps, and about marine life, all the while walking a tightrope so as not to blind the students to reality by giving them stars in their eyes, she was exhausted and somewhat irritable.

And then she had walked into Mahoney's and seen the worst stereotype of a marine.

Damn. She shook her head at her own behavior and turned the corner toward the snug little house that she was renting. The Corps was serious about wanting "a few good men" and women. They wanted the pick of the litter, the few who really had what it took to be a marine. Consequently she had to always be on guard against signing up young people who didn't have what it took, or who had mistaken ideas about what was involved. At the same time, she was being measured by her recruitment numbers. She wouldn't last long if she recruited too many people who couldn't make it through boot camp, but she wouldn't last long, either, if she failed to sign enough recruits.

Anyway, she'd walked into Mahoney's and seen Yates looking like every mother's worst nightmare, and she'd snapped at him.

Dumb. Especially after looking into his eyes. She'd seen that thousand-yard stare too many times in guys fresh out of combat. She should have just left him alone.

She certainly wished she had when he'd buttoned

his tunic and she'd seen the purple heart with cluster, not to mention the other medals. He'd been wounded twice. *Twice!* And she'd called him on his uniform.

Right now she felt about two inches tall.

And she hoped she never set eyes on him again.

Chapter 2

Morning came too soon. It always did. Joe sat up on the edge of his bed, rubbing his eyes, trying to ignore the hammer and chisel that were working on his brain.

Night was his friend. Night was the best time to move safely through enemy territory. He'd gotten so used to living the life of a cave bat that morning seemed like an offense.

Especially when it revealed that he really was in a fantasy world of clean sheets, running water, and hot food right across the street.

There was even a coffeepot on the bathroom counter, with a packet of coffee beside it and two mugs. He could just walk in there and make a fresh pot of drip-brewed. No grounds in it, sitting at the

bottom of a tin pot. He could drink it in comfort, leaning back against pillows instead of sitting on a hard
boulder, or cross-legged on the ground.

It still didn't feel real.

He took a shower first. If that hot water wasn't real,
he didn't want to know it. Head bowed, he stood under
the pounding spray and soaked up the heat, feeling
muscles let go as they hadn't been able to let go in
many months now. Feeling tension seep out of him
and run down the drain with the water. The scar on
his arm was healing nicely, little more than a bullet
nick. The other scars, more serious, were old enough
now that he didn't think about them anymore.

Under the stinging spray, he worked his arm so the
scar tissue wouldn't tighten up, and tried not to think
about anything at all. A blank mind was a man's best
friend.

But his mind refused to stay blank for long.

He needed to go out to the ranch and visit his sister
and her family, but he didn't want to. In fact, he now
wondered why he'd even come back to Conard
County. Habit? Because going home was what you
were supposed to do when you took leave?

Because home was the last place he wanted to go.
It was beginning to occur to him that yanking a man
out of combat and returning him to the civilian world
in a matter of hours was a form of mental cruelty. The
transition wasn't that easy to make. The wind-down
was almost impossible. Since he'd left the Middle East
three days ago, he hadn't really connected with any-

thing around him. He'd been moving through a fog that had been punctuated only by the grief-stricken faces of Kara's family.

He braced his arms against the tile wall behind the showerhead and bent forward, letting the hot stream hammer on his neck and shoulders. The pleasure seemed almost sinful by comparison with what he'd left behind. Hell, even on shipboard, where the life of a marine was at its almost-best, you couldn't stand freely under a shower like this.

The temptation to stay just like that kept him still for a long time. Maybe the hammering of the spray could ease his transition into this strange new world. Maybe he could wash away the soul-deep grime and stain of the past months.

Eventually, though, he made himself get out and dry off. Civvies today. New jeans and a Western shirt he'd bought before boarding the bus in Casper. Jogging shoes because he didn't own a pair of cowboy boots anymore. A ball cap because his cowboy hats were at his sister's house, and he wasn't ready to face that scene yet.

Breakfast at the truck stop across the highway. Just him and a handful of long-haul truckers who didn't know him from Adam. The anonymity was comforting somehow. The only real people in his world anymore were the buddies he'd left behind, marines and some of the insurgents they were working with.

Joe sat at the counter, enjoying real fried eggs, pork sausage and hash browns with another cup of steaming, grounds-free coffee. Hot food was a blessing, and food without grit in it was nothing short of a miracle. As it began to fill his stomach, he started to feel a bit better. Enough so that he decided he was going to have to apologize to Gunnery Sergeant Mathison for his conduct last night.

He noticed the waitress behind the counter was smiling at him. After a couple of seconds, he realized she was a girl he'd gone to high school with. What was her name...Millie? Something like that. Some remnant of manners left from his life before war caused him to faintly smile back and nod at her.

And naturally, that brought her right over to him.

"Hi, Joey," she said almost shyly, using his nickname from high school. "I'm Millie Pestre, remember?"

He nodded, his face feeling brittle. "I remember."

"It's been a long time since you've been around. Where've you been?"

Well, he couldn't tell her the truth. *I've been to war, and have been fighting and killing people in the name of something I've almost forgotten....* "I'm in the military," he said after a noticeable pause. "The marines."

"Oh!" Her eyes widened and said she was impressed. If only she knew. "Are you home for long?"

He shrugged. "I don't know." That much was true. For all he knew, he'd be on the road again tomorrow and spend his entire leave just bouncing from town to town.

Or maybe he'd get his head out of his butt and stop feeling sorry for himself. Because, God knew, in the last few days he'd started to get tired of himself.

"Well..." Millie said, letting the word dangle.

He didn't take the implied invitation. Getting close to anybody, even casually, was begging trouble. He was better off alone.

Millie's smile grew a little forced. "If you need anything, just holler," she said finally, and drifted away.

He returned to his food, thinking that he'd become a nasty son of a bitch somewhere along the way. He could at least have found something polite to say.

Sopping up egg yolk with a piece of rye toast, feeling guilty about every single delicious mouthful he was savoring, he thought that maybe running off to join the marines at the age of barely eighteen wasn't the smartest way to grow up. He could maneuver well within his world, maintaining good relations soldier-to-soldier, but it was becoming apparent he no longer knew how to behave in the world at large.

In fact, his sister, Sara, would have given him a stern talking-to for being so unfriendly to Millie. "Joey," she would have said, "this is a small town and we depend on each other. You be polite, hear?"

Sort of like the way it was in his unit. Bonds formed by interdependency were stronger than steel. This town was that way, he seemed to recall. Even a good feud didn't keep neighbors from coming together in a pinch. But this was different, he told himself. He hadn't been rude to Millie, exactly. He just hadn't wanted to express anything she might misinterpret.

So he was becoming a reclusive boor. The town would just have to deal with it. And wouldn't Sara laugh her head off to know her troublesome younger brother, who'd hated English classes as if they were torture, had picked up the word *boor?*

Thinking about Sara laughing caused him a twinge, and he wasn't ready to feel those tugs and twinges. He didn't want to think about the niece and nephew he hadn't seen in a couple of years now. Kids who surely must be growing up to a more interesting age than the last time he'd seen them. Or about his grandfather, who was getting old and might not be around next time he came home.

Grandfather would want to give him a sweat. Get him to sit in a small lodge with hot stones and steam. Grandfather believed a good sweat would drive out all the evils that plagued a man. Joe had never been quite sure he believed all that Indian stuff, but his brother-in-law, Gideon, had sure taken to it.

So if he went up there, he'd have to do a sweat, and that would mean that he'd spend hours steaming with nothing to think about except the things he didn't want to think about. No thanks.

Throwing ten bucks on the counter, which included an extra-large tip, he left the diner without glancing Millie's way.

He walked back into town, past the stockyards and the auto repair shop, and didn't look either right or left because he didn't want to see anyone he recognized. Not yet, anyway. He supposed if he didn't get out of here by sundown, people were going to start noticing him and wanting to talk to him. He'd changed a lot in nine years, but he hadn't changed *that* much.

He had one goal: the recruiting office on the corner of Main and Elm. The same place where he'd signed his life away more than nine years ago, headed for adventures he couldn't really begin to imagine. Back then the recruiter had been Bill Ebsen, a barrel of a guy with a no-nonsense attitude, a gruff voice and the instincts of a father. Joe wondered why Bill had been replaced with a woman.

Not that Joe had any particular problem with women in the Corps. Nothing like that. It just seemed like an odd choice for a recruiter in this area, where there was only *one* recruiter, not a team.

Of course, given what Gunnery Sergeant Mathison looked like, chances were the marines were getting a lot of interest from those "few good men" the Corps claimed to want.

The thought almost made Joe laugh, the first real humor he'd felt in a while. It fit well with the brisk autumn day, and he decided he could do with more of it. Laughter, after all, even at the darkest of humor, was the best way to cope with most things, including the dissociation he was feeling right now. As long as you could laugh, you were still breathing. And surviving.

That was as much reassurance as he seemed able to give himself now.

* * *

Joe didn't get anywhere near the recruiting station until almost lunchtime. Somehow he spent some long hours sitting on a park bench in the courthouse square, only vaguely aware of the comings and goings around him. The bucolic peace of the day still seemed like a dream to him, something almost remote from his own reality. And thus the minutes had slipped away, lost in some never-never land between past and present.

He was startled when he glanced at his battered watch and realized it was past noon. Maybe, he thought with a sense of self-betrayal, he'd lost this time on purpose, because he didn't want to face the Mathison woman. And he didn't. He hated having to apologize for his misdeeds, especially to someone who didn't seem to have an ounce of understanding in her body. On the other hand, his sister and grandfather had raised him better than that. He owed the woman an apology, and he was damn well going to give it to her.

Besides, he didn't like his mind playing tricks on him. The mere notion made him feel uneasy. His mind, after all, was the only thing in the world he had to rely on.

Giving himself a mental shake, he rose from the bench and headed toward the recruiting station. Maybe she was still there. If she wasn't, he'd just have to come back later.

But she was there, looking as breathtakingly beautiful as his drunken mind last night had thought. Maybe more beautiful. This afternoon she wasn't wearing a hat, and the highlights in her dark hair were almost fiery. Her uniform was tightly tailored to a perfect figure, a figure that stood ramrod straight as he entered the small storefront.

As the door opened, she started to smile, but the smile vanished moments later as she recognized him. Those dark eyes of hers were a warm, sherry brown, warm even as her face grew rigid.

That warmth appealed to him somehow, like a fire on a cold night. He sensed that it was a deep-rooted part of her, not just the accident of a pair of eyes. But her posture was stiff, and her attitude as prickly as a porcupine on alert. He supposed he deserved that.

It also made him feel as awkward as a schoolboy. She waited, saying nothing, refusing even to greet him as the door swung shut behind him, closing out the rest of the world.

"Look," he said finally, resisting an urge to scuff his foot, "I came to say I'm sorry."

"Sorry?" A stiff, unyielding word, offering him no quarter.

The image of Joan of Arc leading troops into battle floated into his mind's eye. "Yeah," he said. "I'm sorry. I was out of line last night."

"Yes, you were."

Hmm. Maybe he was mistaken about those eyes. Maybe that warmth *was* a sheer trick of light. Well, he'd done what he'd come to do, and he didn't have to beg for her forgiveness.

Turning, he started to open the door.

"Marine."

He paused, hand on the knob, wondering if he should just keep going. Instead he turned slowly to face her again.

"Let me buy you lunch," she said. "I was just on my way to the diner."

He wanted to refuse; being close to another human being right now was about as comfortable as having his skin sanded off. But he knew it was her way of accepting his apology, and he knew better than to refuse an olive branch.

"Sure," he said, the word feeling like lead in his mouth.

She bent, pulling her regulation shoulder bag out of a desk drawer. He held the door open for her, letting her pass through into the sunlight, which seemed glaringly bright this afternoon. As she put her key in the lock and turned it, he watched, focusing on the small and inconsequential because it was more comfortable than looking at the larger picture. In silence they went around the corner to the City Diner, commonly known as Maude's.

The place was both familiar and unfamiliar to Joe. It hadn't changed one whit that he could see, but it felt different now. The same regulars, looking older, filled most of the tables, but nobody he had to do more than nod to. There was nobody from school, nobody who'd once been a close friend. The relief was almost overwhelming. Joe wasn't ready to face the questions that would come from those who knew him well, questions like, "Where you been? What was it like?"

Well, except for Maude. Either she'd ask the questions, or she'd act as if he hadn't been gone a day, and was still a skinny eighteen-year-old who put away her burgers and fries as if he had two hollow legs.

There was a booth near the back, and hardly realizing he was doing it, Joe guided Gunny Mathison back there. He didn't want to sit near the windows, where someone might recognize him. He didn't want to be exposed.

She took the urging without comment and, much to his relief, let him sit on the bench that was backed up against the wall, giving him a full view of the diner.

"When I was a little kid," he said, needing to fill the silence, needing to keep her from asking the questions he didn't want to answer, "there used to be a grill over there against that wall. Maude and her husband used to stand there from five in the morning until ten at night, cooking an endless stream of food." He shook his head. "It was some show. I think half the people ate here just to watch the two of them."

"What happened to it?"

Joe shrugged one shoulder. "About the time I was nine or ten, they decided they needed to expand. So they took the space next door and built a kitchen." He managed a crooked smile. "God knows what goes on back there. I suspect she has an army of gnomes cooking for her, but the food is just as good as it always was."

Mathison nodded and reached for one of the plastic-covered menus that were tucked behind the napkin dispenser and ketchup bottle. The diner hadn't yet graduated to steak sauce, and it was rumored the mayor carried a bottle of his own favorite when he came here. If Maude had ever taken note of that heresy, no one knew. Which was unusual for Maude.

Mathison spoke pleasantly enough. "She certainly hasn't heard about the rules for healthy eating."

"No. Rib-sticking is her style."

Those sherry-brown eyes lifted from the menu, and for the first time he got a true inkling of her smile. It didn't reach her mouth, but the humor was there around her eyes. "I'll run it off tonight."

"Yeah." He supposed he needed to start doing that again, too, now that he wasn't running up and down mountains like a goat.

One thing sure hadn't changed: it was Maude herself who came to the table to take their order.

"Gunny," Maude said, with a nod to her. The years hadn't been kind to Maude. Her face looked like heavily lined old parchment, and she'd lost some weight, leaving her skin sagging in folds around her mouth and on her arms. But her eyes were as sharp as ever as they settled on Joe. As sharp and malicious as always.

"Joey Yates," she said, her tone hardly welcoming. "Are you still eating enough to feed a crowd?"

"No, ma'am," he said automatically, the way his sister had always made him address older women.

"Been up to see your sister yet?"

A black feeling filled him, not far removed from rage. Who was this old woman to ask him such a thing? It wasn't as if she were a friend of the family.

"Better get up there," Maude said flatly. "Poor girl has been wasting away from worry over you. What'll you have?"

Joe ignored the unwanted commentary and ordered a steak he didn't think he'd be able to eat. Breakfast, even though it had been hours ago, was still sitting heavily in his stomach. But it would be a shame to pass up one of Maude's steaks. Gunny Mathison ordered one of Maude's steak sandwiches.

When Maude stomped away into her lair, Mathison looked at him. "My first name's Bethany," she said. "Beth."

"I'm Joseph Yates. Just Joe."

She extended her hand across the table and they shook. Cessation of hostilities. Good. The sooner he could forget about this woman and her disturbing eyes, the better.

"Well, Just Joe," she said with a small smile, "we got off to a bad start. I should know better than to come between a marine and his brew. And sometimes I'm a little too, um, stiff."

He liked that she was willing to acknowledge her own faults. Not many people were big enough to do that. Even in the Corps, where utter honesty was expected of everyone.

"It's okay," he said. In all his years in the Marines, he'd never been hassled for having a few drinks when he was off duty. As long as he didn't create a disturbance. But... "I can see your point of view. Let's just forget it."

"Fair enough. It's just that this is such a small town...." She shrugged.

"I know." He looked past her, out the window, unconsciously taking an assessment of dangers, routes of escape and all the rest of it, as if he were in a den of enemy soldiers. The tension between his shoulder blades had been with him for so long now he wasn't even aware of it anymore. Truly relaxing, without the aid of booze, was beyond him, and he didn't even really know it.

Beth spoke. "You have a thousand-yard stare."

The sound of her voice jolted him back into the here and now. Once again he was sitting in a familiar diner in Conard City. "Uh, yeah. I guess." He knew what she meant. He'd first noticed it years ago just after boot camp, when he'd met his first combat veterans. Some of them never learned to relax that stare.

Her next question was simple, and not the one he expected. "Are you going back?"

"I suppose so." Which was the truth. He didn't know for sure, but his unit was still over there. He braced himself for the questions about how long he'd been overseas, and what he had done and seen, but those questions never came. She merely nodded her head.

"I was over there for a while," she offered. "I never got off the ship, though."

Something in her face told him that experience had been bad enough. He knew how it was. Even a ship couldn't keep you safe sometimes.

"When?" he asked finally. Crossing the barrier.

"I was aboard the *Hartridge* when that suicide bomber struck."

He paused, something inside him growing very quiet. "That was bad."

"Not one of the best weeks of my life. I'm sure you heard all about it. We lost twenty-six sailors, and had sixty-four wounded." Her face grew shadowed.

He didn't reply. When words didn't fit, he didn't speak them, and there were no words for what she had probably seen. What could he say, anyway? That he was sorry? No point in it. It was part of being a marine.

"Yeah," he said after a bit. "That was bad."

"I'm sure you've seen worse." She didn't act as if she expected an answer, and he didn't offer one.

"So," she said after Maude delivered their meals and drinks, "you have family around here?"

"Yeah." The answer sounded short, even to him. "My sister's family and my grandfather."

"Are you going to see them?"

"I don't know."

She didn't seem to find that response strange. Nor did she press for any more.

"How long have you been the recruiter here?"

"Nine months." Again the hint of that smile, pushing the shadows away. "A long nine months."

"I can imagine. I used to dream about getting out of here. There's not a whole lot to do."

"I suppose it's great for a family, but..." She shrugged and gave a little laugh. "I'm getting awfully tired of television and movies."

"Oh, you need to take up bowling."

"I got tired of that, too."

He laughed. The sound surprised him. "I hear you. Not exactly the adventure you signed on for."

"It's not that bad, really. It's almost like being on an extended vacation. I don't have a whole lot to do. And most of the time I don't have anyone breathing down my neck. So there *are* advantages. In the winter I manage to get in some skiing, and in the summer I hike in the mountains. It's a good thing I'm not a party girl."

"Have you made any friends?" He couldn't say why that suddenly seemed important. There was no ring on her finger, which said a lot, but...he wasn't interested in that, was he?

"Oh, sure. Sheriff Tate practically took me under his wing. I've met some really nice people at church and at the high school. It's not that I don't have a life."

Of course not. And in her position she'd get to know

a lot of people. She'd have to. But he could still hear the hint of wistfulness underlying her pleasant tone.

It was sad in a way, he thought. The Corps was a tight-knit group, and your unit became your best friends. To take a marine and put her out here in the middle of nowhere like this was to cut her off from the support structure she'd been relying on for years. He felt a twinge of sympathy. In her own way, she must be feeling as much like a fish out of water as he was.

He spoke. "All my buddies are back...there." He caught himself before he spoke the place-name he wasn't allowed to speak.

She looked down at her plate, as if she'd noticed the food for the first time. "I know," she said.

And somehow he figured she did. For a while, they ate in silence, neither of them seeming especially hungry. Maude, he thought, was going to be all over them like white on rice if they didn't finish their meals.

Suddenly Beth looked up. "Wanna go to a movie tonight?"

Chapter 3

Joe wasn't sure why he had agreed. He didn't especially want to see a movie, any movie, especially not one that was billed as "heartwarming and uplifting." Even less did he want to go to a movie with someone else, especially a female someone else.

But he had said yes, probably because she was a marine, too, and marines kinda hung out together, and she had no one else in this town and...

And all the excuses didn't add up to a reason. He'd said yes, and he was damned if he knew why, but since he'd agreed, he would go. At least she'd said she'd meet him at the theater. That felt casual enough. Like friends. The kind of thing he would do with one of the guys.

Which was undoubtedly how she meant it. Marine to marine. Yeah.

He still needed his head examined.

He spent the afternoon wandering around town, checking out old haunts in an effort to bring himself into the present. It was amazing how remote the days of his youth seemed now. Places he'd remembered so fondly now looked strange, different. So far away in time that they might have been someone else's memories. The feeling unsettled him, as he realized that it was true, you couldn't go home again.

Worse, you not only couldn't go home again, but if you tried, you were going to demolish all those happy memories.

Maybe that was part of the reason he was so afraid to go see his sister. Maybe he was afraid that wouldn't feel like home anymore, either. He didn't know if he could handle that. Home, after all, was a place you cherished when you were far away and in danger. It was a place you couldn't afford to lose.

Of course, in the last nine years he'd come home a few times, and nothing had gone amiss before. But this time was different. This time he had brought home a whole new pack of memories. Ugly memories.

And maybe he feared they'd somehow pollute the past, too.

These thoughts, and even darker ones, somehow brought him to the parking lot of the movie theater on the edge of town. He was a little early, but that was all right.

Standing there, he remembered the times he'd come here with his high school friends. All the good times they'd had, all the popcorn they'd packed away. All the good and not-so-good movies they'd seen.

A flicker of curiosity stirred in him as he wondered about his old friends for the first time in a long time. Were they married? What jobs did they have? Children?

He'd lost touch with most of them a long time ago. As far as he knew, none of the ones who had been his really good buddies still lived around here.

Another thing you could never get back: old friendships too long neglected.

Maybe realizing that was part of dealing with his present and recent past. He didn't know. He just knew that he was feeling hollow in a way he couldn't describe. Not depressed. Not whiney. Just hollow. And the dance of his thoughts was probably an attempt to avoid thinking about why he was so empty.

He hadn't felt empty even when Kara had died. Upset, yes. So enraged he could barely see. Deeply saddened. But not empty. He hadn't felt empty until he came home.

Maybe he was just adjusting to the huge changes in himself. He'd be a fool to think combat hadn't changed him at his very essence.

"Hi."

He turned and saw Bethany striding toward him, a smile on her face. "Hi." He managed a smile of his own.

She'd abandoned her uniform for jeans, a lavender Western shirt and cowboy boots. Her jeans and shirt cradled her curves in an eye-catching but not insistent way. At the moment, she looked Conard County born and bred, and nothing like a marine at all.

A ripple of something passed through him, something at once erotic and wistful. For those moments, everything else faded away.

He felt he should buy her ticket, but she insisted on buying her own. Just new friends catching a movie. That was okay.

What the film was about, he couldn't remember by the time they emerged from the darkened theater. What he was aware of, all he was aware of, was her perfume, a subtle, spicy sent, and the sound of her laughter.

"Well," she said with a bright smile when they stepped out into the parking lot, "that was fun. Thanks for keeping me company."

Just like that she was going to be gone. Poof. Vanished. And just like that he knew he couldn't stand it.

"How about getting a drink or a sandwich?" he suggested.

She hesitated, and after the way she'd seen him last night, he could understand why. But then she smiled and nodded. "Sure. Mahoney's?"

"They make a great sandwich."

"Okay. Um...do you have a car?"

He shook his head. "I came into town on the bus."

"Then hitch a ride with me."

As easy as that. And somewhere deep inside, he knew he'd taken an irrevocable step.

Bethany couldn't imagine why she'd invited Joe Yates to join her for a movie. She'd put it down as an instinctive act of charity. But when she agreed to go to Mahoney's with him, she knew something more was going on.

She found him attractive. Absolutely. There was no denying that. A healthy woman with healthy urges, she looked at the tall, muscled, weather-hardened marine with the faintly exotic face and she felt electricity. Parts of herself that she had been ignoring for years seemed to wake up and take notice. And while she wasn't the kind who wanted a quick fling, she actually thought about having one with Joe.

Hmm.

Her hands shook a little on the steering wheel as she realized what she was thinking and where she might be heading. No way. That was a recipe for disaster.

But her insides still quivered, anyway. And being this close to him, she was acutely aware of his scent, of the way his strength seemed barely bottled up by the requirements of civilization. Oh, hell, she'd always been attracted to dangerous men. Hadn't she learned?

Apparently not.

His quietness was making her edgy, too. It wasn't that she need to be gabbing all the time, but so far he really hadn't volunteered much of himself, nor seemed all that interested in getting to know her. So maybe he wasn't interested, and she'd be safe from her own urges.

Somehow the thought didn't cheer her at all.

She drove slowly to Mahoney's as if she dreaded it, when in fact she needed to be far more frightened of being alone in the car with Joe.

But fear didn't come easily to her, not anymore. Boot camp and the years since had taught her that she could handle just about anything. Oh, she might carry a scar or two afterward, but she could handle it. Standing up to her neck in swamp water, feeling like a smorgasbord for mosquitoes and snakes in muggy temperatures that made it almost impossible to breathe, had taught her a lot about her ability to endure. So had later events, events that had nothing to do with mosquitoes and everything to do with guilt.

So she could handle Joe Yates and her feelings for him. She could even handle whatever stupid decisions she might make in the coming hours. And she could handle the consequences. Oh, yes. She was good at handling consequences.

But sometimes she wished she didn't have to handle things. It was a furtive, barely acknowledged wish. One she would never admit to herself. Being a strong, independent woman, especially in a macho outfit like the Corps, demanded that she handle things. *All* things.

Ruck Up, Suck Up And Press On. The Corps' oft-spoken, never written motto. Something you imbibed with the heat, the stench and the fetid swamps of Paris Island.

She pulled into the lot behind Mahoney's and got out of the car before Joe could do anything as stupid as try to come open her car door for her. It was all part of establishing herself as an equal, something that had become part of her nature since joining the Corps. It hadn't taken her long to figure out that if you let them, these guys would put a woman in her place. So she carved out her own place with every breath she took.

Inside, Mahoney's was quiet. Well, it was Thursday night, and it was getting late. She would have headed for the bar, but Joe slid into a booth, giving her little choice but to sit across from him. The high backs on the benches made it seem like a private cocoon, holding the few other patrons at bay.

A waitress with eyes too old for her young face came to take their orders.

"Club soda with lime for me," Bethany said.

Joe smiled faintly. "The designated driver."

"That's me."

"Anything to eat?" the girl asked.

Bethany hesitated. She'd already gone overboard with lunch at Maude's. "Just some pretzels, thanks."

"I want a club sandwich," Joe said. "And a cola."

Bethany was relieved he'd decided not to drink. She didn't want to see him the way she'd seen him last night. It wasn't the drunkenness that bothered her, although she didn't especially care for it. She'd seen plenty of people drunk over the years. What she didn't want to see was the edge it uncovered in Joe, an edge she hadn't seen once in him today.

"I decided to reform," he remarked, as if he knew the direction of her thoughts.

"Reform?" She pretended not to understand.

"Yeah. I'm not going to become a cliché."

She smiled, this time with real amusement. "That's an unusual way to put it."

He shrugged one shoulder. "It's the truth. Marine returns from hell, drowns his sorrows in booze, et cetera. How many times have you seen that one in the movies?"

"Too many."

"Exactly. It doesn't do any good, anyway. The memories are worse with a hangover."

"What memories?" As soon as she asked the question, she knew she shouldn't have, even before his face darkened.

"Let's not go there, okay?"

"Okay," she agreed swiftly. "Stupid question." But she still wanted to get to know him better, so she headed for something that seemed safer. "You grew up around here?"

"Oh, yeah. In another lifetime."

She knew what he meant. Some things changed you so much that it was like there was a permanent marker in your life, a defining line between the person you had been and the one you were now.

He looked down at the wooden table between them

and moved a cardboard coaster around aimlessly. "I'm not sure I know how to have a civilized conversation anymore."

"Sure you do," she said bracingly. "The idea is to talk about all the things that don't matter, like the weather, and the football scores, and who's going to win at Wimbledon or something."

That surprised a laugh out of him, and his dark eyes lifted to her face. "Okay, okay. How about those Packers?"

And suddenly they were smiling at each other with a kind of understanding that, if Bethany hadn't been so mesmerized by how the expression transformed Joe's face, might have scared her, marine or not.

The too-close moment was shattered as their glasses thudded onto the table in front of them. A bowl of pretzels followed.

"Back in a sec with the sandwich," the waitress said.

"Thanks." Joe glanced up at the young woman for a second, watching her walk away. "I have the feeling she was a few years behind me in school."

"That's a possibility."

"But I can't place her." He shook his head.

"Maybe she's younger than she looks."

"Maybe."

"She didn't seem to recognize you, either."

He moved his glass of cola to one side. "I don't look the same."

"Few of us do."

Slowly his gaze returned to her. It was odd, she thought, this feeling that she was having that he kept slipping away from her into someplace in the past. As if he weren't really here with her now. "Have you been home long?"

"A few days."

That might explain it. She remembered her own return, and how out of place she had felt for a while. It was probably even harder for him. She remembered what Maude had said earlier at the diner. "And you haven't visited your family yet?"

"Not yet." Again his gaze drifted away, the thousand-yard stare returning.

"Is there a problem there?"

His attention snapped back to her. "No. Why?"

"I just wondered. Usually when people come home, they visit their families."

"I'm not ready yet, is all."

"I see." But she wasn't certain she really did. Her family was the first thing she had wanted after the bombing, which she still thought of, in her own mind, as The Incident. "Are you afraid?"

It was a good thing she didn't really expect an answer to that question, because she didn't get one. He studied his cola as if the rising bubbles held the answers to the secret of life, and didn't say a thing, even when the waitress put his sandwich in front of him.

Bethany tried to mend the rift, wondering why she'd asked something that was none of her business anyway. "That sandwich looks good. Maybe I'll get one."

"You can have mine."

He started to push his plate across the table, but she stopped him by reaching out and touching his wrist. The electricity that shot through her as her fingertips touched his warm skin was almost enough to make her gasp. But she retained enough presence of mind to say, "No, Joe. You need to eat. You look too thin."

After a moment, he nodded and picked up one triangular piece of the thick sandwich. But he didn't immediately raise it to his mouth.

Feeling as if she were somehow out of place, Bethany forced herself to look around the bar and not at Joe while she nibbled on a pretzel, waiting for the sound of him finally taking a bite.

But the sound that reached her was his voice.

"I'm sorry," he said.

She immediately looked at him. "What for?"

"I'm lousy company. I'm acting like a jerk."

"I was out of line."

"No." His eyes burned into her. "You're trying to be friendly. I'm trying to stop you. I'm being rude."

"Why don't you want me to be friendly?" She almost held her breath, awaiting his answer. She wasn't exactly used to being rejected by men, but it happened sometimes.

He surprised her. "Because I'm still feeling raw. That's why I don't want to visit my family yet. That's why I'm being a jerk. I feel raw."

"I understand." And she did, although more with her emotions than with her head.

"I'm...afraid," he added, as if every word were painful to speak, "that I might...let go."

Then she *did* understand, fully and completely. During and after The Incident, she had often felt she was barely hanging on to her self-control by her bloody fingertips. Trying not to freak out, when freaking out was the only emotional response left in her. She could only imagine that his burden was even greater than hers, and that much harder to hang on to his control.

"Maybe you need to let go," she said quietly.

"Nobody needs to hear this crap. Nobody."

"Maybe not. But maybe you need to spill it."

"It wouldn't do a damn bit of good," he said stonily. "Not a damn bit of good. Anyway, I was doing just fine."

Just fine when? she wondered. Before he'd come home? Before he'd had to face the world away from the battlefield? Before he'd had to remember that once it had been possible to sleep soundly, to eat well, to live a day without being constantly aware you were one split second from death?

Turning, she wagged her hand at the waitress. The girl came over immediately. "Two whiskeys," Bethany told her. "And a club sandwich for me, please."

Joe's expression might have been amused if he hadn't looked so empty. "You're the designated driver."

"I can walk home if necessary."

"I refuse to be a cliché."

"One drink isn't a cliché. And damn it, will you start eating that sandwich?"

"Yes, Gunny." He took a large bite and chewed mechanically. The whiskeys appeared before them. Joe ignored his, for the moment at least. Bethany didn't really want hers, but she lifted the shot glass and tossed it down. It burned all the way, reminding her of a more foolish age when she'd gotten drunk once. Just once. That's all it had taken to cure her of the desire. Her stomach wanted to rebel, but she quelled it with a pretzel.

"Okay," she said, when Joe was working on the second quarter of his sandwich, his mouth safely full of food, "you obviously need to talk to somebody. And you don't want it to be your family. So it can be me. Or it can be a shrink. But you have to talk."

He shook his head and swallowed. "It won't do a damn bit of good. I'm going back."

Something in her stilled, growing quiet and cold. "Why?"

"My unit's over there."

Dumb question, she thought. Of course his unit was over there. Of course he was going back. Why had she even asked? "You still need to dump before you go back to it. You have to dump it or you're going to snap."

"Who made you an authority?"

She bristled. "I realize I never did what you're doing, but I *have* had a little experience, if you remember?''

He didn't say anything, but reached instead for the whiskey. He sipped it, surprising her. Finally he asked, ''Where did *you* dump?''

''All over the shoulder of a psychiatrist. He listened, I talked, and it didn't go into my service jacket because I hunted up a civilian guy and paid for it myself.''

A faint curve lifted one corner of Joe's hard mouth. ''Smart.''

''I'm not stupid. And dumping it was better than kicking the dog, you know?''

''I know.'' Again that distant look came to his eyes. Then he sighed, took another sip of whiskey and swallowed another mouthful of sandwich. ''There was a girl,'' he said after a moment. ''A woman, actually. A United Nations aid worker who was there to supervise the distribution of food. The ruling government arrested her for wearing a cross, but she managed to get away. I met her when she was hiding with the insurgents.''

Bethany nodded encouragingly.

''She was something else, Bethany,'' he said after a few minutes. ''A bundle of fire and determination. Mother Theresa in jeans and a cammie jacket.''

Bethany's heart almost stopped. Somehow she thought that if this was about a lost love, she was going to hurt in ways she didn't want to hurt ever again.

But once again he surprised her. "She was like a sister to me. To all of us. Tough but kind. There isn't much kindness out there. Life's too hard. But she managed to be kind through it all, even when she was starving and cold and whupped. And then she got killed. We were supposed to be protecting her while we carried out our mission and got her to safety, but she got killed."

He shook his head and looked down. Bethany wanted to touch him, to offer comfort, but she didn't dare.

"Anyway," he said, "I got wounded, too. Nothing major. But I escorted her body back to her family in Amsterdam, then came home."

"That must have been rough."

His silence was his answer. He was drifting away again, but this time she didn't have to call him back. He came back all on his own. "Sorry," he said. "My body is here, but the rest of me is having trouble catching up."

"It's okay. It can be jarring to make such a big, sudden change."

His expression suddenly spoke volumes to her, as if he was relieved to know he wasn't just crazy, that what he was experiencing was normal. Nobody, Bethany thought, ever prepared them for these kinds of transitions. And given the he-man mentality of the Corps, it was hardly likely that anyone was going to complain about a readjustment problem.

But she remembered her own readjustment problem,

even though she had had weeks at sea to shift mental gears from the death and mayhem that had struck her ship in the Middle East to the normalcy of life at home. How much worse it must be for Joe, who had spent months at war, only to find himself home in a matter of a couple of days.

"The mind," she said carefully, "needs time to absorb things."

"Yeah." He didn't offer any more, and she didn't press him. All she could do was let him know she was willing to listen if he decided to talk.

But talking was evidently not what he wanted to do now. He took another sip of his whiskey, then another bite of his sandwich. Hers arrived, and while she really didn't feel hungry, she knew she had to eat to balance the whiskey she'd just drunk.

And why had she done that, anyway? To loosen *him* up? Because she hated the stuff herself, hated the fuzzy way it made her brain feel. So many people talked about getting "a buzz" as if it was a fun thing. If it was, she evidently lacked the equipment to enjoy it.

For a while they ate quietly. When he finished his sandwich, Joe ordered another one. It hardly surprised her; he was a big man, and right now he looked a bit gaunt. After his seconds arrived, he started talking.

"I grew up on a ranch," he said. "In the foothills west of here. We were always on the edge of losing everything from the time I can remember. My sister had to take a job as a cop to keep the place."

"That's your sister? Sara Ironheart?"

"Yeah." He looked at her. "You know her?"

"I've met her. She's the only woman deputy here, and once we met at a church social and got to talking about what it was like to be women in men's outfits."

A smile lifted his face. "Yeah. It's not easy. When she first went for the job, the sheriff was okay with it, but some of the guys gave her a really hard time. Funny thing was, Sara was still there when the rest of them were gone."

"Well, she's still there. Part-time now, working as a crime scene investigator with that Dalton guy." Suddenly Bethany blushed. "But you know that."

"That's okay. She's got two little ones she wants to spend time with, and since she and Gideon married, he's turned the ranch around enough that she says she only keeps her finger in so she has something to talk about besides kids."

Bethany laughed. "Well, I can testify to the fact that she has a lot to talk about. I wish I saw more of her."

"Yeah. She's a good egg. For a sister."

Beth caught the teasing note in his voice and realized that Joe Yates was an even more attractive man when he wasn't looking haunted.

"Anyway," he continued, "Gideon turned the place around by boarding and training horses. He's got a spooky way with them. My granddad calls him a horse whisperer. Gideon says all he does is listen to the horse. Whatever it is, it's like magic. So he trains

show horses and cow ponies. Quite a combination.''
He shook his head. ''I swear he could get a wild mustang to stand on its hind legs and whistle Dixie.''

''I'd like to see that sometime.''

''What, the whistling Dixie?''

She laughed again. ''No, the training part.''

''Sure.'' He kind of shrugged the idea away, but didn't exactly say no. ''Anyway, you look at the place now and you can't tell what it was like when I was a kid. We were barely holding it together. Sara had to rent out most of the good pasture to a neighbor for his cattle, and my grandfather had this thing about rescuing mustangs, which meant they had to be fed through the cold months, and Sara worked her butt off. I got a job when I turned sixteen, and started helping out.''

Bethany nodded encouragement.

''I thought we were poor. We didn't have much. But you know what? I never went without a meal. I might have worn clothes from Goodwill when things got tight, but I never went hungry or cold.''

He sighed. ''Then I saw the people in…over there. God, I've never seen such poverty. Or at least such widespread poverty. These folks have nothing at all. Nothing. Not a roof, not a bit of land, just the clothes on their backs and maybe a pot for holding water, or cooking, if they managed to find something to eat. It made me think how lucky I was. And now I'm sitting here eating two sandwiches.'' He started to push the plate away.

"Don't waste it," she said gently. "Throwing that away won't help them. So what did you do? Give them your rations?"

"As much as we could. But the winter…" He shook his head. "I don't know what's worse, the starvation or the war."

"The U.N. is trying to help. And the Red Cross."

"It isn't enough. It's hard to get food to people in outlying areas because there aren't any roads. There are air drops of food, but it's still not enough. God, they need everything. Blankets. Firewood. Shelter. Clothes. Shoes. Food."

"And your friend was trying to help with that."

"Kara? Yeah. It blows my mind that the pigs arrested her."

"Well," said Bethany, feeling almost hesitant, "it's easier to keep people down when they're too hungry to move."

"Actually, it just makes them more desperate. Desperate enough to do something. But the rulers didn't want any food getting to anyone except through them. They wanted it to look like they were the ones who were providing it. Bastards."

Bethany waited a minute or so, to see if he would continue. When he didn't, she said, "You need to eat. Get your strength back up."

Then he asked the most painful question she'd ever heard: "Why?"

Chapter 4

Well, she didn't have an answer for that one, Bethany thought after she drove Joe back to his motel. It was clear he didn't want to go back over there, but it was equally clear he felt guilty as hell about being here.

But she didn't know what she could do to make him feel any better about any of it. There were no magic wands for this one.

On impulse, she turned her car west, and headed out to where she thought the Ironheart Ranch was. She'd never been out that way, but from a few things that Sara and others had mentioned in passing, she thought she knew which county road to take.

The night was already cool, but as she climbed

higher into the foothills, it grew even chillier. Here and there she thought she caught sight of patches of snow, sheltered from melting in the daytime sun by the shadows of rocks and trees.

It was awfully late to be paying a call, and more than once she considered turning around, but she pressed forward anyway. She wasn't a marine for nothing.

Then, just as she was beginning to conclude that she'd gone too far and was probably on the wrong road, her headlights picked out a sign: Horse Training and Boarding.

It wasn't much of a sign—although it was fresh and neat—designed not to catch the attention of mere passersby, but to point the way to those who were already looking for the place. Apparently this business relied on word of mouth.

She turned off onto a ranch road that showed signs of a recent grading to wipe out the effects of the winter. Barbed-wire fence lined both sides of it, not the freshly painted white wood of fancier horse ranches. Already she had the feeling this was a no-nonsense place.

When she pulled into the wide gravel circle between house and barn, she was relieved to see lights on in the downstairs windows of the two-story house, and even a light from the barn. Somebody was still awake. At least she wouldn't scare folks out of their wits by rousing them.

She put the car in Park and turned off the engine.

Just before she slammed her car door shut, the side door of the house opened, and a large man was silhouetted against golden light.

"You lost?" he called.

"I hope not. I'm looking for Sara Ironheart."

"You've come to the right place. Come on in."

Sometimes it didn't pay to rush in where fools dared to tread, and this might be one of those times. Joe might hate her forever for not minding her own business. And she liked Joe. She wanted to see him again. But...she'd also seen how he was hurting, and she didn't think avoiding his family was helping him any.

So she marched forward with squared shoulders until she was standing in the kitchen with the broad-shouldered man whose long black hair was caught in a thong at the nape of his neck, and whose face was stamped with his Native American ancestry. A powerful-looking man who seemed to be at peace with life and unafraid of anything. He, she thought, might be good for Joe. She wondered why she hadn't seen him around town.

"I'm Gideon Ironheart," he said, offering a hand. "Sara's husband."

"I'm Bethany Mathison, the Marine Corps recruiter."

He lifted his eyebrows. "My kids are too young. Don't tell me Sara's taken a wild hair."

"No." She felt herself smile. "I'm here to see her about her brother." At once Bethany realized what that sounded like, and before surprise could change to horror on Gideon's face, she rushed to say, "He's okay. He's not hurt." No physically, anyway. But she didn't want to say more until Sara was here, or at least until she knew this big man would stay calm when he heard what his brother-in-law was going through.

"Well," Gideon said, absorbing the news with barely a change in expression, "have a seat at the table. I was just making some coffee. Sara had to go out on a job tonight, but she called a little while ago. She was probably following you right up the county road."

Bethany accepted his offer, taking a seat at a table that looked as if it had seen generations of wear and absorbed countless conversations, quarrels and good times. She'd never had anything that old in her life, and the age of the piece attracted her. She ran her hand over it, feeling the mars and scars, and the patina of its long life.

"I'm sorry to come so late," she said as he poured them both mugs of steaming coffee, then sat across from her.

"It's not all that late," he said reassuringly. "I'm going to be up most of the night, anyway. I have a mare in foal. And obviously Sara's not in bed yet, and won't be for some time. She always comes in wound up from these things."

"I can imagine. Thanks for being so kind."

"So you know Joey?"

"I met him recently."

"Ah." Gideon's obsidian eyes searched her face,

but he didn't question her further. Somewhere this man had learned the gift of patience, and Bethany was beginning to wish she could ask him for a dose of it. Everything she was doing tonight seemed reckless, and she'd sworn never to be reckless again, not after her last mistake. By the book, that's what she'd sworn to be, and the book said you didn't make impulsive calls on people you didn't know late at night, mixing up in something that was really none of your business.

But here she was, and so as not to scare this family to death, she had to remain. If she left now, they'd wonder what she was hiding. They'd worry.

"I hear you're a horse whisperer," she said, to fill a silence she was beginning to find awkward, even though he seemed comfortable with it.

He smiled. "So it's rumored."

"You don't think you are?"

He shrugged. "I just pay attention to the horses. You have to learn their language. Animals aren't verbal, but they say a whole hell of a lot with their bodies and behavior. There's nothing magical about it, despite what people say. Have you ever had a dog?"

"No, I never had a pet."

"Too bad. People with dogs and cats learn to read them the same way, if they pay attention. What I do is no different."

"Except that you're very good at it?"

He chuckled. "It keeps me in food."

She felt a great liking for this man, and wondered if Joe might ever have been a little like him, before war had affected him. And yet she got the feeling that Gideon's patience and calm arose not from an easy life, but rather from surviving a hard one. There was something in his face that was etched so deep, something hard and painful, that even his calm gaze and friendly smile couldn't wipe it away entirely. That pain was etched on Joe's face now, too, but Joe's gaze wasn't calm. It was nearly empty, sometimes.

That frightened her, she realized. She had only just met Joe Yates, yet she was already coming to care about what happened to him. Maybe caring too much, if she judged by her presence here.

Gideon spoke. "So how did you get to be a recruiter?"

"Well…" She hesitated and smiled wryly. "You have to be gung-ho, you have to look really good, and then the Corps gods have to pick you out of all the applicants."

He laughed. "A by-the-book marine?"

"Of course."

"I guess Joe will never be a recruiter then. He's never been a by-the-book type. I'm surprised he hasn't busted out of the Corps yet, to tell you the truth."

"He seems to be doing pretty well, actually," she mused, remembering the medals that had been on Joe's chest last night.

"Well, maybe they need a mustang from time to time."

She liked that analogy. "I wouldn't have thought of him as a mustang."

"I supposed in military-speak that means something else. But I'm talking about an unbroken horse."

"I knew you were. It kind of goes with what you do for a living."

Again he smiled, but her thoughts were drifting back to Joe, wondering if the mustang had at last been broken. Because to her, Joe seemed perilously close to an edge he might never be able to return from.

"Actually," she said, admitting something she'd never told anyone, "I suspect they made me a recruiter because I'm a martinet. A pain-in-the-butt, by-the-book marine."

Gideon's dark brows lifted. "Why do you say that?"

"It's a long story, but I learned that the rules matter. Even the ones that seem dumb."

"A surprising number of rules are there for a reason," he said. "Even the ones that seem stupid. Maybe Joe finally figured that out."

"Maybe." But she remembered him last night, drunk and wild and ready to fight with her because she'd said he was out of uniform. Now she felt almost embarrassed by the way she had acted, thinking only of the impression he might create in this town where she worked so hard to make the marines always look good. But after getting to know him a bit, she didn't think the man she'd met last night was the real Joe Yates. The one she'd met today had been milder, more reasonable.

And so, so sad and troubled.

She sighed and looked toward the darkened window. The curtains were still open, as if to be inviting to anyone outside.

"There's Sara," Gideon said, rising.

Bethany strained, but couldn't hear anything. "Really? You hear her?"

His eyes glinted. "No, I *feel* her."

Spooky, she thought. Or crazy. But when she looked at Gideon Ironheart, she didn't think he was crazy at all. She wondered what it would be like to be so close to someone you could feel her presence long before you could hear or see her.

Then she heard the growl of an engine. Moments later, headlights pierced the night and bounced off the dark glass.

Gideon went out to greet his wife, leaving Bethany alone in the kitchen. She waited patiently, sipping her coffee, figuring the couple needed a few minutes alone together. Hoping that Joe wouldn't hate her forever for sticking her nose into his business.

Then the Ironhearts came through the door, hands linked. Sara was a quietly pretty woman, a little taller than average, with dark hair caught up on the back of her head. She was wearing the local uniform of Western shirt and boots, but on her belt hung a badge.

"Hi," she said, striding toward Beth and offering her hand for a shake. "Good to see you again, Bethany. Gideon said you're here about my brother?" She pulled out a chair and sat near her, while Gideon got her a steaming mug of coffee.

"Yes," Bethany said slowly. "He's probably going to be furious with me for coming here but...he's in town. I gather he arrived yesterday."

Sara smiled up at Gideon as she accepted the mug of coffee from him. "Thanks, hon." But her smile was gone when she returned her attention to Bethany. "And he didn't tell me he's home. I imagine that's why you're here."

Bethany nodded, feeling that she had made a big mistake. Sara was probably going to tell her that Joe was a big boy now and could make his own decisions. Which was true, and she shouldn't need anyone else to tell her so.

But Sara didn't say that. Instead, she nodded slowly. "What's wrong?"

"He's...well, he's been through a bad time. A very bad time. I think he's trying to avoid...well...I've spent quite a bit of time with him today. We had lunch together, then went to a movie tonight, and afterward had a sandwich at Mahoney's. But he keeps pulling away into himself. As if...I don't know how to explain it. As if he's not really here."

Sara nodded, her gaze flickering to Gideon. "Maybe he needs some time by himself."

"Maybe." She *had* made a mistake by coming here. Sara didn't seem worried that her brother didn't want to see her. Bethany began to feel small and stupid.

"How'd you meet?" Sara asked.

"Last night at Mahoney's. I went in to get a sandwich and he was there." She hesitated, then plunged ahead. "He was drinking heavily, and I...well, I called him on his appearance and we almost got into a fight."

"Now that sounds like Joe," Gideon mused. "Always ready for a tussle."

"But not the drinking," Sara said, frowning. "He knows better than that." She looked at Bethany. "Joey's half Native American. Booze is poison to us."

Bethany nodded, flushing when she remembered how she had ordered whiskeys for them tonight. Stupid, stupid, stupid.

"Joe always avoided it," Sara continued. "We made a point of it while he was growing up." Again her gaze flickered toward Gideon. "I hope he isn't making a habit of that."

"I didn't get that impression," Bethany hastened to say, remembering how Joe had barely touched the whiskey she'd bought for him. She hoped she was right.

Sara's gaze settled on her again. "But you're worried about him."

"Yes, I am," Bethany confessed. "I think he needs emotional support, but doesn't want to reach out for it."

"Maybe," Gideon said slowly, "he's just not ready for the whole fam-damily. Maybe you should go see him alone, Sara. It may be he's just not ready for me and the kids. Or for Grandfather."

"Grandfather," Sara said with a nod. "He can be too damn insightful at times."

"Yeah." Gideon almost smiled. "And he's getting worse with every passing year. Hell, we can't even have a little spat without him making us both feel like idiots."

Sara laughed at that, but it was a quiet, short laugh. "I'll go see him. I can just sort of run into him somewhere. Is he staying at the motel?"

"The Lazy Rest, yes."

"Okay, that's what I'll do. I'll hang out at the truck stop in the morning and run into him."

"Thanks." Bethany rose. "I know I'm being a busybody but..." She trailed off, uncertain what to say.

Sara reached out and squeezed her hand. "Thank *you*," Sara said. "Joey's always had a tendency to bolt inside himself when he's hurting. And it's usually the worst thing to do."

Remembering her own experience after the bombing of her ship, Bethany nodded. She wouldn't have made it through that awful time without her friends.

She said good-night, then drove off into the dark chilly night, hoping she'd done the right thing.

Chapter 5

When Joe walked into the truck stop diner in the morning, the first person he noticed was his sister. And not for an instant did he think this was an accident. Somebody had told her he was in town, and he had a good idea who that somebody was.

For an instant, he considered turning and walking out. But that would hurt Sara, and it would only postpone the inevitable, anyway. Sooner or later, he was going to have to see her.

At least she didn't race toward him and try to hug him the way she usually did when he came home. Ordinarily he wouldn't have minded that kind of greeting, but right now he didn't think he could stand to be touched.

She was sitting at the counter wearing faded jeans, a T-shirt, and a light jacket against the morning chill. She smiled when she saw him and waved him over, the way she might have done with a friend she saw all the time.

That made it easier for him to approach.

"Hi, Joe," she said. "Wanna get a booth?"

"Sure." At least he wouldn't have to wonder who was behind him. He picked the corner booth, backed himself up against the wall. She faced him, setting her mug of coffee on the table before her. He was aware of her searching his face as he scanned the plastic menu card and ordered bacon, eggs, toast and coffee.

Then he couldn't hide behind the menu any longer, and he had to look at her. And looking at her almost seemed to tear his heart out.

"Joe?" she said after a moment.

"Yeah." His voice sounded thick even to him.

"What's wrong?"

"You don't want to know."

"Yeah, actually I do. And you aren't going to shock me. Remember what I do for a living?"

But he was tired of the story, tired of himself, tired of the endless circle of his own thoughts. "How's Gideon? How are the kids?"

"Gideon's doing really well," she said, her face softening. "And so are the children. Tim is growing like a weed and I'm beginning to think he's going to be a basketball player. Dawn is…well, she's four, you know? She loves to play dress-up, and sometimes I'm convinced she was a princess in a past life. Very imperious.''

Joe started to smile. "I can just imagine it."

"Well, if you get around to coming up to visit us, she'll probably treat you like her personal lackey."

His smile deepened, and for some crazy reason he felt his heart lift a little. "You used to be imperious."

She laughed. "No, never. I was just, um, a tomboy. There's a difference."

"So everything is going okay?"

"Better than okay. But you know. I've been writing to you."

She had. And at some point he'd stopped answering. Guilt flickered through him. "Micah and Faith are okay?" Micah was Gideon's brother.

"Oh yeah, they're doing great. Five kids now. And every one of them is the spitting image of Micah, except for Sally." Sally was Faith's child by her first marriage, to an abuser. "Sally looks just like her mom."

"Wow." Joe shook his head, trying to imagine a bunch of Micah clones. Micah was always a silent type, massively controlled. Gideon was more open, more…well, human, than his older brother, who, if Joe were to resort to the beliefs of his ancestors, was probably born to be a shaman.

"And Grandfather?" he asked after a moment.

"Getting on, but still active. I swear that man can see right through me."

"He always could." Which was one of the reasons

Joe was avoiding his family. He didn't know if he was up to his grandfather's all-knowing gaze. "How's life at the sheriff's department?"

"Good. Troubling at times. I'm working on a pretty ugly case right now."

He knew better than to ask her to discuss it. Sara was more silent than a clam when it came to her cases. "And Nate Tate?"

"The same as always. I think he stopped aging ten years ago."

Joe nodded. He and the sheriff had had their run-ins when he was in high school, but he regarded the man with a lot of respect.

His breakfast was served, grease-laden and delicious, but he didn't feel hungry anymore. Maybe because he knew what was coming.

"What about you, Joe," Sara asked quietly. "What about *you?*"

He sighed and picked up his fork, shoving bacon around his plate to avoid answering. He really didn't want to get into this with Sara. He really didn't. "I'll be okay. I think...I think I'm just having trouble switching mental gears from there to here."

"Mmm." Her expression was understanding. "Have you considered getting out?"

"And do what? I'm a soldier, Sara. I don't know anything else." And he didn't want to have this discussion with her. He knew she wanted him to go to college, find a profession. Or even come home and work on the ranch with Gideon. After all, he shared title to it.

But the ranch was Sara's in a way that he couldn't quite explain, and he didn't think he was the type for the bucolic life, anyway. He'd always had a taste for excitement.

Well, until lately. Lately he'd begun to think he might have had enough excitement for a lifetime.

"Okay," Sara said, easily enough. "It's your life and your decision, and I'll shut up. It's just that... Joey, I'm worried about you. I worry about you all the time. Ever since this war started over there, I've been having nightmares." She looked away, and he could see her swallowing back tears.

Cripes, he didn't need this now. His own head was already too messed up. The thought was such a selfish one, though, that shame silenced it almost before it was born. He wanted to hang his head with self-disgust, and at the same time leave town and never come back. This had been a mistake.

But this woman had raised him after their father died. Except for her, he'd have been thrust into a foster home. Instead, she had worked full-time as a deputy, putting her life on the line, and struggling to keep their inheritance intact. He owed her a debt he could never repay.

"I'm sorry, Sara," he said finally. "I'm sorry."

She reached across the table and covered his left hand with hers. On the plate in front of him, eggs and grease were congealing unnoticed.

"It's okay. We all do what we need to. I just wish..."

She looked down and bit her lower lip.

"Wish what?" he asked, deciding he might as well get it all on the chin at once.

"I just wish," she said finally, raising liquid eyes to his, "that you could figure out how to be happy."

Well, she might as well have hit him between the eyes with a sledgehammer, he thought later when she'd finally driven away, leaving him to wander the small confines of Conard City as if walking could exorcize his demons.

She wished he could figure out how to be happy?

The worst of it was, he had thought he *was* happy, at least until lately. But when she'd said that, he had realized she was right. He'd never been happy. Never.

At least not since he'd hit adolescence. He was one of the world's great perpetual malcontents, always chafing to be elsewhere doing some other thing. Even in the Corps. But with the Corps, they kept you too damn busy to do much ruminating, and you didn't have any choice but to do what you were told.

Sure, it had given him a measure of pride and confidence he would never have had otherwise. But...he wasn't happy. He hadn't been happy. He'd been putting one foot in front of the other because there had been no other choice. He was *proud* of being a marine. But he wasn't sure he liked it. And even if he *did* like it, it didn't seem to be making him happy.

Hell.

Maybe it was time he got his head out of his butt and figured out just what *would* make Joe Yates happy. If anything.

Alternatively, he could just end his leave early and rejoin his unit, where he'd be too busy surviving and fighting to think about all this junk.

But some small voice inside him stilled the thought, then rejected it. It was time, it seemed, for Joe Yates to do some thinking.

Finding a bench in the courthouse square, he ignored the chilly air and watched some old men playing checkers on a board placed between them on their bench.

And it occurred to him that someday he wanted to be one of those old men, playing checkers in the sunshine.

Nothing prepared Bethany Mathison for the explosion that burst in on her that evening in her tiny little house toward the edge of town. When she opened her door in answer to the bell, she found Joe Yates standing there, looking like a severe thunderstorm.

"Joe!" she said, taken aback by his appearance as much as his unexpected arrival.

"Where the hell do you get off telling my family I'm in town?"

She looked at him for a moment, feeling her heart sink as she realized she'd gone and screwed up again. Again! By not following the basic rules. Hadn't she learned a damn thing?

"Come in," she said finally, stepping back and opening the door wide. "The neighbors don't need to hear this."

"Damn the neighbors." But he strode in anyway, and she closed the door behind him.

Then she waited, watching a variety of emotions work their way across his face, expecting that at any moment he was going to give her the dressing down she so richly deserved.

Hadn't she learned anything at all? Rules were there for a reason, and there was a basic social rule that you didn't stick your nose in someone else's business. You didn't carry news that wasn't yours to carry. You didn't mix in things in which you had no legitimate part.

And if you didn't follow the rules, you paid for it— or someone else did. And for some reason Joe was looking as if he'd paid for her mistake.

"I'm sorry," she said finally, when he didn't say any more. "I was worried about you."

"Yeah, everybody's worried about me," he said, his voice as hard as steel. "The point was, I didn't want my sister worrying. And now you've shot off your mouth and made her worry. Damn you, Bethany, what gave you the right?"

"Nothing." Nothing except her heart, which cared for him more than it ought to, considering how short a time she had known him.

"You're damn right, *nothing*," he thundered. "I'm screwed up, I admit it. But nobody needs to know that except me. I've been over there fighting a filthy war that doesn't have any rules, a war where even the good guys do bad things. In a place where, if you try to follow the rules, you wind up dead!''

Her heart jolted. ''Your friend?''

''Yeah. Her and hundreds of other people. Do you know what her crime was, Bethany? Sitting here in your insulated world of polished brash and military creases and starch, do you have any idea what can get you killed over there? Her crime, her *crime*, was stepping in to prevent a man from beating his wife to death because her veil fell off in public. That was her crime. You see, she didn't follow the rules.''

Bethany's heart jolted again. Why all this talk of rules? It was almost as if he'd been hearing the echoes of her own thoughts. And worse, he didn't seem to be making any sense. He was saying on the one hand that following the rules over there could get you killed, but on the other that his friend had gotten into trouble by not following them. Where was this going?

But did it really matter? All she knew was that her heart was squeezing so hard it hurt, and her chest was so tight she couldn't breathe. Tears, which she loathed, were stinging her eyes. She didn't want Joe to be mad at her. She couldn't stand it.

He threw up a hand, a gesture so sudden and angry that she almost stepped back. But he wasn't striking at her.

''You're damned if you do and damned if you don't,'' he continued, his voice hard with fury. ''Yeah, living like that screws you up. It screws you up good. But my sister doesn't need to be worrying about it. She didn't need to know I was around until I was ready to tell her. Now she's asking questions I don't want to answer, and she's stewing about me, and it's all your fault.''

Beth couldn't deny that. Drawing a painful breath, she said, ''I was trying to help!''

''Just how was that supposed to help?''

''You need support!''

''I don't need anything. I gotta deal with this on my own. Nobody else can fix your head, Bethany. *Nobody.*''

''Maybe not. But understanding can help.''

''What would you know about it?''

That's when she snapped. ''All right,'' she said, ''maybe you don't like what I did. So what? How dare you tell me I don't know anything about it. I know plenty about it. You think I haven't lost friends? I lost three good friends in the attack on my ship! Three of them. And it's *my* fault they're dead, because if I'd dogged those hatches instead of sending them in to find the wounded, they wouldn't be dead now. I didn't follow the rules, I knew I didn't follow the rules, and they're dead. And you know what I got for it? I got a damn *medal!* I should have been court-martialed.''

Something in his face was changing as she spoke, but she was too wound up to heed it.

''You're not the only person on this planet who's been through hell, Joe Yates. Not by a long sight. You didn't send your people in and then have to kill them. Yes, kill them! Because I finally had to order the hatches *behind* them dogged so the whole damn ship wouldn't go down. I waited as long as I could. I *waited.* And I kept anyone else from going in after them. Do you know how hard that was? When the damn bomb hit our quarters, it was early morning. We had eight people who didn't get out of there, and I sent more in!''

''Bethany…''

''Oh, just shut up. I've had enough of your self-aggrandizing angst. I haven't broken a single rule or regulation since then, except for this time. And you know what? I'm sick of caring so much about people that I do things I shouldn't. I was worried about you. *Worried.* And this is what I get for it. I should know better.''

She pivoted sharply, turning her back on him, wishing he'd vanish into some dark hole and just get the hell out of her life.

''Bethany…'' His hands were on her shoulders, gentle, warm. They squeezed lightly. ''Bethany…''

''We were above the waterline at first,'' she continued woodenly. ''That's what they said. That's why I didn't get court-martialed, even though those hatches are supposed to be closed. Even though I should have closed them right away. But then we started to list from the water we were taking on below, and water started to come into our compartments, and we had to

dog those hatches. We *had* to. And nobody came out.
Nobody ever came out.''

He turned her toward him, and the next thing she
knew she was wrapped in his arms, and her tears were
falling, falling, spilling like water too long dammed,
her throat so tight it felt as if she were being garroted.
Her eyes burned and her head pounded and her heart
hammered…and the tears continued to flow. It had
been a long time since she'd cried over this, and only
in these minutes did she realize how heavy the burden
had continued to be.

Eventually she became aware that Joe was rocking
her gently, murmuring softly, nonsense mostly, things
like, "It's okay…." It would never be okay. Never,
ever. But some things just had to be lived with because
there was no other alternative.

As her tears slowed and began to dry, she began to
feel a bit surprised that he could be so gentle and kind.
Kindness, in particular, was something she hadn't seen
in his makeup, hadn't guessed was there.

Maybe, she thought, she'd been hypnotized by the
marine illusion, the illusion of being tough enough to
handle anything, no matter how painful. Can Do was
another oft-spoken, unofficial motto. The Ruck Up,
Suck Up and Press On mentality you met with if you
evinced any emotional weakness.

And it was even worse for women, because women
were always suspected of not being tough enough no
matter what they did. Any tears she had spilled had

been shed out of the sight and hearing of others, shed with shame for her weakness.

A thought occurred to her, and she lifted her face, looking up at Joe, feeling such a sudden and intense longing that it was difficult to speak. "We're not weak," she said. "We're human."

For a second he looked perplexed, then understanding dawned. "You're right."

"You're damn straight, I'm right. We have the right to grieve, just like anybody else. And when we're grieving, we have the right to lean. I just leaned on you. You can lean on me if you want. Or your sister. But you don't have to be ashamed of it."

He nodded slowly, then he drew her to the battered old sofa she'd bought second-hand because in her job you didn't accumulate furniture unless you had a family, and you certainly didn't get paid enough to buy new furniture, anyway.

It was comfortable, although it did tend to sag a bit in the middle, and it sagged now, easing them together. Bethany started to pull away instinctively, even though she didn't want to, but Joe's arm wrapped around her shoulders, keeping her close.

Never, not once in her life, had she felt such a sense of peace as pervaded her when he held her. It was like coming home after a long journey.

After a moment, her head nestled on his shoulder, and she gave herself up to the moment.

"I'm sorry," he said quietly. "You're right, it's self-aggrandizing angst."

"That was harsh of me," she apologized. "I had no right to say that."

"But you were right about it, anyway. I was getting sick of myself days ago."

"Sick of what? You have a right to grieve."

"I was doing more than grieving. I was sinking into self-pity."

"Hmm." She snuggled closer, hardly aware of what she was doing. "So now it's ruck up, suck up and press on, as if nothing ever happened?"

She felt him move, maybe to look down at her. "Do I detect a note of sarcasm?"

"Maybe three or four notes of sarcasm," she admitted. "I mean...we may be marines. We may have jobs to do, and we may have to do them under unthinkable circumstances. But it's playing a psychological game of ostrich to think those things never hurt us. It's one thing to be tough and keep going. It's another to be emotionally self-destructive."

He didn't answer immediately, but that didn't surprise her. She swallowed a sigh, figuring at any moment he would turn on her again, accusing her of not being a good marine, or the equivalent.

But then he surprised her. "That may be true."

She wanted to look up at him, but didn't dare. "It is true. It took me until right now to figure it out, but now that I have it's as clear as a bell. There's just so much emotional pressure you can hold inside before something has to give. Either you go nuts, or you bury it so well that you become less than human. It's like amputating entire parts of your personality.''

She felt his arm tighten around her shoulders, a comforting squeeze. Comforting, she hoped, for both of them.

''I'm sorry,'' he said.

Now she did look up at him. ''Why should you be sorry?''

''Sorry for what you went through. You know, under pressure like that, we make the best decisions we can. I think I would have done the same thing you did. In fact, I'm sure of it.''

She'd heard the bit about being under pressure before. It was the first thing her C.O. had said to her. But nobody else had said he or she would have done the same thing. Nobody else.

''That's nice of you to say, but—''

''No, it's not nice. It's the truth. The first thing you think of is saving your buddies. I know. I've been in similar situations. Everything else can go to hell, but you gotta save your buddies. You did the right thing. The best thing. You had no way of knowing those marines wouldn't come out.''

''I should have gone in myself!'' And that was the biggest part of the wound, the part she had been trying to deal with ever since. A fresh wave of tears began to spill down her cheeks silently.

''No.'' Joe shook his head. ''You had a responsibility to your unit. You had to stay with the rest of them. You had to keep them in order and be there to take care of them if something else happened. What you *didn't* do, Gunny, was abandon your post."

She closed her eyes, letting the pain take her, allowing herself to feel every aching bit of it. The grief was almost crushing, but she didn't push it away. Some part of her understood that she *had* to feel it.

"I sent three people to their deaths."

"That's command responsibility, Bethany. That's the hell of it."

She nodded slowly, accepting the truth of it. It still hurt, it would always hurt, but when you started to move up the ranks, that was part of the responsibility you took on.

"It doesn't feel any better," she said, her voice broken.

"No, it doesn't." He sighed, and she opened her eyes in time to see him rub his hand over his face. "It sucks, it stinks, it's hell. But it's the reality of what we do."

He turned his head a little and looked at her. His eyes were red-rimmed, but dry, as if he wanted to weep but couldn't. Then he shook his head and looked away again.

They sat like that for a long time, each of them lost in thoughts—thoughts that were probably very similar. Certainly Bethany didn't feel as if she was miles away from Joe. The silence was somehow comforting, soothing, as if understanding linked them at some deep level.

And gradually, something different began to grow

in her. Something heavy and achy. Something that wanted to affirm life even as they were grieving their losses.

Something she tried to tell herself was utterly out of place.

Until his finger caught her chin and tipped her face up. Until his mouth latched on to hers as if he was desperate to drink the vitality of her.

Something wild and long forgotten rose up in her, answering him with all that she was.

Some wounds couldn't be healed. But they could be salved.

Chapter 6

To Bethany, it seemed as if the hunger between them had a life of its own. It grew and raged so fast it was an almost instantaneous conflagration. The ache in her mushroomed until it filled every cell of her body, until her nerve endings felt as if they could bear no more.

She'd thought she'd left hunger and passion of this degree behind her years ago, but now she realized she had never truly plumbed the depths of desire. It was as if some great tidal wave had crashed over her, carrying her away, tossing her wildly with its power so that she no longer knew what was up or down. Robbing her breath from her until she was gasping.

Joe bore her down until she felt the couch beneath her back. Some part of her was loving the fact that he was carried away, too; some part was wondering at the almost animal intensity of her response.

Then thought vanished completely and she became a barely restrained bundle of needs she couldn't deny. Buttons popped; she didn't know whose. Her breasts spilled free with a suddenness that was magical. The bare skin of his chest and back was inexplicably available to her palms, and she soaked up the wondrous sensation.

Not time for thought. Time only to lift her hips to allow him to ease her pants and undies down, a brief tug as her socks disappeared, a glimpse of his incredibly hard body, and then he was on her and in her so deep that she cried out with sheer amazement.

And just as quickly, they tumbled over the precipice together, with deep groans and a stiffening that drew them taut.

Then, of course, there was reality.

Lying beneath him, listening to his panting and hers, feeling his sweat beneath her palms, she momentarily considered digging a deep hole and hiding herself in it. Never, ever had she behaved this way. Never. It was as if something so raw it was scarcely human had burst out of her in a wild explosion.

Keeping her eyes closed, she considered all the ways she could escape. She was embarrassed. What would he think of her now? Oh, God, she couldn't believe how she had behaved. She wanted to crawl away in embarrassment at the way she had utterly lost control.

Oh, God, he was sliding away now. He would look at her, and she would die. How could she have given way like this?

Keeping her eyes closed, so she wouldn't have to read disgust in his face, wouldn't have to see him looking at her sprawled nakedness, she was startled when she felt his arms slip beneath her.

"Where's the bedroom?" he asked, his voice husky.

Her eyes snapped open as he lifted her from the couch. She felt as if she weighed nothing at all. The feeling, which once would have annoyed her, made her feel oddly comforted.

"Straight down the hall on the right," she answered, her voice muffled.

He carried her as if she were precious, his grip gentle yet strong. Turning sideways, he sidled down the hall so he didn't bang her against anything.

Then, carefully, he set her on her feet beside the bed, keeping one steadying arm around her waist as he pulled back the comforter and top sheet.

Then again she was lifted, as easily as eiderdown, and placed on her bed. The covers fell over her, warming her. Hiding her. Then, to both her relief and amazement, he slid beneath the covers with her and drew her close.

"I'm sorry," he said. "That came out of nowhere. I usually show a lot more...uh, finesse."

That was when she realized she hadn't wanted his finesse. That if he had lingered and coaxed her, something precious would have been lost, some barriers never would have crumbled.

She felt more vulnerable and open than she had ever felt in her life. But somehow, lying curled up in his arms, she felt as if that was just how it should be.

Lifting a finger, she laid it across his lips. "It's okay," she whispered.

He kissed her finger and smiled then, and the expression tugged at her heart. He had such a beautiful smile, such a rare smile. It seemed to warm her all the way to her toes.

His hands started to slide over her again, gentle strokes that, much to her amazement, were stoking the fire yet again. But slowly, more gently this time. As if there were all the time in the world, and every second was going to be savored. The ticking of the clock on her bedside table seemed to keep time with her heart.

Then his hand passed over her right shoulder blade. It paused. She knew what he felt, and closed her eyes tight, even though the room was dark. Ugliness.

He moved suddenly, pulling away, and the light flipped on. Then he was back, turning her gently, his fingers tracing the ragged line of the scar. "What happened?"

"When the bomb hit, I was thrown from my berth. I hit the corner of a footlocker." She didn't want to think about that now, but his fingers stroked the ugly line, as if they could erase it.

"How many stitches?"

"Twenty-eight."

"Whew. Anything broken?"

"I cracked my shoulder blade."

"Aw, Bethany…" Then he did something amazing. Bending, he kissed the ugly scar. "You're a hero. You did all that while you were bleeding, with a broken shoulder. You're incredible."

Although she wasn't quite ready to hear that, it was still as if some crevice in her heart healed just a bit.

"I've got matchies," he said gruffly.

Her eyes opened and she looked at him, suddenly no longer afraid of the light. "On your shoulder?"

He pulled the blanket down and showed her his lower left back, a two-inch scar. "Knife."

"How?" she asked. Close combat was rare.

He chuckled. "Mortars were coming in and I dove behind a tree. Stabbed myself with my own damn k-bar. Fortunately, it missed all the vitals."

Moved, she bent and kissed it. "Thank God," she agreed. Then she saw another scar, this one in his side, long, ugly and jagged. "What's that?"

"Bullet graze." This time his face darkened. "Too dumb to duck. I was going to be the hero. Four of my men got killed that day."

Her heart seemed to stop. Twice; he'd come so close to death twice. But of course. What did she think that purple heart with clusters meant, anyway? "Oh,

Joe,'' she said, and kissed him there, too, dropping kisses along every inch of the mark.

"That one hurt like hell," he admitted. "Well, they both did, like being pounded with a hammer. But that one…sheesh. Broke a rib, and like an idiot I kept charging. I should've called in artillery. Instead, I just kept running until I was in the enemy hole. Then I started shooting. They took four of mine. I got…well, some of theirs. At the time it seemed like the right thing to do."

"I can imagine." Her eyes felt hot, as if tears wanted to start again. "And your shoulder?" There was another jagged scar there, in the hollow of his left shoulder, a fresh mark.

"Shrapnel. That was the day Kara was killed."

Bethany sucked in a sharp breath and looked at him. There was no mistaking the grief in his gaze, but he didn't have the hollow look she'd seen before.

Forgetting herself entirely, she pulled the covers back and looked him over. "What about your shin?"

He paused for a moment, as if pulling back from his memories, then laughed. "That, believe it or not, was trying to get into bed on a dark night. I misjudged the end of the bed and walked right into it."

She laughed and turned to kiss the angry red scar, and felt her breasts drifting over his manhood. Felt the hardness of him. A delightful shiver passed through her.

Slowly she turned her head, looking up at him. "Any other scars?" she asked huskily.

"Oh yeah. Every square inch of me is a scar."

There was probably an element of emotional truth in that for both of them, but a breathless little giggle escaped her, and she took him at his word.

Moving downward, she kissed the arch of his foot and felt him shiver. Encouraged, she dragged her tongue lightly over the sensitive flesh, and felt another shiver pass through him. A kiss for each toe—ten, just light little kisses then a lick for each instep. Another for the inside of each ankle, more lingering, more suggestive, until a heavy sigh escaped him.

With the lightest of touches, she dragged her tongue over his shins and the insides of his calves, feeling the tension in his legs until he said, "God, that tickles!"

Another giggle escaped her, but she didn't stop. Knees—sturdy knees—and a quick dart of her tongue around the inside to that exquisitely sensitive place not quite behind. He jerked, and a little laugh escaped her as a sense of delicious power filled her.

She truly had him at her mercy, and she loved it.

When she started to kiss his thighs, he gripped the sheet with both hands and groaned. *Not yet,* she thought. Not yet.

She bypassed his sex in favor of the hollows of his hips on either side. His muscles quivered beneath her mouth, and another groan escaped him. This time he writhed, as if trying to bring his manhood closer. But she eased away, denying him. Her way, her time.

The heat was filling her, too, but instead of weakening her, it seemed to be making her stronger. More wicked. A shower of kisses across his abdomen promised, but didn't deliver.

"Bethany…"

She almost laughed, but somehow she seemed to have lost the breath for that. Higher, teasing, approaching his small erect nipples, then backing away. He writhed and groaned her name again, and this time she did the most teasing thing of all.

She backed away, and started on his hand.

"You tease!" he groaned, but she could hear how he loved it.

The heavy musk of lovemaking filled the air around them as she sucked each of his fingers slowly, taking her time. His palm was sensitive to the touch of her tongue, and the inside of his wrist. As soon as she released his hand, he was gripping the sheet again, fingers digging into the mattress as if he desperately needed to hang on.

The inside of his elbow drew a low moan from him, and she dallied there awhile before moving up his biceps, then on to his neck.

The cords there proved sensitive, too, drawing shudders from him as she kissed, then nipped him gently. And finally, finally, she closed her mouth over one nipple.

He jerked as if electrified, mumbled something about "you witch," as she nipped him, then her world turned topsy-turvy as he rolled her onto her back.

"Your turn," he said, and his dark eyes promised no quarter.

He straddled her, pinning her arms at her sides, and began to tease and torment her with his lips and tongue, giving kiss for kiss. Heavenly kisses, starting behind her ears, causing wonderful shivers to pass through her. Then down to her neck, grazing along the curve of her collarbone, soft dabs with the tip of his tongue in the hollow of her throat, wispy touches of lips taking her pulse. She arched her head back, baring her neck to him, open to her very core.

Now his teeth followed where his lips and tongue had gone, hard little nips that made her wince and growl and moan. Down over her shoulders, breasts, nipples, belly, until his eager mouth found and then avoided her molten, pulsing sex in a way that drew a shuddering cry from the back of her throat. On down her thighs to the backs of her knees, her calves, ankles and feet, his teeth maddening as they dragged across her soles.

"Take me," she demanded. "Take me *now!*"

"Or?" he asked playfully.

"Or I'll make you think Paris Island was paradise."

"Is that a threat, Gunny?"

"It damn sure is, Staff Sergeant. And a direct order. *Take me now!*"

He smiled. "I always follow orders, ma'am."

And with that he crawled up between her legs and used his lips and tongue to drive her to the precipice of bliss and beyond, until her entire world spun and shimmered and exploded in a thousand colors and lights. Her ragged breaths seemed to propel him onward, milking her climax until she felt as if her entire womb must have wrung itself out on his dancing tongue.

"Your turn, Marine," she said, and grabbed his hair, pulling his body upward until once again he plunged deep within her, then wrapping her legs tight around him, so tight he couldn't thrust, but could only accept the pulsing of her inner muscles. She clenched and released, again and again, her thighs still pinning him, until finally he cried out in frustration, an instant before she felt his own pulses explode through her.

As they lay together, gasping, clinging, their skin silky slick with each breath, she reached up and bit his earlobe hard, then whispered, "You do follow orders, Marine."

And somehow it seemed so unbearably right that they both started to laugh breathlessly.

Chapter 7

Laughing with almost carefree abandon, wrapped in blankets against the night chill, they went to the kitchen for a snack. Bethany had lots of snacks on hand, largely because she hated to cook for one. Soon, bags of chips, mounds of chocolate-covered peanuts and a couple of granola bars sat on the table next to a loaf of rye bread and cold cuts, along with other sandwich fixings.

Joe dug in as if he were starved, building a sandwich of epic proportions. Bethany settled for a piece of chocolate.

"You know," he said, "we've got a problem."

Her heart nearly stopped. He was going to tell her this had been a big mistake, and she didn't know if she could bear to hear that now. Not now. Not when she felt as if she couldn't bear to let him go. "What's that?" she finally asked, feeling as if she had to squeeze the words out.

"It's tough for two marines to be married. Different duty stations, long separations…."

"What?" She couldn't believe what he'd just said. "What?" she repeated, sure she had imagined it.

He looked up from his massive sandwich and smiled almost wryly at her. "Maybe I'm jumping the gun."

"Which gun?" She seemed to be growing more confused by the minute.

"The marriage gun."

Marriage. She hadn't imagined it. He'd actually spoken the word. "Umm…you hardly know me."

"True. But I know you enough to know what I feel." His sandwich appeared to lose his interest, and he shoved it aside. "Okay, this is fast. I was never a believer in love at first sight. Until now."

"Love?" At some level she knew she was sounding like a stupid parrot, but she couldn't help it. A deep self-protective urge was refusing to accept that he could mean what he was saying.

"I know it's fast," he said. "But what the hell. I've always leaped in where angels fear to tread. So how about this—I know I'm madly in love with you. But I'll wait six months or a year, until you can figure out if you feel the same. Assuming, of course, that we get to see each other during that six months or a year, which is the problem I'm talking about.''

Her heart was fluttering like a frightened bird as she stared at him, filling her eyes with him, filling her heart with him. But even as she wanted to leap along with him, she knew he was right.

"It's a problem," she agreed.

"Hell yeah." He picked up his sandwich and took a bite. She waited while he chewed and swallowed, almost afraid to start thinking of solutions when the moment seemed so tenuous. Reality said he'd go back to his unit, he'd forget about her and that would be that. Her heart wanted to draw a whole different picture.

He put his sandwich back on its plate and pushed it aside again. "I'm not hungry. I'm too nervous. I'm having a fight-or-flight response right now, and everything is telling me to fight for you, Bethany. Fight as hard as I have to."

"You, uh, don't have to fight," she admitted. "It's just that…we have a problem."

"Yeah. A big one. I mean…" He looked at her, and surprise dawned on his face, as if he'd just understood her. "You love me, too?"

Tension began to ease out of her, and she knew she was going to take another one of her leaps, but this time she was going to risk everything in order to get what she most wanted in the world. "I love you, Joe."

He was up and around the table in an instant, kneeling by her chair and drawing her into his embrace until they were as tightly knit as one. "God, I love you," he said. "I love you. We can work all the other stuff out. We can learn each other and make it together if we just have that. If we're willing to try."

She sighed, happiness beginning to run through her veins, and pressed her cheek to the top of his head. "I love you," she said again, and this time saying it filled her heart with joy. Profound joy.

He moved, looking up at her, and she looked at him.

"So, Mathison, we have a problem," he said. "How do you want to deal with it?"

"The way other couples in our shoes deal with it. We deal with it. We live with it. And we apply for joint assignments until we get one."

He nodded. "I'm willing. It won't be easy but... Bethany, what about kids?"

Kids. Children. Babies. It had been so long since she'd allowed herself to think about that that she'd begun to envision herself as childless for life. A shiver of pure pleasure ran through her. Only in that instant did she realize just how much she wanted children.

"I'd like to have kids," she admitted.

"Me, too. But we can't both be globe-trotting if we have children. Listen, I'll apply for a position as an instructor. Maybe I can get stateside and stay stateside."

"I...could resign." Her heart fluttered again. What a choice to have to make.

He shook his head. "No. Not unless you really want

to. This is your career, too, Gunny. I'm not about to forget that.''

He tipped his head forward, resting it on her shoulder, and sighed. "I'm sick unto death of making war."

"We don't have to decide about that immediately," she said, stroking his hair and kissing his temple. "There's no rush to start a family. We can see how things go, first. Maybe something will pan out. All I know, Joe, is I don't think I can live without you."

He lifted his head and kissed her, then he started laughing exuberantly. "I love you, Bethany. I love you, love you, love you...."

Sometimes the demons still haunted them, but they were married in December. Snow fell like magic dust as they exited the church arm in arm beneath a glistening arch of swords. Both of them had chosen to wear their dress blues for the occasion, a true marine marriage.

The gods of war had chosen to smile on them, for a little while at least. Joe's unit had been pulled out of the Middle East, and after a month's leave, they would both begin their new assignments, at Headquarters Marine Corps in Washington, D.C.

Somehow they knew they would handle whatever came their way, because they believed in each other.

And they had both found their dream marines.

UNDERCOVER OPERATIONS
Merline Lovelace

* * *

This story is dedicated to the men and women who serve
their county—in any and all capacities.

Dear Reader,

To paraphrase an old saying, you can take the man out of the military, but you can't take the military out of the man. Or woman!

After spending the first twenty years of my life as an air force brat and the next twenty-three as an air force officer, I confess the military is in my blood. So you understand why I think warriors make such great heroes and heroines. There's that sense of responsibility to country and comrades, that determination to complete a mission, that touch of reckless daring so necessary to win against all odds.

The events of 9/11 have demonstrated that these qualities reach across economic, social and national boundaries. I salute the heroes, both in and out of uniform, who risked all to save others. And to those now fighting to make the world safer, fly high, stay true and come home safe!

All my best,

Chapter 1

Captain Danielle Flynn had walked into some seedy joints during her eight years in the Air Force. Hitting the bars came with the job in her line of work. But on a scale of one to ten, she'd rank this dark, smoke-filled dive set smack in the middle of Oklahoma's panhandle as a minus four.

The place reeked of spilled beer and old grease. Yellowed posters of half-naked babes touting everything from booze to tractors vied for space with the rust spots decorating the corrugated tin walls. A thin layer of red dust coated every horizontal surface. The handful of patrons wore boots, jeans, sweat-stained ball caps and expressions that ranged from mild curiosity to avid male interest as they surveyed Dani.

Except for one. He sat slouched at a table in the corner, nursing a beer. Eyes narrowed against the smoke, he slanted her a sideways glance, let his gaze roam lazily from her neck to her knees, and went back to his beer.

Dani's inspection was considerably more thorough, and what she saw didn't impress her. Jack Buchanan certainly fit the mental image she'd constructed after reading the information she'd gathered about him. If the bristles shadowing his cheeks and chin were any indication, he hadn't seen the sharp edge of a razor in days. Dark circles ringed the armpits of his blue denim work shirt, and his leather boots wore a collection of scuffs and scars.

Hard to believe this down-at-the-heels crop duster once flew supersonic F-117 Stealth fighters. Or that Dani's father, Colonel Dan Flynn, had risked his life to fly through a hail of enemy fire to pluck this loser from the wreckage of his burning aircraft.

Well, it was time for Buchanan to return the favor.

Threading her way through the tables, Dani slid her hand into her shoulder bag, pulled out a flat case and popped open the top. The Medal of Honor lay nested in its bed of dark velvet. The shiny gold disk embossed with the head of Lady Liberty hung suspended from its blue satin ribbon. The nation's highest award for valor in the face of the enemy, it was given only to the bravest of the brave.

Ignoring a sharp little stab of pain, she dropped the case on Buchanan's table. It landed with a soft thud, barely audible over the chink of glasses and the tinny wail of the radio.

"I'm Danielle Flynn. Captain Danielle Flynn. United States Air Force. That medal belonged to my father."

Buchanan tilted his chair back on its rear legs and pushed up the brim of his ball cap, revealing a thatch of blue-black hair badly in need of a trim. Whiskey-colored eyes surveyed her through the thick screen of his lashes. He made a more detailed inventory this time, taking in her windblown hair, her wilted white blouse, her jeans. His gaze lingered on the Air Force Academy ring on her right hand before lifting to her face.

"You don't favor the old man much."

"So I've been told."

It could have been a compliment or an insult. Dan Flynn had been a big, bluff Irishman, as handsome as sin. Dani had inherited his name, his height and his dark auburn hair, if not his laughing blue eyes and easygoing charm.

Without waiting for an invitation, she claimed the chair opposite Buchanan's. Her long legs tangled with his under the table. He didn't move, didn't alter his sprawl so much as an inch to accommodate her.

"My father was awarded that medal for saving your life, Buchanan. Yours and six others. It's payback time."

One dark brow arched. "That right?"

"That's right."

He toyed with his beer bottle, tilting it in a circle. His fingers were long, blunt. Scars traced fine white lines on the back of his hand.

"Last I heard," he said after a moment, "Dan Flynn was buried in Arlington with full military honors. You want to tell me how I'm supposed to settle accounts with him?"

The pain came again, a quick, sharp hurt Dani suspected would take a long time to dull. Three years after his death, she still missed the man who'd been her friend and mentor as well as her father. She couldn't remember her mother, who'd died in a car crash when Dani was just a few months old. She and her father had been so close, so happy. Even happier when the colonel had married widowed Claire Stevens. For the first time, six-year-old Dani had had a real family. Now…

Now what was left of that family was being ripped apart. Dragging in a deep breath, she spelled out the urgent matter that had brought her from Bolling Air Force Base, just outside Washington D.C., to this corner of the Oklahoma Panhandle.

"You can settle your account with my father by flying his daughter—my stepsister—out of Mexico."

She had to force the words. Each one stabbed into her like a stiletto.

"Patricia's a hydroelectric engineer," she explained tersely. "She flew down to Chihuahua on business three weeks ago, then took a few days' vacation at a mountaintop resort in Copper Canyon. She drove off the hotel grounds one afternoon and didn't return. Her company received a call two days later, demanding five million dollars for her safe return.''

Buchanan's eyes narrowed. The five million had snagged his interest, Dani saw cynically. Somehow, she'd suspected it would.

''I take it her company didn't cough up the ransom.''

''No, it didn't. In an attempt to stop the apparently lucrative business of snatching foreign executives, the Mexican government refuses to negotiate with or allow payment of any kind to the kidnappers. Even if they did, Patricia's company doesn't have that kind of money.''

''Bull!'' Those gold-flecked brown eyes locked with hers. ''Any corporation sending executives abroad these days takes out insurance to cover situations like this.''

''Their policy contains a one million dollar cap. And a clause requiring the host nation's cooperation in all release negotiations, which lets the company completely off the hook.''

His lip curled in disgust. ''They should fire the fool who got suckered in with that policy.''

''They have, but that doesn't help in this particular situation. So I'm using my own assets. I'm offering you a hundred thousand, Buchanan. It's every cent I could pull together.''

She'd expected him to jump at the offer, was surprised when he didn't. She knew darn well he desperately needed cash. He'd walked away from his Air Force career in a last-ditch attempt to save a marriage that went bust anyway. Had walked away from the subsequent divorce with only the clothes on his back. If the information she'd gathered was correct, his sole possessions these days consisted of a dilapidated pickup and the Stearman biplane he'd patched together with chewing gum and baling wire.

"You could buy a new plane with that hundred thousand, Buchanan. An aircraft constructed specifically for agricultural aviation, with computer controlled aerial dispersal systems. Assuming, of course, you want to spend the rest of your life dusting crops."

She hadn't intended the remark quite the way it came out. She understood farm aviation performed a vital and necessary function. Her Air Force bias had just slipped in.

Buchanan didn't rise to the bait, however. Nor did he defend his rapid descent from hotshot fighter pilot to fertilizer spreader.

"A hundred thousand's a good chunk of change," he agreed. "What, specifically, would I have to do to earn it?"

"Specifically, you would have to fly me down to Copper Canyon, hang loose until I locate my sister, and fly us both out."

"Seems to me the United States government would be pulling out all the stops to rescue the daughter of a Medal of Honor winner," he said slowly. "Not to mention the Mexican authorities."

Frustration rose, so thick and bitter Dani could almost taste it. After three weeks of stomach-clenching tension, three weeks of working with the State Department, the CIA, the Mexican authorities and a host of hostage negotiators, three weeks of increasingly desperate measures, she'd run out of alternatives. And out of patience.

"The U.S. has exercised every diplomatic option in the book. The Mexican government mounted several massive search efforts. Five days ago, a joint U.S.-Mexican commando force stormed what they thought was the kidnappers' hideout, only to discover they'd departed the scene less than an hour before. The bastards have a source, apparently. A high-level source. One who tips them off to the government's every move."

She leaned forward, her elbows digging into the stained tabletop.

"This time," she vowed fiercely, "there'll be no leak. No warning. No advance notice of any kind. I want to fly down tomorrow, if you can get your plane ready." Her gaze drilled into his. "I'll pay you half up front. Half when we land back in the States. With Patricia."

Still he didn't grab at the offer. Exercising every ounce of self-control she possessed, Dani waited him out.

"Why me?" he asked when her nerves had twisted tight. "Why not a professional, a soldier of fortune with a small private army to back him up?"

"Because you owe my father. Big time. And because, according to him at least, you used to be one hell of a pilot. It'll take all your skill and then some to put us down in those mountains and fly us out again. More to the point, the resort's in a remote area. A private army, no matter how small, can't go in without tipping off the kidnappers again. So it'll be just you and me, Buchanan. A couple of newlyweds, joyriding around Mexico on their honeymoon."

"Newlyweds?"

Actually, Dani had considered and discarded a number of covers. The area they were going into was a mecca for archeologists, paleontologists and bird watchers, not to mention American developers eager to exploit its stunning natural beauty. She'd decided against assuming any of those occupations, however. Past experience had taught her the most effective covers were the simplest.

A point she kept firmly in mind when Buchanan's mouth curved. It wasn't a pleasant smile, or a particularly flattering one. Yet something crackled in the air between them, and the tension that had tied Dani in knots for so long now took an unexpected twist.

"So what's the answer?" she snapped, annoyed she could feel anything even remotely resembling a sexual response to this man. "Yes or no?"

"No."

The laconic reply tightened her jaws. She waited for him to elaborate, felt a rush of fury when he merely fiddled with his beer.

"That's it?" she demanded. "No sorry 'bout that? No list of reasons why you can't aid the daughter of a man who risked his life to save yours?"

"That's it."

"Dad wasn't wrong about people very often," she said, scorn dripping from every syllable. "Obviously, he missed the mark with you."

She reached for the medal and pushed away from the table. Buchanan's hand whipped out. The hold on her wrist held her suspended half in and half out of her chair. He leaned forward until his face was mere inches from her own.

"I'll bring your sister out, green-eyes. I owe the old man that. But as much as I appreciate the offer to honeymoon with you, I fly solo."

"Not on this mission, Buchanan."

"I do it my way or not at all."

Her jaw locked. Any of the personnel she worked with would have recognized the expression that settled over her face, and instantly found important work that needed doing in another part of the headquarters.

"Not on this mission," she repeated, yanking free of his hold. "We do it my way or you don't get paid."

"Then I guess I don't get paid."

His chair legs scraped the floor. Digging some crumpled bills out of his jeans, he tossed them on the table and tipped two fingers to his hat brim.

"See you around, Flynn."

He sauntered past her, moving with a cocky, confident stride. And, Dani was forced to admit, with a lazy grace that was all his own.

"Yes," she murmured, gripping her father's medal to her chest. "You'll definitely see me around."

She was at the patch of flattened weeds that passed for the local airstrip when the sun broke over the horizon the next morning.

She'd dressed for traveling, in sturdy hiking boots, jeans and a short-sleeved, red T-shirt. A Washington Redskins ball cap confined her shoulder length auburn hair back in a ponytail. Her leather carryall contained a change of clothing, a few toiletries and a nylon windbreaker…along with a few essential tools of her trade.

Leaning against the fender of her rental car, she sipped the coffee she'd picked up at the only gas station in town. The streaks of red and gold shooting across the sky smoothed some of the jagged edges of the tension that had gripped her for weeks now. The Panhandle had a wild beauty all its own, she decided. Acre after acre of wheat fields turning amber with the dawn. The black, low-lying mesas to the north. The Coldwater River cutting a silver curve to the south.

Too bad the current resident of this particular patch of Oklahoma hadn't contributed much to its natural beauty. Shaking her head, Dani scanned the weedy airstrip. A faded windsock hung limply atop a rusted pole. A dilapidated shed marked with a hazard sign was loaded, she guessed, with barrels of insecticide.

The Quonset hut that served as a hangar was definitely World War II vintage.

So was the plane tucked inside.

Dani had done her research. She was well aware that the Stearman N3N biplane inside the hangar had been built in 1940 and performed yeoman service as a trainer for navy pilots. Nicknamed the Canary for its bright yellow paint scheme, this plane and hundreds like her had been sold as excess after the war. Many had then embarked on long second careers as crop dusters.

She was also aware that the Stearman was an extremely stable platform, easy to maneuver, capable of taking off and landing on dirt roads or grassy pastures. Still, the idea of skimming the tops of the rugged Sierra Madres in the back seat of an open cockpit, kept aloft on rickety canvas wings separated by wooden struts, had her sucking down another deep gulp of caffeine.

She'd reached the dregs when Buchanan finally drove up. She could see him coming for a good half mile. His pickup raised a long rooster tail of red dust. Dumping the cold sludge, she crumpled the cup, tossed it inside the rental car and folded her arms.

When he climbed out of the pickup, the canvas flight bag he hauled out of the truck gave her a fierce satisfaction. She'd had her doubts about Buchanan during the long hours of the night, but it was obvious he'd come prepared to fly. Aviation maps stuck out of the sides of the bag, and he'd thrust a brown leather bomber jacket through its handles.

He wouldn't need the jacket to conduct aerial spraying in this heat. He was on his way to the high, cool elevations of the Sierra Madres.

"Morning, Buchanan."

He stopped in front of her. In the dusty dawn, he looked even more disreputable than he had in the bar. And considerably more annoyed. Under the thick black bristles, his jaw had locked tight.

"Maybe you didn't hear me last night. I fly solo."

"I heard you."

His glance shot to the leather carryall at her feet, then back to her face.

"We're wasting time here," she said, preempting the argument she saw forming. "Patricia's mom died just a year after my dad. Trish is all the family I have left. You're not flying down to Mexico without me."

"Oh yeah?" He rocked back on his heels. "Just out of curiosity, how do you plan to stop me?"

"Well, I could call a friend of mine at Altus Air Force Base, just south of here, and have him run an intercept. Or I could call another friend at the FAA and have her pull your certification. Or," she added calmly, "I could take you down right now and have done with this cat and mouse game we're playing."

Damn! She was serious. For a moment Jack actually considered accepting her challenge. The mood he was in this morning, he wouldn't mind a tussle in the dirt. Particularly with Danielle Flynn. The woman had stirred more than his interest when she'd strolled into MacIver's place last night.

This morning, she all but tied him in knots.

Those snug jeans wrapped around her hips and rear like a thin coat of paint. Her cotton T-shirt hugged her slender curves in a way that left little to the imagination, and Jack possessed a *very* vivid imagination when it came to leggy redheads. Deliberately, he squelched the image of Flynn flat on her back in the grass, her legs tangled with his, her green eyes flashing fire.

So she had the neatest, trimmest butt this side of the Red River? So the mere thought of rolling around in the grass with her got him hard? She was Dan Flynn's daughter.

Even without the old man looking over his shoulder, Jack wouldn't move on the woman. His brief contact with Captain Flynn was making it painfully apparent that she'd inherited more from the colonel than her dark copper hair. Jack wasn't about to get up close and personal with another stubborn, hardheaded female. The last one had wrung him inside out before she decamped with a high school band instructor.

A band instructor, for God's sake!

Shaking his head in disgust, Jack invited Danielle Flynn to attempt whatever actions she considered necessary or appropriate. He was going to Mexico. In his plane. Without her.

He was halfway across the grass strip when the ear-splitting report of a pistol stopped him in his tracks.

Directly ahead of him, the windsock whipped around wildly on its pole.

That got his attention, Dani thought in smug satisfaction. Thumbing the safety on the Beretta, she strolled up to join him. Buchanan's eyes were glacial when he turned to face her.

"Was that little demonstration supposed to impress me?"

"No. It was supposed to show you that I can take care of myself."

He studied the Beretta for a long moment. It was a new model, a 9000S, with a fiberglass reinforced techno-polymer frame and two special steel rail inserts for the slide. Compact, lightweight and easy to field-strip, with a magazine that packed twelve lethal 9 mm rounds or ten Smith & Wesson .40 calibers.

Evidently Buchanan knew his way around weapons enough to appreciate this wasn't an ordinary side arm. His face registered suspicion and a grudging respect.

"What do you do in the Air Force, anyway?"

"I'm an undercover agent with the Office of Special Investigations. I'm pulling a headquarters tour at Bolling Air Force Base outside D.C. right now, but I've spent most of the past eight years in the field."

His eyes narrowed. "Any particular reason why you neglected to mention that particular bit of information before now?"

"As a matter of fact, there is. I'm not going into Mexico in my official capacity. This isn't an Air Force operation. The politics of the situation won't allow it.

This is just me, Buchanan. And you. Now I suggest we load up and get this show on the road."

With a self-assurance that said the matter was settled, Dani slipped the Beretta into the holster strapped to her ankle and plowed through the weeds to the Quonset hut. She didn't realize she was holding her breath until she heard a muttered curse and the thud of boots behind her.

She let out a tiny sigh of relief. She would have gone into Mexico alone, if necessary. She'd planned to do just that if she couldn't convince Buchanan to honor his debt to her father. She was congratulating herself on maneuvering him into doing exactly what she'd wanted him to when his deep drawl sounded just behind her ear.

"It'll be tough, but I guess I can force myself to share a bed with you for a few nights in a mountaintop resort."

"Don't get any ideas. The honeymoon bit is strictly for cover."

She tossed her carryall into the back seat of the Stearman and turned, only to find herself caught between the canvas-covered fuselage and a large, immovable male.

"Maybe we need another demonstration," he suggested with a nasty glint in his eye. "Just to lay out the rest of the ground rules."

"Buchanan…"

She could have taken him down. She'd been taught

every defensive and counterdefensive move in the book. But something held her still.

Maybe it was the faint, tantalizing tang of coffee on his breath. Or the tingle just under her skin when his bristly cheek scraped hers. Or the sudden, feminine curiosity that leaped to life all up and down her spine. Whatever it was, it kept Dani motionless as he planted his palms on the fuselage and bent his head.

The moment his lips claimed hers, she realized her mistake. Jack Buchanan subscribed to the fighter pilot school of kissing. He didn't make a slow pass over the target. Didn't perform a careful aerial assessment before engaging the enemy. He swooped in, guns blazing, delivered a full load of armaments and left his designated target with her head spinning and her knees ridiculously weak.

Lord, the man could kiss! Dani fought the urge to rise up on tiptoe, hook her arms around his neck, return fire. Instead, she kept her shoulders against the canvas and her hands fisted at her side. When he raised his head, it took everything she had to infuse her voice with cool disdain as she threw his words back at him.

"Was that supposed to impress me?"

A grin flashed across his face, transforming the rugged planes and angles into something dangerously close to handsomeness.

"No, but it sure goes a long way to making up for the buzzing in my ears from your pistol shot."

Dani refused to admit that the buzzing in *her* ears had nothing to do with the shot. She wouldn't give

Buchanan the satisfaction. Besides, she wasn't about to let this man distract her. Not with her sister's life hanging in the balance.

Still, she couldn't decide whether she was more relieved or disappointed when Buchanan tossed his flight bag into the front seat and kicked aside the wooden chocks.

"Let's roll this baby out and get her fueled, green-eyes. This looks to be one helluva flight."

Chapter 2

Dani had never flown in an open cockpit plane before. Six hours into the flight, she was pretty confident she never wanted to repeat the experience.

Granted, skimming along at fifteen hundred feet was incredibly exhilarating, with the air rushing, silky soft, in her face and scattered cumulus clouds puffing up like mounds of whipped cream in the ocean of blue all around her. The Stearman's 220-horsepower engine purred like a kitten, so the noise wasn't bad. And flying at little more than eighty miles an hour, Dani could swipe the occasional oil spray from her goggles, lean into her shoulder harness and see the patchwork of farms, towns and cities below in precise detail.

Unfortunately, the Stearman's slow speed, ability to

fly well below radar and capacity to land on any semi-level surface—all of which made it the perfect aircraft for this mission—also made for a *long* flight. Once they were out of the Oklahoma Panhandle, Texas rolled by beneath the double wings for hour after hour. The flat, dusty plains around Amarillo. Lubbock's cotton fields. Midland-Odessa's Permian oil basin, with black metal derricks bobbing up and down like giant grasshoppers as far as the eye could see.

At the first refueling stop, Dani unhooked her harness, climbed out and made a dash for the bathroom to get rid of her coffee. The messages scrawled above the urinal raised her brows. The sink was so filthy she figured her own germs were safer than any she might pick up from touching the faucet. She returned outside and waited patiently while the airstrip manager drooled over the Stearman.

At the second stop, there were no bathroom facilities of any kind, crude or otherwise. Nor did an airstrip attendant make an appearance. A cell phone call to the number painted on the fuel tank gave the location of the key and permission to pump away. Buchanan left two bills folded under a rock to pay for the gas.

Thankfully, their third stop was a city airport just outside Fort Stockton, with a real tower and a restaurant. Dani climbed out of the Stearman on rubbery legs as a knot of people gathered to admire the biplane.

''She's decked out in navy colors,'' an old-timer said with a catch in his throat. ''Just like the trainer I soloed in at Pensacola in '43.''

"Glad to see you didn't gut the old girl's front cockpit and fit her with a fertilizer hopper," another commented. "From the nozzles you've installed under her wings, I'd guess you disperse chemicals *and* seed?"

"Not just seed. I also spray dry material to speed up snowmelt on golf courses and small grainfields," Buchanan explained. "Had a contract last year to clean up an oil spill along the Lower Colorado."

"No kidding? That was you? You did a damned good job, from what I heard. Used MT-64 dry microbial pellets, didn't you?"

Left completely behind by the abrupt transition into the technicalese of aerial applications, Dani heeded her stomach's rumblings and made for the restaurant. She was halfway through a heaping platter of enchiladas and french fries, both swimming in scorch-your-eyeballs Texas chili, when Buchanan finally joined her.

"That looks good," he told the waitress. "I'll have the same. And iced tea."

Grimacing, Dani watched him dump six packets of sugar into the quart-size jug of tea that was delivered a few moments later. She refrained from commenting on his sweet tooth, but did remark that she hadn't realized agricultural aviation had taken on such a variety of dimensions.

Buchanan slanted her a cynical glance. "I'm not surprised. I formed the impression last night that you don't hold the profession of crop dusting in high esteem.''

''Not as high as flying fighters for the United States Air Force,'' she admitted. She played with her fork, eyeing him curiously. ''Do you miss it?''

''The Air Force or flying fighters?''

''Either. Both.''

''Not particularly.''

She digested that while he tipped his head back and took a long swallow of his tea. Despite her determination to remain focused on the mission and not the man, Dani couldn't help noticing the weathered skin, the square jaw, the strong column of his throat. He wouldn't be bad if he scraped off those bristles and trimmed his hair, she admitted silently. Not bad at all.

Sternly, she banished the thought and probed deeper. ''My father said you were one of the best pilots in his squadron.''

''Yeah, well, Dan Flynn knew how to wring every last ounce of performance out of his men and their aircraft.''

''Did you ever consider going back into the military? You're what? Thirty-two?''

Actually, he would turn thirty-three in a few weeks, but Dani saw no need to let him know she'd put together a file on him.

''Given the million or so the Air Force spent training you,'' she commented, ''they might entertain a waiver.''

''They might, if I was interested in one.''

His heaping platter arrived. Several forkfuls disappeared down his throat. She knew she should let him enjoy his meal in peace, but the career officer in her wouldn't let go.

"So why aren't you interested?"

His shoulders lifted in a careless shrug. "What I'm doing suits me fine."

"But…"

"There are no buts, Flynn. Not in my mind. I'm my own boss. I spend as many hours in the air as I can cram in. I take the contracts I want and turn down those I don't."

"You can't prefer tooling around in a World War II vintage plane to flying jets!"

"You think so?" Annoyance put an edge to his voice. "I like flying low and slow. I like throwing my plane into a loop or a hammerhead stall whenever the mood strikes me. I like landing on runways so short I have to plow into someone's backyard to stop. There's nothing that compares to the feel of that old rag-wing's stick in my hand. Nothing."

Except maybe the feel of Danielle Flynn's mouth under his. The thought jumped uninvited into Jack's head and wouldn't jump out.

Damn! He couldn't remember when a woman had gotten to him like this. Even his ex hadn't delivered this kind of quick, hard punch to the gut. Their courtship had been rocky, their marriage even rockier.

And that, Jack reminded himself grimly, was a lesson he wouldn't soon forget. Couldn't afford to forget.

Now that he'd arranged his life exactly the way he wanted it, he wasn't about to let some intense, intent career-type take it apart again. Scowling, he dug into his enchiladas.

"Eat up," he ordered curtly. "We've still got a good five hours of flying time before we reach this mountaintop resort of yours."

It took Dani exactly one flip of the biplane to understand that Buchanan was not happy with her for challenging his present career choice. Two to bring her lunch back into her throat.

She closed her eyes to the crazily tilting horizon, gritted her teeth as the harness straps gouged her shoulders, and shouted into the intercom. "All right! You've proved your point. You like throwing your plane into loop-de-loops."

"Those were barrel rolls."

"Whatever," she growled. "Unless you want recycled french fries and chili all over your damned plane, I suggest you fly straight, Buchanan."

The grin he shot her over his shoulder was positively evil.

Dani still hadn't quite forgiven him when they touched down on a dirt airstrip high in the Sierra Madres some five hours later. Unsteadily, she clambered out. Her bottom was totally anesthetized from sitting so long, and she was sure the harness straps had carved permanent creases in her shoulders.

While Buchanan made arrangements to service the

plane with the attendant who ambled down from the hotel perched high on an escarpment above them, Dani rolled her neck to relieve the kinks and did a slow 360. The sun was slipping behind the mountains to the west, but the beams shooting through the towering peaks illuminated a stunning landscape.

This was Copper Canyon. Barranca del Cobre. Not really a single gorge, but a network of canyons slicing through the Sierra Madres. An area four times larger than Arizona's Grand Canyon, with dizzying changes in elevation and flora that ranged from cactus and sagebrush to cedar and pine. Filled with cascading waterfalls. Staggering cliffs. Verdant valleys. Sprinkled with prehistoric cliff dwellings, abandoned gold and silver mines, and isolated villages inhabited by the shy, dignified Tarahumara people.

And marked by steep, almost inaccessible arroyos. Hundreds of them. Maybe thousands. Any one of which could hide a ragtag band of kidnappers.

Grimly, Dani dug into her carryall for the plain gold wedding band she'd purchased to complete the cover, and slipped it onto her ring finger. She glanced up to catch Buchanan's ironic gaze, shrugged, and led the way up the steep incline to the resort.

The main lodge of the Posada Barrancas clung to the side of the cliff like an eagle's aerie. Two dozen or so individual casitas were scattered along the canyon rim on either side of the lodge. Inside the lobby, timbers held aloft a soaring ceiling, and the sharp tang of pine resin drifted through two-story sliding windows left open to the spectacular vista.

"I'm Danielle Flynn," she told the receptionist. "I called in a reservation."

"*Sí, señora*. We have the reservation for you and the *señor*." A warm smile lit her face. "May I congratulate you both? We at Posada Barrancas are honored you chose to spend your honeymoon with us."

"Thank you."

"We've upgraded you, compliments of the house. Here are the keys to our best casita. And this key is for your Jeep. You must be careful when exploring the canyon, though. The roads are very narrow and steep."

Dani accepted the keys, her throat tight. Patricia had been driving one of the hotel's green-and-white-striped vehicles the afternoon she was kidnapped. It took some effort to toss off a casual query.

"A woman I know stayed here a few weeks ago. Patricia Stevens? Perhaps you remember her?"

At the mention of her stepsister's name, the friendly smile fell right off the receptionist's face.

"*Sí*. I remember." Chewing on her lower lip, the girl glanced around the lobby. "Señorita Stevens was here. She...she left."

That's all the girl would say. Or could say, probably. The hotel had no doubt put a tight lid on word of the kidnapping to avoid adverse publicity. Dani could only hope she had better luck in the villages nestled in the valleys below.

Neither she nor Buchanan spoke during the short ride via golf cart to their casita. But once the bellhop had showed them the amenities and left with a hefty tip, Buchanan gave a low, appreciative whistle.

"Now *this* is the way to fly."

Dani had to agree. The furniture was all natural wood—smooth, polished pine; white oak; native birch peeling bark in long, curling strips. Fabric woven in colorful Mexican designs covered the chair and sofa cushions. Aztec and Mayan statuary decorated the walls, interspersed with exquisitely woven basketry.

But dominating all was the view. It was, quite simply, magnificent. Tall, sliding glass panels formed one entire wall and framed a panorama of rugged mountains just turning purple. The doors opened to a railed balcony that hung suspended over a sheer, thousand-foot drop.

The bedroom proved even more stunning. A king-size bed sat on a raised platform surrounded on three sides by glass. Sleeping on that platform would be like floating on air, Dani thought, or in an eagle's nest. Not for the fainthearted. Or the acrophobic.

And not for her. Her plans for the next few nights didn't include sleeping.

"You can have the bedroom," she told Buchanan. "I'll take the sofa in the sitting room."

"Fine with me."

He could have offered at least a token protest, she thought wryly. He made up for it—somewhat—by giving her first dibs on the shower. She jumped at the chance to wash away twelve hours of open cockpit flying, along with the serious aches in her lower regions.

"Thanks. I won't be long. *Too* long," she amended with a huff as she got her first glimpse of the gleaming spa just off the bedroom.

"Do you want me to order something from room service while you're in the bathroom?"

She dragged her rapt gaze from the circular stall with its floor-to-ceiling, all-round jets. "What?"

"Want me to order from room service?" he repeated. "I figure we should stay in. Since we *are* newlyweds..."

He let the sentence trail off provocatively, but Dani was too enthralled by the gleaming gadgets in the bathroom to do more than flap a hand.

"Okay. Sure. Whatever you want. Just go away, Buchanan. Please, go away."

He gave a small snort. "This honeymoon is starting to remind me a lot of my first."

Startled, Dani swung around and stared at his back as he strolled out. The former Mrs. Buchanan must have lacked a few necessary hormones, she thought. Or brain cells. Had the woman really turned Jack Buchanan away? On their honeymoon? The mere thought of tumbling onto that decadent bed with the man raised goose bumps all over Dani's skin. If he made love with anything close to the same skill he kissed with...

Whoa! She'd better derail that train of thought before it left the station. She wasn't here to test the mattress on that sybaritic bed. Or to indulge in erotic bedroom exercises with a scruffy crop duster. She was here to find her sister. Only to find her sister.

Closing the bathroom door, Dani stripped down, padded into the shower stall and turned the water jets to full blast.

Jack stood at the tall windows, trying his damnedest to ignore the muted buzz of the shower. Trying even harder not to picture in precise detail the wet, naked body of the woman caught in the crossfire of those jets.

He should be exhausted. Should be feeling those twelve hours at the stick, with only short breaks for refueling. Instead, the urge to strip off and join Danielle Flynn in that glass cubicle kept him wound tighter than the Stearman's engine coil.

She bothered him. Big time. Not just physically, although thinking about the way her mouth had tasted under his was enough to put a hitch in his stride. What really bugged him, though, was that he couldn't figure her out.

Last night, he'd pegged her as an uptight, ring-knocking academy grad. This morning, she'd damned near shot off his ear before calmly announcing that she was breaking all the rules by mounting her own rescue operation. Jack was pretty sure the OSI wasn't going to appreciate one of its agents going into a potentially dangerous situation alone, without authority or backup.

She had guts. He'd give her that. Just like her old man.

He emerged from his turn in the shower some time later to find her examining the contents of domed serving dishes laid out on a wheeled serving cart. He'd ordered fish for both of them, a local trout, crusted and served with a red salsa, black beans and chorizo. If the dishes tasted half as good as those heavenly scents wafting across the room promised, he'd made an excellent choice.

"I didn't think I could eat again after this afternoon's aerobics," she commented, her nose twitching appreciatively as she raised another dome.

"Barrel rolls are fun, aren't they? Wait until you experience your first hammerhead."

"Which I hope happens, oh, maybe never. I've decided—"

She broke off, her eyes widening as she turned and caught her first glimpse of him showered, shaved and minus three days' growth. Her reaction drew a rueful grin from Jack.

"I caught a few too many bugs on the way down," he admitted, dragging his hand across his chin. "The whiskers had to go."

Oh, man!

Dani sucked in a breath, sincerely wishing he'd left both the whiskers and the bugs in place. She'd suspected Buchanan might pack quite a punch under his bristles, but she'd seriously underestimated its potency. With his midnight hair slicked back and those golden eyes glinting through those sinfully thick black lashes, he could give the Baldwin brothers a real run for their money.

Shaking herself out of her temporary trance, Dani passed him a plate. They ate at the table set beside the soaring windows. Outside, dusk deepened to night. A few pinpricks of light pierced the darkness. Not many. Aside from a few scattered villages, the canyon was sparsely populated. Which could make tonight's task relatively easy or incredibly difficult.

"So what's the plan?" Buchanan asked as he speared into his trout. "What do we do now?"

"Right now, we don't do anything."

We being the operative word in the equation. Dani had plans for the rest of the night, but they didn't include her dinner companion.

At his questioning look, she shrugged and forked into her fish. "Tomorrow morning we'll drive down to the village and nose around. The kidnappers must have a local base. Someone's supplying them with both information and food. I intend to find out who that someone is."

She intended to do more than that, but she was a professional. She hunted down bad guys for a living. Considering all she hoped to accomplish tonight, she couldn't risk taking along an amateur.

Since she suspected Buchanan might have a different view of the matter, Dani schooled herself to patience for another hour or so. Finally, he cracked a yawn, hooked his hands behind his neck for a body-twisting stretch, and surprised her with another chance at the eagle's nest.

"Sure you don't want the bed?"

"It's all yours."

His glance drifted to her mouth. "We could share."

"I don't think so."

"You might be making a mistake here, Flynn."

She didn't miss the underlying message. He was talking about more than getting naked and sweaty on that wide, inviting mattress. He wanted in on whatever she was planning.

For a moment, she was tempted to take him up on his offer. On *both* offers. An hour or so spent testing the bedsprings with Buchanan would no doubt do wonders for the tension crawling along her spine. And it would certainly help to have someone drive the Jeep while she operated the specialized piece of equipment she had tucked in her carryall. Convenience, however, wouldn't make up for the danger she'd be exposing him to.

Shrugging, she turned aside his offer. "It wouldn't be my first mistake."

But it could very well be her last.

Dani had time for that one thought and that one thought only when a menacing figure lunged out of the darkness at her an hour later, just as she was about to climb into the white-and-green-striped Jeep.

Chapter 3

It took only a single, fleeting glimpse of the figure in black for Dani's training and instinct to kick in simultaneously. Dropping her carryall, she flattened her right hand into a throat-crunching blade. Her left knuckled into a fist that might have seriously rearranged the man's facial features if she hadn't recognized his set, angry face.

"Buchanan!" Her breath hissed out. "You damned idiot! Don't you have more sense than to creep up on a trained operative like that?"

"If the trained operative had let me in on her plans for the night," he shot back, "maybe I wouldn't have had to creep up on her."

He crowded her against the Jeep, all hard, angry

male. Dani had handled bigger and badder men, but she had to admit Buchanan could project a particularly nasty air when he wanted to.

"You want to tell me where you're going, green-eyes?"

"No."

His jaw locked. So did the powerful body pressing hers against the Jeep's fender.

"Wrong answer," he said softly, dangerously. "Try again."

She gave in. *Not* because he intimidated her in any way, shape or form, but because she'd already wasted too much valuable time.

"I'm going to conduct a little reconnaissance."

"And you didn't tell me because…?"

Dani saw no need to sugarcoat the matter. "Because I didn't want you getting in my way."

She could feel his anger singeing the ends of her hair.

"Do you really expect me to sit around twiddling my thumbs while you scour the canyon on your own?"

"That's exactly what I expect. Your part in this operation consists of flying me into Mexico, providing a convenient cover where necessary, and flying me and my sister out. I'll handle the rest."

"Wrong again."

"This is what I do," she insisted, trying for calm and rational. "I'm trained in specialized surveillance techniques. I brought along a piece of very high-tech equipment that lets me—''

''I'll drive.'' He bit out. Obviously he wasn't buying calm *or* rational. ''You play with your high-tech toy.''

''You're not listening, Buchanan. I don't need you for this part of the operation.''

''Tough. You've got me. Grab your stuff and get in the Jeep.''

Okay. Fine. She'd warned him. He didn't have a clue what he was getting into, but she suspected he wouldn't find it anywhere near as much fun as joysticking a Stearman around the clouds.

Despite the James Bond mystique, the truth was that ninety-nine-point-nine percent of undercover operations consisted of pure drudgery. Manning listening posts. Monitoring electronic emissions. Following up on tips from dozens of different sources in the hopes that one might actually produce a solid lead.

Occasionally, only occasionally, did operatives get to play Lone Ranger and charge in to the rescue. With any luck, Dani thought grimly, tonight might just be one of those occasions.

It wasn't.

She and Buchanan spent the hours between midnight and dawn cruising the narrow, winding roads that cut through the canyon. After the first few hairpin turns, Dani ignored the dark precipices plunging straight down from her side of the Jeep, and concentrated her attention on the hand-held, heat-seeking scanner she'd "borrowed" for this mission.

The powerful device was a derivative of the active-passive defense systems developed by the military to guard missile silos and nuclear aircraft. In those systems, strategically deployed sensors detected any approaching source of heat, however slight. Holographic images of the heat source would then paint on screens in the control center. If the heat source got close enough to actually trigger alarms, security forces would respond, but they'd know whether they were responding to a stray jackrabbit or a possible saboteur.

The scanner Dani aimed across the dark canyon used the same technology. Its sensitive beam pierced the darkness and picked up any heat source registering a specified number of degrees above the surrounding cliffs and rocks. The images that appeared on the screen were small, but astonishingly detailed.

She zeroed in on a mule deer curled up around her fawn under a pine tree. What looked like two coyotes on the prowl. An owl swooping down on a scurrying creature. Isolated farmhouses tucked in the narrow valleys, with assorted farm animals asleep in their pens or roosting in henhouses. An occasional village clinging to the side of a mountain.

Painstakingly, Dani swept each farmhouse for signs of something, anything, out of the ordinary. An armed guard at a door. Sentries posted at the farm's perimeter. She recorded the coordinates of each village in the scanner's computer for return, daylight visits. But it was the cliffs above the farms and villages that drew her most intense scrutiny.

Despite the failed attempt to rescue Patricia, government authorities had gathered some useful intelligence. By far the most significant piece had come from a Canadian executive who'd escaped some months before Patricia was snatched. The kidnappers had kept him hidden in caves, he'd told authorities. He'd also confirmed that they moved often to escape detection. Always at night.

Inch by inch, grid by grid, Dani swept the dark cliffs across the valley. She stayed hunched over the scanner, her eyes glued to the small screen, as Buchanan navigated the tortuous, winding roads. The tight switchbacks and steep curves restricted the Jeep to a slow crawl. By dawn, they'd covered only about ten miles of a series of canyons that stretched for more than a hundred. And they'd surveyed just the east-facing cliffs. They'd have to cross to the far side of the valley to survey those facing west.

When Dani finally tucked the scanner inside the carryall and slumped wearily against her seat, Buchanan hooked his arm over the steering wheel. Eyes narrowed, he studied the sun rising above the rugged escarpments stretching endlessly in both directions.

"Driving these dirt roads isn't going to hack it. Not if you want to find your sister this year."

"The only other options are horse or mule," Dani retorted. Her back ached and her eyes felt as dry and hard as peach pits, but she was darned if she'd give up after just one night. "I doubt they'd prove any faster."

"We've got a plane at our disposal. We should use it."

"In these narrow ravines? At night? With no terrain-following radar or sophisticated navigational aids? You can't be *that* good a pilot!"

The grin he flashed her said it all. "Sure I am."

"Get this straight, Buchanan. I'm not climbing into that sorry collection of canvas, baling wire and bubble gum you call a plane and swooping sideways through these gullies and ravines in total darkness."

"Chicken?"

"Yes!"

"Well, you've got twelve hours of daylight to work up your nerve. What do we do until then?"

Firmly resolved to use those twelve hours to convince Jack of the idiocy of night aerial surveillance in a forties-era Stearman biplane, Dani hooked a thumb over her shoulder. "We drive back to the hotel, snatch a few hours sleep, then hit the villages."

That was the plan, anyway.

Dawn was exploding into bright, brilliant morning when Jack parked the Jeep outside their casita. Scrunching her eyes against the dazzling sunlight, Dani trudged inside and dumped her leather tote on the table. Puffs of red dust billowed from the bag, adding to the layers already coating her face and clothes.

"Mind if I grab another quick shower before you claim the bedroom?"

"Be my guest."

Stripping off, she set the water to just below scalding and stepped inside the glass booth. Hot needles pierced her body from every angle. Sighing in pure delight, Dani dropped her head back and let the water drill through the tension that had gripped her day and night since Patricia was snatched. It took awhile, but she finally worked up enough energy to soap down and shampoo up.

Wrapping herself in one of the hotel's bath sheets, she plopped down at the built-in dressing table and grimaced at the creature in the mirror. Her cheeks glowed bright cherry from wind-chafing during yesterday's flight. Last night's activities had drawn road maps in the whites of her eyes. Her hair... Well, at least the dust was out of the red tangles.

Flicking on the wall-mounted hair dryer, Dani adjusted its flexible neck to blow down without scorching her scalp, and set to work dragging a comb through the sodden mass.

That was where Jack eventually found her. With her back slumped against the bathroom wall. Her hair a red sail rippling under the force of the blow dryer. Sound asleep.

He'd knocked. He'd give himself credit for that, at least. And he'd called her name. When he'd received no response and cracked open the bathroom door, he'd even spent a good ten seconds debating whether he should pull it shut again.

But he'd never made any claim to sainthood, and Danielle Flynn draped only in a sagging bath towel could tempt the archangels to sneak a peek. Besides, he couldn't just leave her to sleep sitting up.

Or so he told himself as he strolled into the bathroom and cut off the dryer. If she'd stirred then, or flickered so much as an eyelash, he would have just waited with a wicked grin for her eyes to open. When they didn't, he let himself enjoy the view for several more satisfying moments before he scooped her into his arms.

Her lids drifted up at that point. Glazed with sleep, her forest-green eyes filled with confusion. "Buchanan? What are you doing?"

"Taking you to bed."

Jack anticipated a dozen possible reactions to that provocative remark. A sudden tensing of her body. An icy demand that he get real. Or maybe one of the lethal karate chops she'd been ready to lay on him last night. To his surprise, she merely snuggled against his chest.

"Thanks," she mumbled into his shirt. "The couch is too short for you, but maybe if you scrunch up..."

The sleepy murmur gave way to a long sigh as he stretched her out on the downy comforter.

"Two hours," she muttered. "I'll just sleep two hours."

With that mumbled vow, she rolled over and buried her face in the pillow. The towel rolled with her—

more or less. Jack's lungs squeezed as he took in a curved spine. A rounded bottom cheek. A long, smooth leg.

When he could breathe again, he dragged his gaze away, gave the wood-framed couch in the sitting room a considering look and tossed a mental coin.

Dani wasn't sure what pulled her from total oblivion. She knew her internal alarm clock hadn't pinged. No way could she have slept for a whole two hours. Her body still desperately craved sleep.

Nor had she sensed danger. No external alarms had gone off, either. Her instincts told her that whatever had wakened her posed no immediate threat. So she lay still, letting her mind rev up to full power. Slowly, she absorbed the hazy light. The damp towel tangled around her body. The heavy arm draped over her waist.

The *very* heavy arm draped over her waist.

It lay across her, casual, possessive, altogether too intimate. Dani could feel Buchanan behind her now, a solid wall of warm flesh. The damp towel separated them. Barely.

She remembered sitting under the blow dryer. Remembered going horizontal. And she was sure she remembered a gruff promise of sorts.

"Buchanan?"

When the wall behind her made no response, she poked it sharply with her elbow.

"Buchanan!"

He jerked awake, tightening his arm instinctively, and grunted an inarticulate, "Huh?"

Locked against him now by an iron band, Dani twisted her head. His chin, clean-shaven last night, already showed a dark shadow.

"What happened to our deal?"

"What deal?"

"You were supposed to bunk down in the living room."

"Oh. Yeah." His head dropped back to the pillow. His arm loosened a mere fraction. Drawing up his knees, he nested her bottom on his thighs. "This is better."

Much better. Dani could admit the truth when it slapped her in the face. Or in this case, the butt.

"Go back to sleep," he mumbled into her damp hair. "We've still got a good forty minutes."

Dani spent the next forty minutes reviewing her game plan for the coming day, counting the dust motes dancing in the sunbeams and fighting the most ridiculous sense of pique.

Here she was, in bed with the man. Naked, except for the damned towel. His ribs pressed into her bare back with every rise and fall of his chest. The bristly hair on his thighs tickled the undersides of hers. She could feel the warm wash of his breath on her cheek. Feel, too, the hard curve of his arm tucked just under her breasts.

The bath sheet had long since ceased to act as a

protective shield. It was now more of an irritant, still damp, still twisted under her in hard ridges. Wiggling discreetly, Dani tried to smooth the lumps.

They wouldn't smooth. Buchanan's weight added to her own and kept the oversize cotton towel pinned in place. Frowning, she tried again.

"Careful, Flynn."

The warning was low and rough and went a long way to soothing Dani's feminine pique. The growing bulge on the other side of the towel eliminated the rest.

It also set off the internal alarms that had been silent up to now. Her heart began a wild rhythm, hammering against her chest with heavy, erratic thumps. Nerves danced under her skin everywhere Buchanan's hard body contacted her own.

She knew she had exactly two options at this point.

She could roll over. Go front to front with him. Fan into fire the sparks they'd been striking off each other since she'd walked into that smoky dive two nights ago.

Or she could roll away. Stay focused on the urgent business that had brought her to Copper Canyon.

With a sharp sting of regret, Dani gathered the towel against her breasts and swung her legs over the side of the bed. Behind her, Buchanan flopped onto his back. She speared a look over her shoulder and felt her stomach clench. For a man with only a rickety biplane and a rusted pickup to his name, he looked—and acted—like he owned the world.

Hands hooked behind his head, his body lean and tanned against the white sheets, he gave her a look that made goose bumps pop out all up and down her spine. ''Next time, we'll finish what we've started.''

It took some doing, but she managed a cool smile. ''You think so?''

''I know so.''

She couldn't help laughing. He looked so smug. And so damned sure of himself. She almost hated to burst his bubble.

Almost.

Buchanan's tantalizing promise hovered in her thoughts all day. As if to add to the simmering turmoil he'd created in her mind, he played the honeymooner to the hilt.

Each time they parked the Jeep and climbed out to explore one of the villages Dani had circled on her map, he draped an arm around her shoulders. Anchored side by side like the newlyweds they were supposed to be, they ambled through the dirt streets and explored the local markets.

While she discreetly pumped the locals for information, Jack maintained their cover by purchasing gifts for his new bride. Some were mere trinkets. A wooden flute carved with fantastic shapes. A nest of intricately woven baskets. A small but obviously fecund soapstone figurine.

''The ancients believed this goddess bring babies,'' the Tarahumara Indian who sold it explained. With a shy smile, she rubbed the figure's grossly distended stomach. "Many, many babies."

"Good," Jack said solemnly. "We want many, many babies."

"Speak for yourself," Dani muttered under her breath.

Nevertheless, she tucked the goddess into her pocket. But when they stopped at an open-air market just after lunch, and Jack picked up a beaten silver bracelet studded with bits of tourmaline, she drew the line. Or tried to.

"How much?" he asked the native craftsman.

The man named his price, and Dani murmured a quick protest. "It's too expensive."

"The stone is the same color as your eyes," Jack said with a shrug, reaching into his back pocket for his wallet.

"You should at least try to bargain!"

"Why? I want you to have it. Our friend here wants to sell it. A few pesos won't change that. Right?"

Thus appealed to, the silversmith nodded in agreement. "It is a good price, *señora*. The stones, they are very clear and bright."

"Yes, they are."

Dani felt herself weakening. The bracelet really was gorgeous. The primitive designs stamped into the silver swirls hinted at Barranca del Cobre's past. The rough-cut bits of quartz shimmered in the sunlight.

"Do these pieces come from around here?"

"From the caves above the village where my wife's

uncle lives, *señora*. I used to get many such stones there before the…''

He caught himself. A guarded expression dropped over the broad planes of his face. It was, Dani thought with a sudden kick in her pulse, the same careful wariness that had wiped the friendliness from the hotel receptionist's eyes.

''Before the what?'' she prompted.

The artisan glanced around, fingering the fringe of his colorful serape. ''Before the caves became unsafe,'' he said finally, choosing his words with obvious care.

She wanted to probe further, but he pocketed the wad of bills Jack passed him, bundled up his wares and scurried away. Her every nerve taut, Dani stared after him.

''Did you see his face?''

''I saw it.''

''He's scared. Just like the receptionist at the hotel.''

''The thugs who kidnapped your sister must have a pretty extensive network of spies.''

''They do,'' she replied, her stomach clenching as she remembered the tip the bastards had received just before the commando raid last week. ''I'm going to nose around, see if I can pick up the name and location of this wife's uncle's village.''

Jack's gaze roamed the square and snagged on a tin-roofed cantina. ''Okay. While you do that, I'll check out the home brew.''

Dani's mouth thinned as she watched him stroll across the dirt square. So much for not sitting idly by, twiddling his thumbs! Disappointed and more than a bit disgruntled, she worked the square.

When Buchanan sauntered up to her some time later, she'd verified the name of the artisan, but was still trying to pin down the exact location of his wife's uncle's village.

"It's about twenty miles from here." Jack informed her. "I've got rough directions. Best guess is that it will take four hours to drive there on these winding roads." Slipping a hand under her elbow, he steered her toward the green-and-white vehicle. "Let's get back to the hotel and rev up the Stearman."

"Wait a minute." She dragged her heels and brought him to a halt. "Before I climb into a Jeep *or* a plane with you, I want to know how many beers you downed before you solicited this information."

"Two bottles."

She had no idea how much of a punch the local brew packed, but Buchanan didn't show any signs of inebriation. On the contrary, the glint in his eyes signaled he was ready for anything.

As if to prove the point, he curled a knuckle under her chin and dropped a swift, hard kiss on her mouth.

"You drive. I'll fly."

Chapter 4

They located the remote village an hour later. Just in time, too. The sun hung low on the horizon, casting long shadows that almost swallowed the handful of huts clustered at the base of the cliffs. Another twenty minutes or so and they would have been searching the narrow valley in darkness.

Not a prospect that filled Dani with wild enthusiasm. She wasn't particularly anxious to put Buchanan's claim of being able to fly blind to the test. Twisting in her harness, she studied the sheer rock walls they'd just swooped by, and pressed the button for her intercom.

"I want to scan the cliffs above the village. Can you take us down a little closer on the next pass?"

Silly question. Of course he could. Gulping, Dani clutched the sides as he aimed the Stearman straight up, spun her on her tail and plunged back down. The valley that had seemed semi-navigable at best just seconds ago suddenly closed in on all sides.

While Buchanan fought a series of vicious updrafts and ninety-degree twists, Dani did her best to level the scanner at rock precipices above the village. The slicing wind and dizzying, tip-tilted angles defeated her. After the second pass, she was forced to admit defeat.

"I can't hold the scanner steady. We'll have to land and conduct the surveillance on foot. Where's the nearest airstrip?"

"According to the charts, there's a dirt strip about five miles farther up the valley. But I think I can get us down a little closer than that."

He banked, taking the canary-yellow trainer into a steep turn. A moment later, he aimed for a small, flat plateau almost lost amid the surrounding peaks. Dani squinted through her goggles at the scruffy oaks and twisted piñons dotting the plateau. True, there was a clear patch among the scrub—a very *small* clear patch!—but it ended abruptly in a sheer drop at the far edge of the escarpment.

"Buchanan! Tell me you're not going to try to land on that anthill!"

"Not to worry. This baby can stop on a dime and give back nine cents in change. You'd better check your harness, though, just in case."

She didn't like the sound of that. At all.

"Jack! Wait! I don't think this is a good idea!"

Her nervous shout got lost in the wind. Either that, or Buchanan simply ignored it. Working the controls with both hands and feet, he leveled off and throttled back. When they were still a good fifty yards from the flat mountaintop, he killed the engine completely.

A sudden, soaring silence surrounded them, the same stillness that must envelop hawks and eagles when they glided on the wind. Dani might have appreciated the profound quiet more if she wasn't convinced that the Stearman would go into a nosedive several yards shy of the designated landing site. She dropped the scanner, scrunched it tight between her boots and clutched the sides of the cockpit with white-knuckled fists.

They skimmed in mere inches above a piñon clinging to the edge of the cliff. The wheels hit once, bounced up and came down with a thump. Dani pushed out a shaky sigh of relief, then sucked it back in again as the plane kept right on rolling. If her paralyzed brain cells had been capable of emitting a signal at that point, she would have squeezed her eyes shut. As it was, all she could do was stare in fascinated horror at the empty void looming dead ahead.

Finally—*finally!*—they fishtailed to a stop. Buchanan fiddled with the instruments, climbed out of the front cockpit and nonchalantly strolled forward to peer over the edge of the plateau. He ambled back a few moments later, wearing a thoroughly satisfied expression.

"We're right on target. The village looks like it's only a mile or so away."

Thoroughly rattled and trying hard not to show it, Dani climbed out of the cockpit on rubbery legs. "That means the caves are, too."

"So what's the plan?"

"Give me a minute, okay? I'm still waiting for my stomach to catch up with the rest of me."

He looked genuinely wounded. "You weren't worried, were you? I told you the Stearman could stop on a dime."

"I'll feel a lot better if you'd tell me she can take off again on the same ten cents. With—assuming we get lucky!—a third passenger."

"That shouldn't be a problem."

"*Shouldn't?*"

"Well, I might need to siphon off some fuel. How much does your sister weigh?"

"About the same as I do, give or take a few pounds. Or she did, the last time I saw her."

The last of Dani's shakiness disappeared, edged out by the hollow, helpless feeling that had haunted her for the past three weeks. She'd listened to the taped interview with the Canadian executive who'd escaped his kidnappers, knew what indignities and deprivations he'd suffered.

But Patricia was tough, Dani reminded herself grimly. She couldn't have made it in the mostly male, ultramacho world of hydroelectric engineering without developing survival skills. Besides which, Daniel

Flynn had made sure both his girls could protect themselves.

"Okay," Dani said, pulling in a steadying breath, "here's the plan. You stay and guard the plane. I'll work my way down the cliffs, using—"

"Dammit, I thought I made myself clear last night! We're in this together, Flynn."

The anger that flared hot and swift gave Jack his first hint that he might be in over his head. The idea of Dani climbing down those cliffs to take on a band of kidnappers put a kink in his gut. The fact that she'd intended to go it alone completely infuriated him. Conveniently forgetting that he always insisted on flying solo himself, he barked out an order.

"Help me push the plane under those trees."

"Look, Buchanan—"

"Now, Captain!"

Her arm whipped up in a mock salute. "Yes, sir!"

Simmering with irritation, he positioned her behind the left wing and lined up on the right. It took both of them to angle the biplane around and back it tail-first under the shelter of a piñon. While Dani gathered loose branches to cover the nose, Jack hauled over two good-size boulders and jammed them against the wheels.

"That should keep her," he pronounced.

Reaching into his canvas flight bag, he pulled out a Glock. Dani's brows snapped together as he popped the magazine, checked the load and slapped it back in again.

"When did crop dusters start carrying police specials with crosshatched grips and laser sights?"

Shrugging, Buchanan holstered the Glock, unbuckled his belt and slid the weapon around to the small of his back. "I can't speak for the rest of the profession, but I never leave home without one. Ready?"

"Ready."

Not fifteen minutes later, Dani was forced to call a halt.

This narrow slice of Barranca del Cobre didn't run to soft, purple dusks. Once the sun dropped behind the mountains, dark shadows speared across the cliffs. Seemingly in the next minute, inky darkness coated the peaks, the valley and everything in between.

Anticipating a night operation, Dani had tucked a set of night-vision goggles into her gear bag. Even with their powerful capabilities, however, a night descent was just too darned dangerous. Besides, she'd brought only one set. No way was she letting Buchanan navigate in the dark. Biting down on her frustration, she insisted they climb back to the plateau.

"We'll grab a few hours sleep and try again come dawn."

Going back up was easier than going down. Dumping her bag beside the fuselage, Dani kicked away some of the concealing scrub while Buchanan dragged out the packed chutes, the seat cushions and his brown leather bomber jacket.

"It won't be the first time I've bedded down under

this baby's wings," he acknowledged, arranging the chutes and cushions into a rough mattress. He seemed to take it as a matter of course that they'd sleep side by side.

Remembering his husky promise to finish what they'd started, Dani opened her mouth to inform him this wasn't the time or the place for a roll in the seat cushions. The chill breeze dancing along her arms had her shutting it again. The temperature would drop considerably before dawn. It only made sense to share body heat.

But that's all they'd share. There was too much at stake and she was too darned close to her objective to lose her edge now. With that thought firmly in mind, she dropped down on one knee and fumbled in her bag. She'd left most of her spare clothes at the hotel, but the silver bracelet was in the bag, tucked away for safekeeping. Nudging it aside, she rummaged around for the toils of her trade.

"You sack out," he instructed. "I'll take first watch."

"We can both sack out. I, uh, requisitioned a supply of electronic sensors for this mission."

With a flourish, she extracted a package of wafer thin, dime-size disks wrapped in electrostatic plastic, and what looked like an ordinary sports watch.

"These babies are simple, silent and highly effective. If anyone or anything steps on them, the wrist receiver emits an electrical pulse. This little contraption has jolted me out of sleep more than once,'' she admitted wryly.

He hunkered down beside her while she unwrapped the disks. ''How do you activate them?''

She moved his fingers until he found the slight ridge on the underside of one. ''You just slide this little tab to the right, then sow the sensors at ten or fifteen foot intervals.''

''Got it. I'll plant a half-dozen on the goat path we just climbed up. You sow some around the far edge of the plateau, just in case.''

Torn between amusement and irritation, Dani glanced up at his shadowed face. Evidently you could take the pilot out of the Air Force, but not out of the habit of command.

Ten minutes later they were back at the plane. Buchanan made himself comfortable on the seat cushions, taking up more than his fair share of space. Hopefully, he eyed her leather carryall.

''Any chance your magic bag of tricks contains anything edible?''

''As a matter of fact, it does. I raided the bar in our room before we left this morning. We have chocolate bars. We have Spanish peanuts. We have individual rounds of Gouda and cheddar. Crackers. What I'm guessing are smoked beef strips. Bottled water, and...'' she squinted at the label on a tall, slender jar ''...cocktail onions.''

''Doesn't sound like we'll starve.''

''In one night? Hardly.'' She tossed him the can of

peanuts. "Besides, you went through survival training. Didn't they teach you to make a meal on beetles?"

"Beetles, mosquito larvae and the occasional snake or two." Popping the top on the can, he scooped out a fistful of peanuts. "What about you? Did you have to crunch down bugs in spy school?"

"A few," she admitted, firmly repressing all thoughts of those weeks of Survival, Evasion, Resistance and Escape training. SERE did *not* rank among her favorite memories.

While they made a serious dent in the cheese and crackers, the night deepened around them. Shivering, Dani pulled on her nylon windbreaker. The thin layer of protection lessened the bite but generated only minimal warmth. She left Buchanan shrugging into his beat-up leather jacket, and ducked behind a tree for a few minutes. When she returned, he'd taken full possession of the seat cushions.

"Think you can make room for two there?"

She caught a gleam of white teeth. "If we squeeze up tight."

Dani hesitated. For a brief instant, she felt just like Little Red Riding Hood standing before the big bad wolf.

Which was totally absurd. The wolf hadn't even *tried* to sink his fangs into her this morning when she'd cuddled up against him on a nice, soft mattress. He wasn't likely to do so tonight, when they were both fully clothed and bedded down on a mountain, for pity's sake.

Which just went to show how little she knew about wolves. Or Buchanan. She'd no sooner wiggled into a comfortable position when he pounced. So to speak. It was actually more of a roll than a pounce, but it tilted the cushions and wedged her against him.

"You're not contemplating anything stupid, are you?" he growled.

Her heart skipped a beat. With his mouth only inches from hers, she was contemplating a number of things, almost all of which were monumentally stupid. From the way he'd phrased the question, however, she guessed he wasn't entertaining the same carnal thoughts she was.

"Such as?" she asked, just to clarify matters.

"Such as slipping off the way you tried to do last night and tackling those cliffs on your own. I'm a light sleeper, remember?"

"I remember," she said coolly. "If I do decide to slip off, I'll make sure you're out for the count."

"Wrong answer, Flynn." The irritation that had roughened his voice earlier surged back. "When are you going to accept that we're a team?"

"Oh, I don't know. About the same time you do, I suppose."

"What's that supposed to mean?"

"It means, Mr. I-always-fly-solo, that we both possess certain unique skills and don't necessarily feel the need to consult with each other about how to employ them…even when one of us is sitting in the rear cockpit, ready to toss up her cookies."

"Still hacked off about that landing? I got us down, didn't I?"

"Yes, you did. I just wish you'd let me know what you plan to do *before* you do it next time."

He thought about that for a few moments, his eyes unreadable in the darkness that surrounded them.

"All right. I'll give it a shot. Here's the plan rattling around in my head right now. First, I'm going to kiss you. On the lips to start with. Then I'm thinking seriously about unzipping your jacket, tugging off your T-shirt and jeans and kissing the rest of you."

Dani's mouth opened. Snapped shut. A dozen flip retorts flashed into her mind, but she didn't utter any of them for the simple reason that Buchanan had already bent his head and was initiating Phase I of his plan.

She braced herself for another fighter pilot-type attack, was all prepared to laugh it off and put an end to matters before they went any further. Instead of swooping down with guns blazing, however, the sneaky devil glided in and merely brushed her lips with his. Slowly. Gently.

So slowly, she had time to absorb the taste of salty peanuts along with the rich scent of leather and healthy male. So gently, she un-braced and allowed herself to relax.

That, of course, was exactly the incentive Buchanan needed to implement Phase II. His head angled. His mouth fastened hard and sure on hers. One hand tunneled into her hair, tangling in the windblown strands, and held her steady while his tongue began a dark, sensual exploration.

Dani thought about calling a halt at that point. She urgently needed to stay centered, to concentrate all her focus on the coming dawn.

Yet dawn suddenly seemed so far away.

And Buchanan was right here, right now.

She fought a fierce, silent battle with herself and lost. Her palms flattened on the worn leather, slid up to hook around his neck. Her tongue danced with his, slowly at first, then with increasing greed. She closed her eyes, shutting out the silhouette of canvas wings and the swaying piñon branches just beyond, allowing Buchanan to dominate her mind as well as her senses.

All too soon, she was ready to move from her mind and her senses directly to her body. Or more correctly, to move on to his. The hands she'd hooked behind his neck unlocked and made a slow trip south, stopping momentarily at each button along the way. His belt buckle gave after a tug or two. His jeans unsnapped with a small pop.

He lifted his head, his breath coming hard and fast. "This team business works both ways, green-eyes. You want to tell me what's next on your agenda? Just so we can coordinate our activities, you understand."

Dani understood. He was giving her the choice. As far as she was concerned, there was only one. It was right there, under her palm, hard and straining against his zipper.

"The first item on my agenda," she said on a low, husky note, "is this."

She pressed the heel of her hand against the ridge and felt a leap of feminine delight at his instant response.

"Then," she murmured, "I thought I might try this."

Her fingers found the zipper tab and worked it down. When she dipped inside the open waistband, he gave a little grunt and went stiff all over.

After that, they abandoned the pretense of following any sort of plan. There was a wild rush to shed their clothes, an urgent tangle of arms and hips and legs. Jack retained just enough sanity to grab his flight bag, fumble among the charts and assorted jumble for a condom, and sheathe himself before Dani's greedy mouth and hands sent him straight into a tailspin.

With his muscles coiled, his entire body taut with need, he kneed her legs apart and positioned himself at the entrance to her slick, wet core. As eager as he, she hooked her calves around his and canted her hips to meet his thrust.

She was every thrill Jack had experienced in the air and on the ground, all rolled into one incredible woman. When he tried to throttle back, she pushed him harder and faster. When he drove into her with the force and rhythm of a piston, she gasped, stiffened and locked him deep within her.

The earth was falling away beneath him when her

entire body arched. A groan ripped free from far back in her throat.

"Jack! I can't...hold...back!"

"Then don't!"

With a rush of primitive satisfaction, he took her over the edge. Satisfaction gave way to a momentary sense of masculine power while Dani spasmed around him. Then she shuddered, gripped him tight with arms and legs and drove him right off the planet.

She woke him hours later the same way she had the morning before—with a low hiss and a sharp jab to the ribs.

"Jack!"

The hiss barely penetrated his consciousness, but the sharp elbow got his attention. He jerked, tightening his arm around her instinctively, and blinked awake. Before he could grunt out a demand to know what that was all about, she whispered an urgent warning.

"Quiet! The sensors have picked up some kind of movement."

He went still, listening intently. The wind sighed through the tree branches. An owl hooted in the distance. Nothing else disturbed the quiet.

"What was it?" he murmured.

"I'm not sure."

He threw a quick look over his shoulder. The distant glow of dawn gilded the peaks to the east, but their private patch of mountaintop remained bathed in darkness.

Suddenly, he heard a sound. The faint scrabble of a paw or a hoof—or a foot!—on rock. Caught by the wind and carried up to the plateau.

"Sounds like something's climbing up toward us," he whispered into her ear. "Could be a deer or a mountain cat."

"Could be," she agreed grimly. "Or it could be that someone saw the plane come down and has decided to check it out."

That particular thought had occurred to Jack, too. It was hovering foremost in his mind when another rattle of stones broke the stillness. No doubt about it. Someone or something was climbing up the cliffs below.

Both he and Dani sprang into swift, silent action. With a lithe twist, she shed his protective arm and the leather bomber jacket he'd tucked around her while she slept. Hastily, she scrambled into her clothes and grabbed her Beretta with one hand, the scanner with the other.

Jack yanked on his jeans, shoved his feet into his boots and snatched up the Glock. A heartbeat later, they were crouched low and racing for the edge of the escarpment.

Chapter 5

Buchanan cut through the darkness with the silent, lethal grace of a panther. Dani had worked with a number of operatives during her years as an undercover agent, but had to admit the ex-fighter pilot seemed to possess the instincts of a born hunter.

Twenty or so yards from the edge of the plateau, they took up positions designed to provide maximum concealment and an unobstructed line of fire. Dani crouched behind a bush that gave off the pungent stink of turpentine. Jack dropped into a fissure in the rock.

The sun was gold-plating the peaks to the east, but the predawn light had yet to sweep across the plateau. Squinting through the darkness, Dani communicated with Jack by means of hand signals. Together, they worked out a rough plan. She would aim the scanner, Jack the Glock. She'd raise one finger to indicate she'd picked up the heat source. Two to signify it appeared to be of the two-legged variety. Three...

Three meant it was armed and potentially dangerous. In which case Dani would remain concealed, allow the source to climb onto the plateau and let Jack get the drop on him—or them!—from behind.

Pure, undiluted adrenaline pumped through her veins. The receiver strapped to her wrist was pulsing like mad now. Their uninvited guest had tripped at least a half-dozen sensors.

Dani gripped the small scanning device with sweaty palms, willing herself to calm, forcing air into her lungs in measured breaths. Still, every nerve in her body jolted when she heard another scuffle of foot on stone, followed by a grunt.

No, not a grunt. More like a gasp. A harsh, ragged intake of breath laced with panic. Or desperation.

Her jaw tight, Dani aimed the scanner directly toward the sound. A green blip appeared on the screen. She stabbed one finger into the air to let Buchanan know she'd picked up the heat source. A moment later, the blip took on shape and definition, and a second finger shot up.

With startling clarity, the scanner tracked the figure that heaved itself onto the plateau and lay flat, panting. It was definitely of the two-legged variety, wearing what looked like ragged cotton pants and a fatigue-type shirt. Dani's throat closed as she made out the green-and-black camouflage spots on the shirt...and the automatic rifle slung over the man's back.

Grimly, she jabbed a third finger into the air.

She was just about to drop the scanner and aim the Beretta when the man lifted his head. Dani gaped at the screen in disbelief, blinked twice to make sure what she was seeing wasn't a mirage.

It wasn't!

With a wild whoop, she abandoned both the scanner and her concealment and charged full tilt at the prone figure.

"Trish!"

Fifteen yards away, Jack registered the name but didn't take his finger off the Glock's trigger until their uninvited guest lurched to her feet.

"Dani!"

The newcomer threw herself forward, laughing and crying at the same time. The two women collided and wrapped their arms around each other in a ferocious bear hug. Total chaos ensued, with more exclamations, more hugs, and both sisters firing questions like bullets.

"How did you find me?"

"It took some doing. How'd you get away?"

"I had one of the guards take me outside the cave to go potty, and I decked him. Are you part of another government task force? They gagged me, dragged me off kicking and fighting, just moments before one hit last week."

"No, no task force. How many kidnappers are there?"

"Ten that I saw." Her jaw tightened. "They wore ski masks whenever they came into the caves, but I'm pretty sure I can identify at least three from various tattoos, broken teeth and the names the others let slip. Those bastards are going down."

Standing in the shadows, Jack could only admire the woman's astounding resilience. She'd just decked an armed guard and scaled a sheer cliff in the dark, yet she was ready to go back and take them all on. No wonder Dani and her stepsister were so close. Their old man had molded them into hard, tensile steel. Remembering the colonel's efforts to do the same with him, Jack smiled and shoved his Glock into its holster.

The movement caused Patricia's head to whip around. She stabbed a swift, narrow glance into the shadows.

"Who are you?"

"Jack Buchanan."

"Formerly U.S. Air Force," Dani supplied. "Now a private pilot."

Enough light was filtering over the peaks for both the hostage and her would-be rescuer to get a good look at each other. While Jack noted a tumble of mink-dark hair and high, sculpted cheekbones, Patricia took in his bare chest, unsnapped jeans and unlaced boots.

Her gaze zinged back to Dani and performed a quick inventory of tangled red hair, a T-shirt pulled on wrong side out and sockless feet shoved into hiking boots.

"Well, well," she murmured, fixing Jack with a longer, considering glance. "This is interesting. I don't recall Dani mentioning you before. Just how long have you two known each other?"

"Long enough." A wicked grin pulled at his mouth. "We're on our honeymoon."

"What?"

"It's a long story," Dani interjected hastily. "One we don't have time to go into right now."

Patricia sobered instantly. "You're right. The guard I conked has no doubt come to by now and sounded the alarm." She did a quick scan of the plateau. "How did you get up here, drive or climb?"

"Neither. We flew. Jack's plane is tucked under those trees over there."

Her sister's jaw dropped. "You landed a plane here? On this mountaintop?"

"Hey, it wasn't my idea."

Patricia closed her mouth, opened it again, looked around once more. Knocked completely out of her cool, she shook her head.

"We...we heard a plane buzz the cliffs earlier, but we thought... That is, the kidnappers thought it was another government search plane. They figured it would touch down at the airstrip north of here, and sent two men to check it out. That's why I climbed *up* instead of down. I was afraid I'd meet those two on the way back. But I never dreamed...never imagined..."

"Why don't we talk about it later?" Jack suggested, shepherding them toward the Stearman. "I need to dump some fuel and you need to—"

"Oh, hell!"

Dani's exclamation stopped him dead. His stomach did a swift roll as she glanced down at her wrist.

"Is that gadget telling you what I think it is?"

She nodded, her face grim. "We've got more company."

"How long?"

"I'm guessing five minutes."

Swiftly, he calculated the odds. Eight, maybe ten heavily armed men against one Beretta, one Glock, the rifle slung across Patricia's shoulders.

Well, he'd been in tighter spots. One in particular would remain burned in his memory for a long, long time. Daniel Flynn had extricated Jack and six other crew dogs from that disaster. He would extricate the old man's daughters from this one.

"Good thing the Canary doesn't have to warm up to sing," he said, breaking into a run.

Patricia shot Dani a perplexed look. "Canary?"

Dani didn't have the heart to go into details. Three or four more steps, and Trish would be able to discern for herself the size and shape of the bright yellow biplane. And its age.

Sure enough, her first glimpse of the aircraft brought

Patricia stumbling to a halt. Utter disbelief blanked her features.

"*That's* how you got up here?"

"That's it," Jack confirmed cheerfully, kicking aside the brush piled in front of the nose. Two quick heaves moved the rocks away from the wheels. Tramping over the various items of clothing still scattered under the wing, he thrust one chute at her and the other at Dani.

"Okay, ladies. Squeeze into the rear cockpit and strap yourselves down."

Dani guessed she might—*might!*—erase the memory of their takeoff, say, sometime in the next century.

Thanks to its many overhauls, the Stearman's 220-horsepower engine coughed a couple of times, burped once and revved up to full power. The ensuing roar shattered the dawn. Frantic birds thrashed out of the bushes. A startled deer bounded across the far edge of the escarpment. And Dani was sure she heard shouts. Close by.

Too close.

Wedged tight in the rear seat, she squirmed around for a better angle. As Jack taxied out from under the trees, she kept the Beretta aimed at the spot where Patricia had flung herself over the edge. Beside her, her sister leveled the semiautomatic rifle at the same spot.

Jack took the Stearman right to the edge of the escarpment, so close that the tail rudder fanned sky as the plane swung around. Patricia sucked in air.

The Stearman lurched into a roll. Gathered speed. Bumped across the rocky surface.

Dani sensed immediately the plane was too heavy. She was sure they'd blow a tire. Or bust a strut. And they were moving too slowly! Craning, she tried to see around Jack's bulk to gauge the distance still remaining.

A burst of gunfire from Patricia's semiautomatic rifle almost shattered her eardrums. She whipped her head back around, saw two men dive for cover and another duck back down below the edge of the plateau. Calmly, she took aim with the Beretta.

The bastards never got off a single shot. The two sisters maintained a steady hail of fire, keeping them pinned while the Stearman bumped and lurched toward absolute nothingness. Suddenly, the ground dropped away beneath the plane's wheels. Sheer momentum kept the biplane moving forward. Five yards. Ten.

Then it sank like the proverbial stone.

Patricia gave a small shriek, dropped her rifle with a clatter and wrapped her sister in a stranglehold. Dani couldn't breathe, couldn't hear for the roaring in her ears, couldn't see a thing except the tendons cording Jack's bare shoulders and neck as he worked the controls.

It probably took only a few moments until he brought the nose up and they were flying straight and level, but those were the longest damned moments of Dani's life. Patricia's, too, judging by the stream of rather colorful invective she let loose. Buchanan didn't help matters by twisting around, giving them a thumbs-up and grinning.

Incredulous, Patricia shouted into Dani's ear, "The idiot looks like he actually enjoyed that."

"He probably did."

"Where did you find this guy?"

"In a bar in Oklahoma."

"And you *married* him?"

"No. That's just the cover we're using here in Mexico."

Shoving back her wildly whipping hair, Patricia eyed Jack's naked back. Her gaze slid from his broad shoulders to her sister's inside-out T-shirt.

"So does he perform as well in the sack as he does in the air?"

"Better, actually."

Scrabbling around with her boot, Dani found the radio headset and slipped it over one ear so she could communicate with Jack via the intercom without shouting herself hoarse. With the other ear, she listened while Patricia recounted the details of her harrowing weeks in Mexico.

The morning ground haze gradually dissipated, but as they headed north a bank of gray clouds drifted up to obscure the sun. The Sierra Madres wound and twisted below them, too close at times for Patricia's comfort. Her ragged nails gouged canvas on more than one occasion until the mountains began to flatten into rolling foothills.

Dani had just convinced herself they were home free when she caught a high, faint whine. Frowning, she coiled around to squint at the sky behind.

That small black speck was probably a hawk.

Lord, please let it be a hawk!

She tracked it for another few minutes. That's all it took to determine the black blob was, in fact, a small plane. And that it appeared to have vectored in on them. Sighing, she repositioned the headset and keyed the intercom.

"How far to the U.S. border?"

"Another twenty minutes or so. Why?"

"We've got company. Six o'clock and closing fast."

Jack twisted around and squinted at the aircraft.

"Could they be part of the gang who kidnapped you?" Dani asked her sister urgently.

"They could. I heard them talking about a plane they kept at that airport north of the caves." Her lip curled. "They bragged about buying another one with my ransom money. Supposedly, they equipped it with more armament than a Sherman tank."

Dani relayed the information to Jack, who absorbed it with a tight jaw. He eyed the horizon ahead and made an instant decision.

"Hang on. We'll cut into those clouds and alter our course to see if they follow."

They did.

The Stearman emerged from the billowing white mist and dropped so low it almost skimmed the foothills.

A moment later, the small turboprop swooped out of the clouds and dived after them. Small bursts of red shot from its wing. Tracers cut through the sky not fifty yards behind the biplane.

"Damn! They're firing on us."

Jack jenked the stick, sent the bright yellow Canary into a steep climb, and flew back into the cloud bank. While he coaxed the Stearman to every ounce of speed she had in her, Dani reached for the radio switches.

It was time to call in the cavalry. Or in this instance, the United States Air Force.

A quick flick of the switches dialed up a special frequency that broadcast to all Air Force bases within radio range. The closest, she knew, was Laughlin, just a few miles across the Rio Grande.

"Laughlin tower, this is Charlie-echo-mike-three-two-two. Do you read me?"

Her heart hammering, she waited for confirmation. Static crackled through the headset for what seemed like forever. Finally, the calm voice of the controller cut through the screechy noise.

"This is Laughlin tower, three-two-two. We read you loud and clear. How did you obtain this frequency?"

Dani ignored the sharp query and cut right to her message. "This is Captain Danielle Flynn, United

States Air Force, transmitting a code forty-five. Do you copy, Laughlin? Code forty-five.''

There was a short, startled silence. She could imagine the reaction in the tower. Only agents assigned to the Office of Special Operations could transmit a code forty-five, and then only in the most dire emergencies.

''We copy. Code forty-five. Stand by while we verify.''

Swiping the condensation from her eyes with her forearm, she threw a look over her shoulder and saw only a reassuring wall of gray mist.

''What's the nature of your emergency, three-two-two?''

''We have a bandit on our tail, firing at us.''

''State your present location, altitude and speed.''

Jack supplied the information, which Dani relayed to the tower. They were still over Mexican airspace, but closing on the border fast. Laughlin tower confirmed their position.

''Be advised we have two F-16s from Cannon transiting our airspace. We've received authority to divert them to perform an intercept. They'll meet you at the border.''

''If we make it that far,'' she muttered, switching to intercom mode.

The murmured comment broke through Jack's fierce concentration. He'd put himself in the place he'd learned to go during aerial operations, a small, enclosed capsule where his mind received input from dozens of different sources, processed the data with the speed of light and directed instant action. Wrenching himself out of the capsule, he took a deep breath and keyed the mike.

"We'll make it, green-eyes. This baby's got some tricks left in her that will surprise you. So do I, for that matter. I intend to demonstrate a few when we get down."

His reward for that bit of outrageous bravado was a choking laugh. "Thanks for the warning, flyboy."

"Just trying to stick to my end of our bargain and keep you apprised of my plans," he drawled. "You two strapped in good and tight back there?"

"Yes. Why?"

"Looks like the cloud bank is thinning up ahead. It's show time, ladies."

Dani aged at least two lifetimes in the ten minutes or so before the F-16s swooped down out of the clouds.

In those heart-stopping, eye-popping moments, Jack performed every aerobatic maneuver in the book and, she was convinced, invented a few new ones. He put the Stearman on its tail, on its nose, on all four wingtips. He rolled it, banked it, looped it, stalled it and somehow managed to keep it out of their pursuer's gun sights.

When the F-16s appeared, the bandit tucked tail and ran like hell. Patricia whooped and wrapped her sister in another stranglehold. Jack did pretty much the same when they finally glided onto the runway at Laughlin.

Dani exited the cockpit in a graceless stagger and fell off the wing into Buchanan's arms. Oil spray coated her face. No self-respecting rat would have nested in her tangled, wind-whipped hair. Yet the gleam in Jack's eyes made her feel like she'd just come up with the winning Power Ball ticket.

"You make one helluva combination copilot, flight engineer and tail gunner, Flynn. Your old man would have been proud of you."

"He would have been proud of you, too," she said softly. "Consider any and all debts paid in full."

Dragging his head down, she closed the account with a long, lip-locking kiss. When Jack raised his head again, his eyes had deepened to molten gold.

"Funny," he growled. "I have a feeling the tab's just starting to run up."

Before she could probe that interesting comment, he set her on her feet and reached up to help Patricia. Her sister's knees wobbled, but she managed a shaky grin.

"Thanks. There were a few moments back there when I wasn't sure if you knew what you were doing."

"Well…"

"Stop! Don't shatter the illusion! Let's just agree you're one fine pilot."

The F-16 pilots echoed Patricia's sentiments when they touched down some time later. They climbed out of their jets and strode across the concrete, their parachutes flapping at the backs of their knees.

"That was the damnedest aerial maneuvering I've ever seen," a tall, tanned major exclaimed. "Where did you learn to fly like that?"

"Same place you did."

"You're Air Force?"

"Former Air Force. I strapped on an F-117 for a few years before I traded it in for an open cockpit."

"Hell, man. You ought to think about going back into fighters. We're training a whole new generation of pilots. You could sure teach them a thing or two."

Dani agreed. So much so that she left Jack in a borrowed shirt, surrounded by representatives from the CIA, the Border Patrol and the State Department, and slipped away to make a private, very personal phone call.

It was late afternoon before the government agencies had finished with them. Early evening when Patricia finished wolfing down her first full meal in weeks, pleaded an urgent need for a bubble bath, and retreated to a suite in the luxurious hotel where she insisted her company put them all up. With what the company had saved in ransom, she declared, they could also supply her and her rescuers with a new wardrobe.

Ever efficient, she even called a local department store and arranged for a selection of designer sportswear to be delivered first thing in the morning. That done, she retreated to a mound of scented bubbles.

Dani opted for a steamy, bone-melting shower instead of a soak. Wrapped in the hotel's thick terry robe, she knocked on the door to the connecting suite.

"It's open."

She pushed through and smiled at the sight that greeted her. Jack lay sprawled on the king-size bed, his hands laced behind his head. Showered and shaved, he wore only a strategically placed towel.

"I've been waiting for you."

Her glance grazed the interesting bulge under the towel. "So I see."

He waggled his brows. "Care to try your hand on the stick?"

Groaning, she shucked her robe. "That *has* to be the sorriest pun I've ever heard."

"Give me time," he said with smug confidence, rolling her naked body under his. "I can do worse."

He could.

And he did.

Laughing helplessly at his completely outrageous, incredibly erotic aeronautical metaphors, Dani rolled, banked and performed a series of aerobatic feats that left her limp, sweaty and exhausted.

Boneless and replete, she sprawled across his chest while his fingers lazily combed the dark red hair spilling over her shoulders.

"Jack."

"Mmm?"

"I made a call this afternoon. To my boss."

"I bet he wasn't real happy with you for going into Mexico without authorization."

That qualified as the understatement of the millennium. Dani had hung up the phone feeling remarkably akin to pancaked roadkill.

"He did have a rather strong opinion on the matter," she admitted. "Once he calmed down, though, he agreed to pull a few strings."

"Is that right?"

His voice held only lazy curiosity. Suspecting that was about to change, Dani raised her head.

"He's got friends in high places, Jack. He's going to get them working a special review board to see if you qualify to return to active duty."

The idle movement of his fingers stilled. The sleepy satisfaction in his eyes evaporated. Dani had anticipated surprise, maybe even anger that she'd taken the initiative without consulting him. What she didn't expect was the sardonic twist to his lips.

"You're definitely your father's daughter."

Stung, she jerked her head back. "What's that supposed to mean?"

"It means the colonel only understood one way of life, too. For all his heart and courage under fire, he could be as narrow as you are in that regard."

"Come on, Buchanan!" Pushing upright, she gathered the tangled sheet around her. "I know you said you like being your own boss and jockeying around whenever and wherever you please, but…"

"What's the matter, Flynn? A crop duster's good

enough to sleep with, but not take out in public, is that it?''

''No, of course not! But you could do more!''

''And maybe I'm doing exactly what I want to do.''

His stubborn refusal to admit he was wasting his talents infuriated her.

''Fine! You're doing just what you want to do. So where does that leave us?''

Disengaging, she rolled to the side of the bed and yanked on the terry-cloth robe. Her fists clenched around the ends of the tie belt. She waited, *willing* him to say something. Anything! When he didn't, hurt piled on top of her anger.

''Sorry we got our signals crossed, Buchanan. I thought we might actually have something going here.''

Spinning on her heel, she marched to the open connecting door, sailed through and slammed it shut with enough force to rattle her bedroom windows.

Chapter 6

Buchanan departed the hotel at the crack of dawn the next morning.

Patricia brought Dani the news. Eager to catch up on world events, she'd gone down to the newsstand in the lobby to grab a copy of every news magazine and paper on the racks.

"When I walked out of the newsstand, Jack was climbing into a cab," she informed her sister.

Dumping her armload of goodies, she plopped into one of the chairs set around a square table littered with the remains of a room-service breakfast.

"He didn't look happy," Patricia related. "Neither do you, for that matter. What gives? After the interesting sounds I heard coming through the wall last night, I figured you two would be sleeping in this morning.''

''Things didn't work out.''

''Things? What things?''

Shrugging, Dani sloshed more coffee into her cup and shoved the carafe toward her sister.

''We have different goals. And different opinions about Buchanan's current occupation.''

''Just what *does* he do? When he's not ferrying undercover agents down to Mexico to rescue their sisters, that is.''

''He's a crop duster. He also contracts for some oil spill cleanup and ice-melt.''

''And that's bad because…?''

''Because he could probably get a waiver to go back on active duty, but refuses to consider it.'' Scowling, Dani planted her elbows on the table. ''Dad once told me Jack Buchanan was one of the best pilots he'd ever flown with.''

''Uh-oh. No wonder the poor man decamped at first light. I would, too, if I had both you and the colonel coming down on me.''

Patricia grinned at Dani's offended expression. ''I loved Dad as much as you did,'' she added. ''More, maybe, because I wasn't his natural daughter, but he took me straight into his heart, warts and all. I wasn't blind to his faults, though, any more than he was to mine.''

''Which specific fault are you referring to?'' Dani asked stiffly.

"Dad lived, breathed and slept Air Force. So do you, kiddo. There *is* life outside the military, you know."

"Oh, that's great coming from the woman who left her fiancé literally standing at the altar. Let's see, what was the crisis that time? Oh, yes. I remember. You had to zip over to China and work an emergency fix to the power grid supplied by the Yellow River Dam."

"Okay, okay. I'll admit that wasn't exactly my finest hour. What does it prove, except that we both need to reassess our priorities?"

"Maybe."

"Maybe, my left foot." Reaching into a wicker basket, Patricia helped herself to a cherry Danish. "Think about it. How many chances does a woman get to have a man like Buchanan teach her aerial maneuvers?"

Not many.

It took Dani several weeks to acknowledge that fact. She spent her nights tossing and turning and generally being hacked at Buchanan. Her days she spent at OSI headquarters, pushing paperwork. Her boss had decreed that every field agent had to serve at least one sentence at headquarters, so they'd appreciate their freedom in the field.

She was working her way through a stack of site surveillance reports when one of her fellow agents strolled into her office and hitched a hip on the corner of her desk.

"Hey, Flynn, who was that crop duster who flew you down to Mexico?"

"Buchanan. Jack Buchanan."

"Bingo! I knew I'd heard his name somewhere before."

Dani's inner alarms started pinging. Harrison headed the counterterrorism division at OSI headquarters.

"Before what?" she asked tensely.

"Before I saw the guy mentioned in this morning's operational report. The op rep just hit the In box. You might want to take a look."

"Thanks. I will."

Nodding, he sauntered out. Dani was already at the keyboard. She punched in her security code and waited impatiently while the video input device confirmed her identity. Seconds later, the latest operations report painted down her screen.

She read it through twice. Incredulously the first time. Furiously, the second.

Signing off, she stormed down the hall to her boss's office.

Chapter 7

The bar reeked of spilled beer and old grease. The odors enveloped Dani the moment she stepped inside, along with the stink of stale cigarette smoke. Ignoring the murmurs of interest she stirred among the handful of patrons in boots and jeans, she threaded a path through the tables.

The man slouched at the corner table watched her approach with no sign that he recognized her. His gaze made a slow descent, taking in her pink T-shirt and thigh-hugging jeans.

Dani stopped beside his table. "I want to talk to you."

He tipped his chair back on its rear legs. His whiskey-colored eyes were unreadable.

''That right?''

The deliberate drawl pulled at nerves already stretched wire thin.

''That's right,'' she snapped. ''Outside, Buchanan.''

His chair remained at an angle. He made a lazy circle on the table top with his beer. Dani got the message. Gritting her teeth, she ground out a single syllable.

''Please.''

He followed her into the Oklahoma night. The hot wind sweeping across the Panhandle had already coated her rental car with red dust. Buchanan didn't appear unduly worried about transferring the dirt to his rear as he leaned against the fender.

Dani planted herself in front of him and cut right to the chase. ''Why didn't you tell me you're FBI?''

His shoulders rolled in a careless shrug. ''Like you, I didn't go down to Mexico in an official capacity. Who I work for wasn't pertinent.''

''It wasn't pertinent?'' Her voice spiraled up a full octave. ''It wasn't *pertinent?*''

The fury that had simmered inside her since she'd discovered Jack's real status exploded. She still couldn't believe the FBI had recruited him right out of the Air Force. Or that he used his crop duster cover to travel without the least suspicion throughout the Texas-Oklahoma region. *Or* that he was the agent who'd recently unraveled a terrorist plot to seed lethal biological toxins into chemicals sprayed by U.S. agricultural aviators.

"Dammit, Buchanan! You let me make a complete fool of myself."

He cocked a brow, forcing her to a grudging concession.

"Okay, okay. Maybe I did that all on my own."

She dragged in a deep breath, caught between her anger and the need that had brought her back out to this hot, dusty corner of Oklahoma.

"I guess what really torques me," she finally admitted, "is that you let me walk away from you that night in Del Rio."

"I was coming after you."

She tipped her chin, glaring at him in the dim light thrown by the single, bug-speckled light. "Oh yeah? When?"

"When I stopped fighting the inevitable and accepted that a bossy, take-charge, super-efficient undercover operative was about to turn my life upside down."

"Really?" She tapped a foot in the dust. "Are you there yet?"

His mouth curved. "Almost."

Her heart skipped. She felt that crooked grin all the way to her toes. The tension that had wrapped around her neck and shoulders eased its tight grip.

"What's it going to take to convince you?"

"Not a whole lot, green-eyes."

He reached for her then, his big hands folding around her upper arms, and drew her closer. She found a comfortable spot with her knees tucked between his and her hands splayed against his chest. Moonlight winked on the silver bracelet that banded her left wrist.

"Let's start with a kiss," he suggested, "and see where it takes us."

Dani knew where it would take them. She'd been there before. Sure enough, the hard, hungry feel of his mouth on hers sent her right into a spinning, dizzying, stomach-clenching hammerhead stall.

TO LOVE AND PROTECT
Lindsay McKenna

* * *

This story is for the men and women
of our armed forces. Thank you for your
dedication and patriotism.
We have freedom because of you.

Dear Reader,

I was thrilled with the opportunity to write a brand-new MORGAN'S MERCENARIES story for this collection featuring two other great writers of military fiction. I haven't written about the Coast Guard for a while, and so I felt this was the ideal time to do so! As many of you know, I write stories that are close to reality. I've been through volcano eruptions, earthquakes, hurricanes, tornadoes and just about any other kind of natural disaster you can think of. Having had the opportunity to work closely with the Coast Guard over the years—fly in their helicopters and Falcon jets, ply the Atlantic aboard their cruisers and go on SARs (search and rescue missions) with them—I feel honored to write about these brave men and women.

Too, I'm always thrilled to see Morgan in action. In this particular story I sent a man and a woman from Morgan's team to Hawaii, a place I've visited many times. I hope you enjoy this love story, which shows how life can sometimes offer us a second chance in the most unusual of ways.

Warmly,

Lindsay McKenna

Chapter 1

*H*ell was one word in particular that Lieutenant Brie Phillips could appreciate more than most. Especially now, she thought as she sat on the wooden bench between the lockers of the women officers' ready room, her hands clasped between her thighs. Hanging her head, she stared at her long, thin hands, the blunt-cut nails, her mind and heart churning with turmoil, her stomach tightening. She had arrived at the U.S. Coast Guard station on Kauai, Hawaii, a month ago on a new assignment, not realizing her ex-husband, Lieutenant Niall Ward, was already on board. Up until now she'd managed to avoid seeing him. But she knew it would be inevitable that she'd be assigned to his flight duty roster. There were only so many pilots at the station, and they all flew with one another on a rotation system. Now her number was up and Brie was still reeling from the shock.

Yes, hell had a new and galvanizing meaning to her. Hell was the fact that starting tonight, for a twenty-four hour tour of duty, she'd have to be his copilot on a search and rescue helicopter. Hell was the fact that in about five minutes she'd have to leave the safety of the women's ready room and go out to the mission planning room where everyone was gathering. Hell was having to face Niall again, after all this time.

Looking at the Chase-Durer watch on her right wrist, a timepiece that many military aviators wore because it had many essential features a pilot needed, Brie tried to force out a full breath of air. When she got emotionally tense, she breathed shallowly and her gut tightened.

"Relax, will you?" she muttered to herself between thinned lips. Her eyes narrowed as she looked around at the gray metal lockers. The place was quiet. Painfully so. But then again, it was 1800 on a Sunday evening. No one stayed around the Coast Guard station unless they were scheduled for weekend duty. How she wished she was at her bungalow up near Princeville, on the northern coast of this beautiful, green paradise.

"It *was* paradise," Brie muttered. Until she'd found out that Niall was stationed here. In the two years since her divorce, Brie had lost touch with him after the first year—on purpose. Having contact with him had proved too painful to her heart. The last thing she wanted now was to be reminded of the awful, crushing agony she'd experienced with him and had barely survived. Yet, somehow, Brie knew, she was going to have to reach into the deepest parts of herself as a woman and bear this new burden.

At twenty-nine, Brie thought she'd been through everything. But this latest twist in her life was one that she could never have conceived: she never imagined she'd be stationed with her ex-husband. Now she would be forced to fly with him.

Worse, Brie had been told there was an emergency search and rescue to fly tonight in the face of a major hurricane that was bearing down on the island chain. The winds were already at fifty miles per hour, and at eighty, their helicopters would be grounded, unable to fly in such furious weather and rain.

Heart thrashing painfully in her chest, Brie unclasped her hands and rubbed the damp palms against the bright neon orange of the single-piece flight suit she wore.

"Get up, Phillips. You've got to act professional at this mission briefing." She wondered how *he* would handle their first meeting. Shutting her eyes, Brie felt shaky inside. She wanted to cry. Oh, how had her life become so tangled like this? Hadn't enough happened to her?

Fortunately, she had her Native American beliefs to give her strength. Though her father was an Anglo, her mother's side was Cherokee. Raised by her anthropologist father and her medicine woman mother, Brie had grown up in a matriarchal environment where women were encouraged to be anything they dreamed of being.

Right now, she needed to believe that the Grand-parents, benefic spirit beings who worked directly with the Great Spirit, had her best interests at heart. Brie recognized her present predicament as a test. Even though she wasn't a medicine woman, she was the eldest daughter of one and would have been trained in those healing arts if she'd desired it. Instead, Brie had wanted to be a buzzard, a bird honored by her people, and spend her life flying gracefully on the unseen currents of Father Sky, far above his beloved Mother Earth. As a child, she would lie stretched out for hours on a grassy knoll in the mountains of North Carolina, where she was reared. Hands behind her head, she would watch through half-closed eyes as any number of buzzards, which flew in a family, spiraled high above her.

Well, she'd gotten her wish to fly; she was now a Coast Guard helicopter copilot. And one of the best. She was due to become a full pilot shortly. Because Niall was a full-fledged pilot, she would have to work with him. And she was worried that if he bore any anger toward her, which was possible, he could stop her from progressing. Would he do that?

"Get up," she commanded herself. Standing, she went through her usual perfunctory preparations. Opening her locker, she got out her life vest, put the knife into its sheath and double-checked to make sure all her gear, such as flashlight, food bars, whistle, emergency radio and beacon, were all there and working properly. It was time to go. It was time to be an SAR Coastie.

Brie quietly shut her locker, then turned and left the small room. The highly polished, white tile floor gleamed beneath the fluorescent lights above. The passageway was empty; the doors on either side were locked. Everyone was gone who could be gone on this miserable, rainy Sunday night. They were home making sure there were protective boards across their windows, and doing whatever else they could to prepare for Hurricane Eve, which was being forecasted as a level-five storm with lethal possibilities.

Tonight Brie was going on a top secret mission with her ex-husband, in the middle of one of the potentially most brutal hurricanes that Kauai had seen in the last ten years. How could her luck get any worse? And how was she going to handle being in the same room, much less the same cockpit, with Niall after not seeing or talking to him for two years?

Lieutenant Niall Ward tried to still his chafing anxiety. He sat in the mission briefing room, hands tense on the armrests of the chrome-and-wood chair as he wrestled with the idea of the coming confrontation with Brie. Just thinking of his ex-wife sent his heart pounding wildly in his chest. He lifted his hand and wiped at the sweat on his brow. How was Brie after all this time? he wondered. Was she well? He had a hundred questions about her. At war with his anxiety was his anger over the fact that Brie had abandoned him at the most critical moment in his life. He was reminded once again that he could not rely on anyone—not his family, not even the woman he had loved. Brie hadn't trusted him when things turned nightmarish for them. She had asked for a transfer to another station just when things got bad. He would never forgive her for that transgression, just as he could never forgive his real mother for putting him up for adoption. He could trust no one. Even the couple who had adopted him at age two had done nothing to build his faith in others. His adopted father was an alcoholic who'd divorced his wife three years after Niall came to live with them. Niall became a latchkey kid, living with his single adopted mother, who worked long hours to keep food on the table. His biological mother stepped back, briefly, into his life when he was seven years old. A year after that, his biological father had, too, showing up unexpectedly from time to time, like a painful shadow, until Niall had graduated from high school.

Niall did not look back on his childhood fondly, and as a matter of fact had gone off to college mostly to get away from the whole sordid scene at first opportunity. He'd found a far steadier and reliable family structure when he'd joined Coast Guard aviation at the college. Here he felt safe, cared for. People were attentive to his needs in a way he'd never really experienced before. It was better than what he'd started out with, at least, and he was planning on a thirty-year career with the Coast Guard as a result. Here, Niall fit in. He was wanted. He was praised. He was looked up to.

Niall had found out that Brie was being transferred to his station about a week before her actual arrival. He'd been in shock when he had first heard the news from someone over in the personnel department. And then his traitorous heart, which had never stopped loving her, sang with a joy that had brought unaccustomed tears to his eyes. Tears, of all things! Niall had cried when— He stopped himself. No, he didn't want to go there. Never again, if he could help it. The anguish was too great; the cross too heavy to bear, the guilt all-consuming. Shaking his head, he drummed his fingers nervously on the arm of the chair.

Need of her warred with his guilt. Wanting Brie was like wanting air to breathe for Niall. They were divorced, but his heart had never taken that legal piece of paper seriously. Just when he thought he was over her, that he could get on with his life and leave the tragedy of their divorce behind him, Brie had been assigned to his station. Now, the memory of her abandonment stung him once again. It was as if Brie were pouring more salt into the open wound of his life by coming here. A part of him was wary of working with her in the cockpit. He'd have to stay on top of things more than normal, because he couldn't trust her. He'd never flown with her before, either. Husbands and wives assigned to the same station never flew with one another.

Of course, Niall had no control over where Brie would be assigned; he was an SAR pilot, and at the end of each two-year tour of duty, search and rescue pilots were sent to another station. Kauai was one of them. Niall had never thought he'd see Brie again, because the Coast Guard had many stations across the U.S. More than enough to keep distance between them. Somewhere, though, the higher-ups in the Coast Guard had made the assignment without realizing they were a divorced couple. Working with Brie was going to play havoc on Niall as nothing else could.

Rubbing his eyes, he took a deep, ragged breath. Hearing footsteps, he felt his heart leap in his chest. Was it Brie? His fingers curled in anticipation on the arms of the chair. Licking his lower lip nervously, he sat up tensely and waited.

Two men entered the mission room. One Niall recognized as Lieutenant Rod Nichola, the OOD—officer of the day—who had responsibility for the twenty-four hour watch at the station. The other...Niall's face split with a sudden smile. Instantly, he was on his feet, his hand extended as Morgan Trayhern, the head of Perseus, the supersecret organization in the CIA, entered the room.

"Sir," Niall said with enthusiasm, "it's good to see you again."

Morgan turned and looked at the Coast Guard pilot. His serious features warmed immediately. Thrusting out his hand, he murmured, "Niall. How are you? I didn't know you were scheduled for this black ops. That's excellent news. We're in good hands, then."

Gripping Morgan's hand, Niall pumped it with sincerity. "I didn't know this was a black ops we were being called in for, sir." He released Morgan's hand. Niall had worked for Morgan shortly after his split with Brie. The special undercover assignment had taken him away for three months, and Niall had needed the bone-jarring, dangerous mission to wipe the agony and loss from his heart.

"Have a seat, Niall," Morgan invited. He turned. "Where's your copilot?"

"She'll be here shortly," Lieutenant Nichola told him as he went to the mission planning table, a square surface with maps spread across it.

Eyebrows raising, Morgan said, "She? A woman? Good."

It was known that Morgan liked to pair male and female pilots because of their complementary skills.

Just as Morgan turned toward the table, Niall saw Brie enter. She stood there, looking around uncertainly until their eyes met. And then she froze. Niall thought she looked even more beautiful than he could ever recall. Brie was already in the one-piece, neon-orange flight suit, her vest secured across her upper body. But he could see she still had that graceful, swimmer's figure as she stood before him, her red hair in a chignon at the nape of her neck and her normally ruddy complexion drained of color as she spotted him.

Unable to stop the emotions clamoring inside him, Niall could do nothing but stare into his ex-wife's large, expressive blue eyes, which reminded him of the pristine beauty of the glaciers he'd seen on his Alaska assignment. The beautiful turquoise-blue of her eyes seemed unearthly to Niall, almost mystical, and he had always been mesmerized by it. Maybe *she* was unearthly.

His heart surged with a keening cry of joy at seeing her once more. Yet the cold reality of her abandonment, the memory, as icy as a glacier, washed over him. His mouth thinned and hardened, and he glared back at her.

The shock of seeing Niall once again slammed into Brie like a mighty ocean roaring full speed into a stone jetty. Rocking slightly in reaction, she tried to ignore his narrowing gray eyes, which studied her with ruthless intensity. At thirty-two years old, Niall was even more handsome than she could recall. He came from Black Irish stock, and his hair, though military short, shone with blue highlights. Standing six feet tall, he had a powerful athletic body and broad, square shoulders. There was nothing defenseless or vulnerable about him as he stood there staring back at her, more like an enemy than a friend.

What else could she expect from him? Brie felt his anger and saw it in his gray, stormy eyes. He had a wonderful mouth made for kissing, one she had lost herself in so many times in the past. Now it was thinned with anger, telling her that she wasn't welcome here—not by him.

Tearing her gaze from Niall, Brie tried to shore herself up, and walked confidently over to the table. She introduced herself to the distinguished-looking man with silver at his temples who stood there, looking dapper in a gray pinstripe suit. But as he smiled warmly at her, shook her hand and introduced himself as Morgan Trayhern, she felt chilled, as if ice water was pouring over her.

She had never met Morgan Trayhern before. The only thing she knew about him was that he was the reason Niall had left her in her hour of need. In truth it was Niall who had volunteered to take the three-month black ops assignment for this man. But as she released Morgan's hand, she saw genuine gladness in his eyes that she was here, as a pilot, on this mission. Brie had to give him credit, at least, for not being prejudiced against women in the cockpit.

"Let's have a seat here, shall we?" Morgan said to the pilots, and gestured for them to sit down at the planning table.

Rod shut the door quietly and joined them.

Morgan stood and spread out a map after handing them the black ops mission manuals. "Here's what we have going down and why you were called in to help us," he said. Opening his own manual, he turned to the first page. "One of the mercenaries with my organization, Perseus, has gone undercover. Burke Ormand is our operative and he's been posing as a crewman aboard a tuna boat by the name of *Jellyfish*. It's really a drug runner in disguise. Burke has been wearing a wire to tape evidence against the drug lord, Torres Rebaza, who owns this trawler, and his younger brother, who is the skipper. Rebaza owns ten tuna clippers that ply the Pacific waters. His real cargo is cocaine, which is dropped out at sea by long-range airplanes flying from Mexico. The coke is packed in buoyant, watertight bales, which are picked up by the trawlers and stowed below.''

Morgan turned the page, to a colored photo of the mercenary. ''We've found all this out because of Ormand. Once a tuna trawler gets the cocaine aboard, the crew continues to fish, putting the tuna in storage freezers where the coke's hidden. When they come in to the dock at Kauai to offload their tuna cargo, the cocaine stays—until after dark. Torres then sends his men in a van to pick it up under cover of night.'' Looking up at the pilots, he added, ''The problem is, we've lost contact with Ormand. The boat was going to find shelter on a small island, Tortoise Isle, a hundred miles north of Kauai, and sit out this hurricane— at a place called Half Moon Bay. We know the *Jellyfish* made it to safe harbor at that part.

''The radio that Ormand is wearing is a special state-of-the-art model,'' Morgan told them. ''This radio has a button on it that, if pressed, sends out a signal to us—meaning that Ormand has been found out. It's basically a cry for help. If we'd received that signal, we'd have mounted a rescue effort immediately.''

"But you didn't get that signal?" Brie asked.

Niall looked up. Brie's voice was husky and confident. He recalled that alto voice sweeping through him, recalled hearing her cry out in ecstasy as he'd loved her and they'd spun on ever widening wings of pleasure in one another's arms. *Stop it. Stop. You can't do this to yourself.* Tearing his gaze from Brie's clean profile—her slightly curved nose, high cheekbones and oval face indicating her Native American heritage—he stared down, unseeing, at the manual in his hands. Niall had had no idea how hard it was going to be to remain immune to Brie. Anger flared through him. She might be a temptress to him, but she'd also abandoned him. He had to remember that fact.

"That's correct, Lieutenant Phillips. We received no signal.''

"Is it possible they killed him and threw him overboard, and that would explain why you didn't get the signal?" Brie pressed.

Morgan nodded. "You're very astute, Lieutenant." He grinned wryly. "I like people with your kind of mind. You think ahead and look at the possibilities. Sure you wouldn't like to work for me instead of the Coast Guard?''

Managing a thin smile, she said, "No, sir. I'm happy here, thank you." Brie quelled the anger she irrationally felt toward Morgan Trayhern. Her anger should, by rights, be directed solely at Niall, she knew.

Morgan hadn't ripped him out of her life; Niall had volunteered for the mission. He'd run again. It was a pattern with him: any time life got too dicey, too emotionally painful, Niall bailed out and ran. Just as he'd run out on her during the worst emotional crisis of their lives.

"Well, should you change your mind," Morgan teased lightly, "you just let me know."

"Yes, sir."

Turning his attention back to the mission, Morgan said, "Ormand is either already dead, or possibly, the device wasn't pressed and he's fine. The fact that we haven't received a signal could also be weather related."

"Or," Niall suggested, "the device malfunctioned? Plus if Ormand was discovered, he might not have had time to press it. That's another possibility."

"That's correct, Niall," Morgan affirmed. Paging through the manual, he said, "So here's what I need from you two. I need you to fly a fake SAR mission, which will be broadcast over the airwaves so your flight pattern doesn't raise suspicion. We're going to put the latitude and longitude about twenty miles away from Tortoise Isle. That's the point you'll fly to. The reason you'll do this is because we had a backup system built into Ormand's device. The second button has only a twenty-five mile range. A special radio device has been installed in the helicopter you'll be flying. You'll turn it on, fly around the island and see if you can pick up Ormand's second radio signal. If you don't, then he's probably all right. Or dead. If you do pick it up, then you will radio me back here, and we'll send out a special rescue unit from Perseus to pick Ormand up and blow the cover on the operation. You're not equipped to take on a ship load of drug runners by yourself. I don't want to raise suspicion by sending in a rescue team. Sending you in won't make them jump.''

"So, our fly-by is just that," Brie said. "We don't have to affect a rescue if Ormand's beacon is signaling us?''

"That's correct," Lieutenant Nichola said. "Coast Guard doesn't normally get mixed up in a dangerous drug mission like this. Especially not tonight, because of the hurricane. The winds are increasing. You're going to have enough of a job just seeing if you pick up the signal. Even if all goes well, it's a hundred-mile flight to and from that isle on a nasty night and heavy winds and rain.''

"Nice to know we aren't going to be shot at," Brie said dryly. She glanced at Niall and her heart clenched. He was studying her critically. What was the look in his eyes? Need? Desire? Anger? Brie couldn't be sure. Her hands shook slightly as she thumbed quickly through the rest of the manual. Above all, she couldn't allow her personal feelings to get in the cockpit with him. Two years had given her time to let her bitter feelings subside and a new maturity replace them. But her heart was thumping wildly in her chest. How badly she wanted to say to hell with everything and simply sit down and talk to Niall, at length. Snorting softly, she decided that was a lost cause. The biggest thorn in their marriage had been a lack of communication. Niall had simply run away when things got bad. He had come from a one-parent family, and his adopted mother was rarely around while he was growing up. He wasn't used to relying on others and so he closed up emotionally, like a proverbial clam. Brie had had three years of hell with him, trying to get him to open up and be emotionally accessible to her. Like a lot of men, Niall didn't know how to talk on a personal, intimate level. Just when things were getting good in their marriage, and he was starting to open up, disaster had struck—the worst kind.

"Questions?" Morgan asked as he twisted around and looked at each of them.

"I have none, sir," Brie said. "Looks pretty straightforward from here."

"No, sir," Niall told him. "This is probably going to be a long, boring flight fighting headwinds and gusts, getting thumped around out there."

Grinning, Morgan said, "I suspect you're right, Niall." His smile disappeared as he looked from one to the other. "I want you to know we're grateful you'll do this. Our mercenaries are our highest priority, and I don't want to lose a single man or woman on an assignment if we can help it. I'm deeply appreciative of your and the Coast Guard's help on this."

Niall stood. He smiled at Morgan. "We're glad to help, sir."

Brie closed the manual and made notes in her flight log. Her heart was beating hard now. Within minutes, she'd be in the cramped cockpit with Niall, elbow to elbow with him. The last place in the world she wanted to be.

Chapter 2

Niall's mouth was dry as they sat in the helicopter outside the well-lit hangar. Wind gusts shuddered against the fuselage, where they were dry and protected as the rain poured down around them. The atmosphere in the cockpit was tense, to say the least, as he ran through the preflight checklist with Brie in a clipped, professional tone. Her own voice was cool and detached sounding as she responded. Outside, in front of them in the rain, the crew chief waited to give them the signal to start the engine.

"We're set," Niall said gruffly, closing the checklist and stowing it in a nylon net pocket on the side of his seat.

"Yes." Brie winced inwardly. She didn't mean to

sound robotic, but she couldn't help herself. Being this close to Niall, squeezed into a narrow cockpit with him, was tearing her up emotionally. As she tightened her harness and put on her fire-retardant Nomex gloves, her hand accidentally brushed against his just as he reached up to flip on a set of switches on the instrument panel. Instantly, Brie jerked her hand away, as if burned.

Hurt soared through Niall. And then anger. He reminded himself that Brie was no longer his wife. They were no longer intimate. She couldn't be trusted. She'd thrown away their marriage in one act of abandonment.

"I'm not going to bite you," he snapped with unconcealed irritation. Jerking the chin strap of his helmet so that it fit more tightly beneath his clenched jaw, he saw her look toward him. Her eyes were huge with shock.

"No?" Brie's voice became accusatory. "You did once before."

Rocking internally from the anger tightly throttled in her low-pitched, husky tone, Niall pressed his lips together. "Let's just get this show on the road, shall we? I don't like this any more than you obviously do." *Liar.* His heart ached. How many nights had he lain awake, tossing and turning and thinking of Brie, of what they'd had—and lost?

Stung, Brie tore her gaze from Niall's dark and shadowed features. How terribly handsome he was. His face was narrow, with a strong chin and high cheekbones. He was proud of his Irish heritage; it was the one thing that he'd managed to salvage from his lousy childhood. His birth mother, Fiona Ward, had visited him once, when he was seven years old, and told him his father was Irish. Brie also knew Niall's birth father was an alcoholic. Seamus Farrell had married Niall's mother to escape Ireland's poor economy, and then left her as soon as he found out she was pregnant. Seamus had been a dark, morbid cloud floating in and out of Niall's life from age eight onward. About the only thing he'd given Niall was his name and his dark good looks. When Seamus waltzed drunkenly back into Niall's young life, he'd torn him up, emotionally. Those short visits had been rare, explosive and heartrending.

She recalled how, one night, Niall had told her the story behind his name—how his father wanted him to have a name of an heroic Irish chieftain. Niall, in Celtic, meant "brave" or "chief." Seamus had wanted his son to amount to something, to be heroic, to do something important with his life because he himself hadn't. All Seamus Farrell could do was spin colorful and exciting yarns about hopes and dreams.

Brie knew that Seamus Farrell's affair with alcohol was his undoing, and that he'd placed all his hopes and dreams in Niall. That was so unfair. She had seen how Niall had ordered his life around his father's unrealistic expectations and pipe dreams. At age eighteen, Niall went to court to have his last name become Ward, after his mother. He wanted no trace of his father in his life—not even his last name. But Niall had inherited one of Seamus Farrell's worst faults: running when things got bad. Seamus didn't have the maturity or responsibility to see things through to the end, and neither did his son. Niall had forsaken Brie, just as Seamus had forsaken his mother—at a time when both women had needed their men the most. Yes, father and son were alike in that area, unfortunately. It had been the main reason for Brie's divorce from Niall.

Within moments, the blades of the orange-and-white helicopter began to turn, faster and faster. The trembling and shaking was soothing to Brie; her raw nerves settled down and grew calmer as she relaxed, snugly ensconced in her seat. As the pilot, Niall sat in the right-hand seat. Normally, they'd have a swimmer and a crew chief on board. Because this was not a standard search and rescue, they had neither. They were alone in a tight little space, and Brie's heart was pounding unrelentingly in her breast. Niall was so close! Her heart screamed out in anguish, in need of him. Brie fought the feeling.

Outside in the slashing rain, the crew chief gave the signal for them to taxi to the takeoff point. The Lihue Airport, which served civilian flights as well as Coast Guard aircraft, was well lit in the blackness as Niall notched up the power and the helo began to trundle slowly forward.

Just the movement of the helo soothed more of Brie's fractious state. She was busy monitoring the dials, her gaze sweeping from left to right across the console. Her job as copilot wouldn't be too demanding on this trip. It would be a pretty dull and boring flight in one respect. In a way, Brie was glad this was a black ops mission because she didn't want the pressure and stress of a rescue at sea on top of everything else she was presently experiencing.

Within minutes they were airborne and heading out over the inky darkness of the Pacific Ocean. Niall guided the helicopter to three thousand feet and leveled off. The aircraft rocked and jostled from the gusting fifty-mile-an-hour winds, which slammed into them repeatedly. His grip on the cyclic and collective was firm and steady. Rain slashed across the windshield. It was impossible to see very well and they were flying blind. Niall's constantly roving gaze never left the control panel in front of him. For now, they had to fly on instruments only. To try and fly visually in this deteriorating weather would be folly. Helicopters over water created a special visual illusion for pilots at the best of times, and if they relied on their eyes instead of their instruments, they could crash.

"Bad night," Brie muttered unhappily, trying to defrost the icy tension in the cockpit.

"Yeah, it is," Niall grumbled. *In more ways than one.* He yearned to say something neutral, something less acidic, but his anger was spiking, and hurt writhed within him like a wounded snake.

Frowning, Brie felt a chill go through her, despite the special one-piece suit she, like Niall, wore over her normal flight suit. It was highly insulated and waterproof, so that in case they crashed into the chilly ocean, they wouldn't die of hypothermia—at least not right away. Even though the Pacific currents were balmier around the Hawaiian Islands, the sea wasn't that warm and a person could die of exposure. The suit was bulky and ill fitting. Normally, Brie sweated in it, but the chill working its way up her spine caught her attention. As she moved the flight log aside and placed it behind her seat, she couldn't shake the bad feeling she had.

The pleasant green glow of light from the cockpit panel was the only illumination in the inky night surrounding them. Even though the helo shuddered and shook, the roar of the engines was muted to a degree by her helmet. Niall's profile was stern and tense looking. Flying in this weather was not easy. Every few seconds the helicopter would shimmy and shake, fighting the powerful up- and downdrafts created by the hurricane. Or it would slide sideways, to the right or left. Niall had his hands full trying to keep the chopper on an even flight path.

Tucking her lower lip between her teeth, Brie wondered if she should offer to help fly the mission. Usually, pilot and copilot would trade off on long flights. Especially on nights like this, when battling the storm took all of the pilot's attention, creating high stress levels. Even the best of pilots could become fatigued, their senses dulled. Then it became dangerous for everyone on board.

To heck with it. She sighed and said, "If you want me to take over at any point, let me know."

Niall responded instantly to her low, husky tone. Brie had a voice he'd loved from the moment he'd met her, so long ago. It was like warm, melting honey flowing soothingly, like a balm, across his tense body. Hearing her voice always calmed his fractious state. A Type-A personality, Niall was always highstrung and often stressed out. Brie was a Type-B personality—low-key and easygoing. She seemed to be able to cope with demands in a completely different way.

"Maybe," he muttered. "I'll see how it goes."

Well, at least he was talking to her. Brie felt a little of her tension dissolve. His tone was less abrasive. Less accusatory. "Nasty night," she commented, hoping to tamp down the tension still lingering between them.

"Yeah, helluva night." Giving Brie a quick glance out the side of his eyes, Niall saw her face soften as he spoke to her. She was so damned attractive. All woman. He remembered holding her—how rounded and soft and velvety she felt in his arms. *Stop it. Stop remembering.* Niall fought himself. Fought the past, which was now glaring into his present world and life. He wanted to run, but there was no place to go, no place to hide from her or their unhealed past.

Spreading the map across her thighs, Brie studied it in the pale green light. Green was restful on the eyes, the best color for night work. To use a flashlight would destroy their night vision. On this flight, she was the navigator, and she gave Niall coordinates and told him to change course. "You ever been over Tortoise Isle?" she asked then.

Shaking his head, he said, "No. Closest I've come to it was an SAR about six months ago, roughly twenty miles south of it. A yacht got in trouble in heavy seas in that area, took on too much water and called in a mayday to us."

"You ended up rescuing the crew?"

"Yeah, parents and a kid."

She smiled slightly. "I'm sure they were glad to see you show up."

Nodding, Niall tried to keep focused on his flying, watching the instruments. He didn't want to engage Brie in conversation. A sudden, violent gust of wind slapped into the helicopter. Hissing a curse, he got the chopper back under control, but only after they'd dropped a good fifty feet. His stomach had lurched up into his throat. He'd heard Brie gasp. Did she question his ability to fly now, too? Anger riddled him.

"Stop acting like a greenhorn student pilot, will you? I don't need any jeers or cheers from my copilot."

Brie glared at him. His face was set like stone and she saw perspiration dotting his furrowed brow. A memory of how they had argued came back to her. Lips tightening, she withheld the angry salvo she was going to fire at him.

Brie knew this flight would be tough on any seasoned pilot. Looking down at the map, she continued to give him navigation information, as appropriate. Looking at her watch, she saw that in another thirty minutes they'd be at the twenty-mile mark they were heading for. On the console she saw a small black box that had been hooked into their electrical and electronic systems. Turning the dial to the specified position, Brie switched the machine on.

Their fuel was being eaten up rapidly by having to fight the massive headwind, but Brie knew Niall had calculated how much would be needed for the flight. Still, she thought, studying the gauge, the fuel was lowering rapidly. That worried her, but she said nothing. The heater was on in the cockpit and that, plus the all-weather suit she wore, kept her warm.

"We're going to arrive at Alpha in ten minutes," she told Niall as she looked at her watch. Alpha was the twenty-mile limit point. If there was no signal detected, it meant they could turn around and fly back to base.

"Okay," he grunted. The helicopter was wobbling and shaking in earnest from the constant beating of the hurricane's winds. "If I didn't know better, I'd say we're hitting seventy- or eighty-mile-an-hour gusts."

"Yes, I agree." At eighty miles an hour, a search and rescue was called off. "Want me to contact meteorology?" Brie knew that if she did, and they confirmed that the winds were at maximum, the mission would be canceled. They were almost on target, and to turn back now would be such a waste. But that was Niall's call to make, not hers.

Shaking his head, he said, "No. Just send a radio report of our position now."

"Roger." Brie picked up the radio and gave their position in latitude and longitude, then signed off.

As her gaze flicked across the panel, she saw the needle that indicated engine heat shooting into the red zone. If an engine overheated it could burst into flame or worse. the power of the hurricane was a terrible stress on the engine. "Niall..."

Before Brie could say anything more, there was an explosion, the sound like a cannon going off around them. Automatically ducking her head, Brie saw sparks and then fire shooting out above the cabin. Instantly, the helicopter began hurtling downward.

A curse ripped from Niall's lips. He grabbed the cyclic and collective hard and frantically worked the yaw pedals beneath his booted feet. "Call in a mayday!" he croaked. His mind whirled. A bad ball bearing could have caused this situation.

The engines stopped. The chopper's blades floundered, then waffled unsteadily in the gale-force winds.

They were going down. Down into the black, unseen ocean below.

Brie grabbed the mike on the radio and thumbed it on. She made the call.

The helicopter was sinking like a rock! They were at thirty-five hundred feet. She heard Niall grunt. Valiantly, he worked the yaw pedals to straighten out the flailing helicopter. Brie found herself jerked violently back and forth as he fought to gain the upper hand on the plummeting aircraft. They were going to crash! The thought was the last one Brie entertained. After making the call, her mind went into overdrive. The station had a last mayday fix on their location. They would send someone out to rescue them.

But first they had to survive the helicopter crashing into the ocean, and climb out before it sank and took them down with it. A helicopter didn't float. It was like a huge boulder in the sky, with four blades to keep it aloft.

Brie's mind flicked over egress procedures. Escape from a helo was via the sliding door on the starboard side of the fuselage. She would be responsible for getting out of her harness first, to make her way back to it before they sank and couldn't escape. Her other responsibility was to not only open the door, but retrieve the uninflated life raft hanging on the bulkhead opposite it.

Abruptly, the instruments went dead, because there was no electricity being generated by the spinning blades and engine. The cockpit went black. They were being slammed around. The harness straps bit deeply into Niall's tense shoulders as he tried valiantly to pull up the nose of the helicopter. They were sinking fast! He had no idea of their altitude or when they'd hit the water. He could see nothing out the windows. Rain slashed around them, preventing him from a visual. They were blind. Completely blind. And they were going to crash. Would they survive? Suddenly, in that second, all his anger toward Brie was ripped away.

Niall didn't want her to die! She was too beautiful. Too kind. Too loving… In the next moment, he bitterly regretted how their marriage had turned out. If only… If only they'd had a second chance! But that was impossible now.

Brie sucked in a breath as the helicopter, nose up, slammed into the Pacific Ocean. The aircraft screeched and grated as it hit that massive and invisible wall of water. A second later, pain shot up her back and into her head from the crash.

"Get out!" Niall roared.

Instantly, Brie fumbled with her harness closures, trying to release them with her gloved fingers. Seconds dragged like hours. *Come on! Come on!* Lips pursed, she scrambled to find the openings.

The helicopter lurched and her hands flew away from her body. Slamming into the side panel, Brie gasped. Quickly, blindly, she sought the harness closure once more and tugged at it, trying to get it open. Yes! Unsnapping her harness, Brie twisted around and lurched between the seats toward the cargo area behind.

Landing hard on her hands and knees, she found saltwater splashing up around her. Gasping again, she struggled to stand. The aircraft was turning slowly, like a wounded whale. It was listing to port, groaning. She could hear the metal being torn by the fingers of the greedy, grasping ocean. Water sloshed ankle deep around her boots. Unable to see anything, Brie fumbled along the fuselage panel, hunting wildly for the door latch. *There!* Hands shaking, she pulled on it.

Jammed! It was jammed from the crash. "No!" Brie cried. "It's jammed! I can't open it, Niall! Help me! Help!" Her voice was swallowed up by the burping, gurgling sounds of water entering the wallowing helicopter, which listed even more as it bobbed in the waves.

Behind her, Brie heard Niall groping his way out of the cockpit in the unforgiving blackness. His hand hit her hip and he gripped her hard. The aircraft tipped more to port, almost upside down.

"The door!" Niall gasped. "Open it!"

"It's jammed!" Brie cried. "Help me!"

Fumbling, Niall held on to her, wrapping his left arm around her waist to stop them from being thrown against the side of the chopper. Thrusting out his right hand, he followed her arm to where she was holding on to the door, and slid his gloved fingers through the latch.

"Let go," he ordered, breathing raggedly.

Instantly, Brie pulled her hand away, and fell backward. Slamming into the port side of the helo, she practically had the wind knocked out of her before she fell to the deck.

Cold and numbing saltwater enveloped her. Briefly, she was underwater, but getting her feet under her, she surged upward. Coughing violently, eyes stinging, she tried to stay upright. If they didn't get out of here in a few seconds, they were going to drown. The helicopter was beginning to sink.

With a curse, Niall wrenched back with all his weight and strength. The door was starting to give. Again he jerked at it. Water was gushing in past him now, nearly sweeping him off his feet. One more pull...

The door finally screeched and slid open.

"Brie!" he screamed. "Where are you?" He turned and clung to the door opening as the helo rolled completely over on its port side.

"Here!" Brie scrambled upward, with the raft held tightly in her left hand. Somehow she'd managed to release it from the port fuselage. "The raft! Here's the life raft!" she yelled. "Take it! Take it!"

Niall grunted as his groping hand struck the tightly rolled pack that contained the dingy. Brie's hand was locked beneath the strap. He hauled both toward him in a feat of strength that would have been impossible without the adrenaline beating wildly through his bloodstream now.

Blindly, they leaped off the helicopter's lip and into the grasping, cold waters of the ocean. Niall had a firm grip on the shoulder of Brie's flight suit. He kicked out hard and fast to get away from the aircraft as it burbled and started to slide downward. The sucking, spinning whirlpool left in the wake of the sinking helicopter pulled powerfully at their heavy, waterlogged boots.

Water deluged Niall. He went under, his hand still

tight on Brie's shoulder. No way was he going to let her go! But his flight boots were like concrete weights, pulling him down.

Instead of fighting to surface, he fumbled for the cord of his life vest. When he jerked on it, the vest instantly inflated. That alone helped pop him to the surface.

The roar of the ocean surrounded Niall as he shot above water. Air! He could breathe! Sobbing for air, he anxiously tugged at Brie again, hauling her upward. When she surfaced, he heard her cough violently.

"Inflate your vest!" he cried hoarsely. With it deployed, they wouldn't have to try and swim to keep their heads above water. He heard the hissing sound that told him it was inflating. Again Brie choked and coughed.

Niall's fingers ached from holding on to the shoulder of her weather suit. But never would he let her go. Never. Raising his other hand, he pulled Brie against him, so they were face-to-face, body-to-body. If for even a second, he let her go he knew he'd lose her in this storm. The violent surging of the waves would quickly separate them and they'd never find one another again.

"The raft!" Brie choked out. "We've got to inflate it!" And she fumbled for the releases.

Managing to get the flashlight attached to his vest flicked on, Niall did the most important thing next. There was a special hook and nylon cord, located on the front of each vest. He took his hook and fastened it securely to the front of Brie's vest, so that no matter what happened, they couldn't be separated by the angry ocean. With her attached to him, he trained his flashlight beam on the raft she was still holding on to with a death grip.

Releasing the straps, he found the valve that would initiate inflation. The moment he pulled it out, a loud hissing began. Within minutes the flotation device blew up into a yellow rubber raft.

Brie gave a cry of joy as the raft inflated fully. That meant it hadn't sustained any punctures or cuts during the crash or egress. It was a small, two-person raft with barely enough room for both of them, but with it, at least, they had a shot at survival.

"You first," Niall shouted above the roar of the ocean. Wind and rain splattered his tense face. He helped Brie clamber awkwardly into the raft. She floundered drunkenly, the weight of the suit pulling her downward, making each of her efforts seem to be in slow motion. Her flight boots were filled with water, making it hard to maneuver. Setting his hand beneath her buttocks as she threw her arms over the side of the raft, Niall pushed upward with all his strength. Brie slid unceremoniously into the raft, arms and legs akimbo. The three-foot lifeline went taut as she turned and reached out to help him climb on board.

"Give me your hand!" Brie cried, straining toward him. In the light of the flashlight tucked in Niall's vest she could see that his tense face was glistening with seawater. His eyes were hard and narrowed. Brie felt his large hand wrap around one of hers. In moments, he had hauled himself into the raft. Safe! They were safe!

Gulping unsteadily, Brie watched as Niall maneuvered his bulk to balance the raft so it wouldn't overturn. There was a special hook and tether line that could be attached to their life vest. Hands shaking badly, Brie got the device and snapped it to the front of her vest and then Niall's. That way, if they were washed overboard by a huge wave, they wouldn't lose their raft.

Niall saw Brie attach the raft tether to his vest. Her hands were shaking badly as she fastened the device. He saw the terror in her pale face, visible beneath her helmet. The weather was cold. The wind beat against them. It shrieked and moaned, sounding like a wounded animal in horrible pain. Niall knew by her expression that Brie wanted to cry. Without thinking, he shut off the flashlight and turned to settle down in the raft. Blackness engulfed them immediately. Then he blindly reached out to her.

"Come here," Niall urged gruffly, placing his arm around her shoulders and drawing her into his arms. Brie came without fighting. She didn't stiffen or try to pull away. To his surprise, Niall felt her arms slide around his torso. She rested her helmeted head against his and he heard her gasping.

"Go ahead," he said harshly against her cheek, "cry. We made it. We made it, Brie…." And Niall choked back a sob himself.

Darkness surrounded them. Niall clung to Brie as much as she clung to him. The wind was howling, sometimes a soul-shattering shriek. Rain slashed and cut at them. He turned his face toward hers, their helmets protecting their vulnerable flesh to a degree. It was cold. Much colder than he'd ever imagined. Glad to be wearing the Mustang Suit, Niall felt his pounding heart begin to slow over the next few minutes. Just having Brie in his arms was all he needed at this moment. She felt soft and curved in all the right places, just as he'd remembered from so long ago.

Brie let the tears come as she clung tightly to Niall. She needed his confidence and strength right now. They'd nearly died. If he hadn't gotten the door open, they'd have drowned already. The reality of their narrow escape from death avalanched through Brie. She felt Niall patting her shoulder awkwardly in an attempt to comfort her. Rainwater slashed relentlessly against her face, mingling with her tears. Crying was a relief valve for Brie. They were alive. *Alive.* And Niall was holding her. Even in the midst of this unfolding nightmare, his strength, his touch, soothed her shock and the fear of nearly dying. As she huddled against him, glad for the solidity of his strong, male body, Brie found herself wanting to let all the hurt from the past go. Why, oh why, couldn't they have talked it out? Why did he have to run away?

The raft surged upward and they both tensed. Brie felt Niall's hands tighten around her like steel bands, to protect her from the unseen threat. They were riding a huge wave skyward at a terrific rate of speed. And then the raft slowed.

Brie gave a cry of terror. She realized that the wave was probably twenty or thirty feet high, and the raft was riding it upward. If they didn't crest it, the wave would crash over them, hurtling them back into the sea. If that happened, they'd be flattened, like bugs under a flyswatter, by tons of water crushing down upon them. It would throw them out of the raft. They'd drink a lot of seawater. They might drown.

"Easy…easy…" Niall whispered harshly. He felt Brie tense. Felt her hands work frantically around his torso, as if to hold on even more tightly. They were riding a huge, vertical wave, and he knew the consequences. Would they crest it or not? Holding his breath, he felt the raft slow even more. They had to be near the top of the giant.

The roar around them heightened. It sounded as if they were standing in an echo chamber, with a jet engine screaming at them. For a moment, in the blackness, Niall felt as if he was in limbo, between two worlds. Without being able to see, he had no idea what was happening around them. Tightening his arms around Brie, he waited out the long, tortured seconds as the raft slowed to nearly a standstill.

The burbling, rushing whoosh of water foaming around them happened within moments. And then the raft took in gallons of water as the wave boiled and vomited around them. Niall didn't try to get rid of the water; he knew the raft would float even if it was full.

Relief rushed through him. They'd crested the monster wave.

"It's okay," he whispered tautly to Brie. "We crested it. We're all right, sweetheart...."

Chagrin filled him as the endearment slipped out of his mouth. Niall wondered where the hell that had come from. Brie had been his sweetheart; it was his pet name for her. And now, in a moment of real crisis, it had come flying out of his mouth. What the hell.

There was too much going on, Niall decided as he eased his grip on her slightly. The raft was sliding gently now, down into the trough before the next wave. Not all waves were such monsters. But in a hurricane in the middle of an ocean, some could reach twenty or thirty feet with no problem at all. Sometimes even higher.

"Okay?" Niall asked, as she eased back slightly. He still kept his arms around her because, despite their past, he wanted to protect her. Although he couldn't see her, he could feel her. Brie felt good to him. She felt like home.

Bitterly Niall reminded himself that he had no home. He never had. And now they had crash-landed and were drifting aimlessly in the largest ocean in the world. Had the Coast Guard station picked up their mayday before they crashed? Or would they die out here in each other's arms?

Chapter 3

"It's going to be all right...all right..."

The husky, emotion-laden reassurance drifted into Brie's awareness, easing her terror-stricken state. She lost track of the roller coaster movement of the raft. The roar of the ocean was overwhelming and constant. Salt spray whipped across her face, stinging, painful and cold. Most of the time she kept her eyes tightly shut. If she opened them, they filled with the salty water and burned—and with the salty tears streaming down her cheeks.

Oh, how Brie had dreamed of Niall holding her so tightly against him. This wasn't how she wanted it—not in a hurricane-driven ocean, where she wasn't sure if they were going to live or die. But just the act of clinging to him, feeling his strong, comforting arms around her, his sandpapery cheek pressed against hers as they were tossed wildly about in the blackened night, made her feel safe.

Brie knew they weren't safe. She knew Niall couldn't tell with any certainty that they'd be all right. Still, the husky sound of his voice was balm to her shocked soul. Never in all her life had she anticipated such an incident occurring. She was a pilot, sure, and she trained weekly for just such a crash, but somewhere in the back of her mind, Brie had felt it would never happen. Well, it had. And in the worst kind of weather situation.

Her arms were wrapped around Niall's torso. The raft wobbled and bobbed violently. Spray and white froth would rocket across them like icy bullets fired from an unseen enemy in the inky night. They had initiated their individual radio beacons, small transmitters on their vests that would send out a mayday signal. However, the radius of the transmission was limited to a five-mile area. Any fixed-wing aircraft, such as the Coast Guard C-130 Hercules, a medium-size transport plane, would have to penetrate that zone in order for the instruments on board to pick up the mayday signal. That was their only chance for detection, their only chance for rescue from this watery hell. No other aircraft would be able to fly through eighty-mile-an-hour winds, through squalls and violent up- and downdrafts.

Niall shut his eyes and clung strongly to Brie. She

felt so damn good to him, despite the terrifying circumstances. The worst moment for him had been when he thought he was going to lose her in the sinking helicopter. Relief pumped violently through his heart that she had survived and was here, in his arms, as he'd always wanted her to be once more.

Talking was impossible right now. Each time the raft slid upward, he knew it was climbing torturously toward the crest of some giant, unseen wave. In a way, Niall was glad it was night, because if he saw those monster waves during daylight hours, he knew he'd be scared to death. Never had he been in such a situation. If there was anything good about it, it was that Brie was here with him.

In another hour, dawn would come. Daylight would help them in many ways. As he keyed his hearing, Niall thought the howling screech of the wind might be lessening. He knew from their last plotted position that they'd been flying very close to the center of the gathering hurricane. If only they could get into the eye! That would mean no rain for a while, only smooth, quiet ocean and a good chance to be rescued. However, there was no guarantee they'd make it into the eye; they were totally at the whim of the ocean.

"Are you okay?" he asked, raising his voice near her left cheek. Brie's helmet covered her ears, and Niall knew he'd have to shout for her to hear him. He felt her arms loosen a little as the raft slid slowly down into an unseen trough.

"Y-yes…just scared."

He laughed bitterly. "Makes two of us..." He'd nearly said "sweetheart" again, but caught himself this time. Why did his traitorous heart want to gift her with that endearment?

"Are you okay, Niall?"

Shrugging, he said, "I think I am. I wrenched my shoulder opening that damned door."

"I'm sorry I couldn't get it open."

"I didn't think I would, either. It was really stuck. The crash jammed it." His lips came to rest against the cool firmness of her cheek. He wanted to touch her, wanted to kiss her, but fought the wild, spontaneous urge. Using their dire situation as an excuse, because they had to be close in order to hear one another, he said, "We're going to be okay."

"Liar."

He smiled a little. Then the raft bobbled, climbing another unseen wall of water. Niall held his breath. His arms automatically tightened around Brie. When the raft bobbled, and sea spray whipped across them, pummeling them like boxers, he knew they'd crested it. Breathing out in relief, he felt Brie sag in reaction, too. "I'm sorry I got you into this mess," he told her.

"This isn't your fault. I pulled the duty. You had nothing to do with the flight pilot roster."

"If I could, I'd have flown with someone else." He realized what he'd said. Before he could correct his mistake, he felt Brie stiffen in his arms.

"I'm sure you would have," she said, her voice sad.

Hearing the tears in her voice, Niall castigated himself. He was rattled by the crash. Adrenaline was still pumping strongly through his veins and he wasn't monitoring what he said. Knowing his words had hurt Brie, he scrambled to try and patch up the mistake.

"No...I didn't mean it that way, Brie. I really didn't."

"Considering that I haven't heard from you for two years, I think you did. No letters. No phone calls to see how I was doing..."

Anger seared him. "Well, you didn't exactly communicate, either."

"I did more than you did, Niall." Her voice quavered with anguish. "I sent you cards the first year. Six of them. They were all returned by you, unopened. At least I tried. And yeah, when you didn't respond, I did stop trying to talk with you. Blame me if you want."

Closing his eyes, Niall felt anger and sadness wind through him. "I—just couldn't, Brie. I was too hurt...."

"You ran, Niall," she charged, her voice brimming with escaping emotions. "You always run when life gets tough. That's how you survive. You run!"

Her voice was angry. Filled with grief. Niall felt Brie's words slice through his pounding heart. Another deluge of icy salt spray hit them, and they were soaked once again. Even now, they were arguing. "Look," he rasped, "you were the one who told me to leave after...well, after..."

"After I lost our baby," Brie sobbed. She couldn't

help herself. The trauma of the crash had stripped her of her normally cool composure. Now, with Niall holding her, one leg wrapped tightly about hers so she wouldn't fly out of the life raft, his closeness had divested her of all the armor she had built around herself after the loss of their baby. Choking, Brie tried to recapture her escaping grief over the loss. Oh, how long had it been since she'd cried for her loss of the baby? *Too long.*

"*You* were the one who ran out on me. *You* abandoned me in my worst hour of need, Niall!" Her voice cracked. Brie opened her eyes. She could see nothing in the blackness, but she felt his cheek against hers. His chest heaved against her breasts, and she could feel the tension gather in him. "I had just lost the baby. I was in the hospital crying, and you volunteered for a black ops with Morgan Trayhern. You just up and left! You ran out on me just like your father ran out on your mother!"

Helplessly, Niall worked his mouth, but no sound came out. He couldn't protect himself from her torn words, the hoarseness of her voice. He felt Brie's hands opening and closing frantically against him. "I didn't run out on you," he said at last. "The assignment came up."

"So? Why did you take it, Niall? Why?" Her voice grew even hoarser. The raft wobbled dangerously as the sea swelled around them. Another wall of spray deluged them. Brie could feel the water slopping back and forth around their bodies in the bottom of the raft.

There was no way to bail it out, and it didn't matter; the raft would continue to float anyway. Right now, all Brie wanted to do was escape Niall. Her rage strangled her, and she wanted to hurt him as badly as he'd hurt her by walking out on her that way.

"Because you didn't need me, that's why, Brie," he growled.

"I didn't need you?" Her voice rose, incredulous. Stunned at this revelation, Brie lay there against him, her spongy mind working over his admittance.

"Look," Niall said in a raspy voice, "we need to stop arguing. We're at risk right now. We could die any moment. Let's just conserve our energy for now, okay? We can talk more after we get rescued." He slid his hand upward, against the back of her helmet, and forced her head down on his chest. "Just lie here against me," he ordered thickly. "I'm not running now."

"You would if you could walk on water and get the hell out of this life raft right now, Niall. But you can't."

He laughed unsurely. "No, I can't walk on water. I'm too damned bad and dark."

Brie surrendered. She was too tired, too stressed and terrified of dying to continue fighting with him. Death wasn't an option to her. Niall was right: they had to conserve themselves in every way. Rescue might come…or it might not. Or rescue might come too late, depending upon the hurricane's antics. They had enough food and water in their life vests to sustain them for forty-eight hours, and that was it.

Closing her eyes, Brie tried to stop feeling, tried to stop thinking of Niall's words and charges. He didn't think she *cared* about him? Of course, since he had run out while she was in the hospital recovering from the miscarriage, Brie had never had a chance to speak with him. When Niall had come back three months later, he was a walled-up warrior who refused to talk about their loss. Their marriage, at that point, had rapidly disintegrated into two strangers living under the same roof. The loss of the baby was too painful for either of them to bring up. Brie admitted now that it was probably due to the depth of their grief and loss that they hadn't been able to talk honestly and at length with one another.

She felt herself spiraling downward. Within minutes, she lapsed into a broken sleep in Niall's sheltering arms, feeling safe even though her world was being twisted apart.

Gray dawn light greeted Niall's sore, scratchy eyes as he slowly raised his head from his light sleep and looked around. Disoriented at first, he sat up from his prone position in the raft, sending the few inches of water in the bottom swilling around his legs. The growing light revealed many things. First he noticed that the ocean was calm, the swell of waves less than one or two feet in height. Secondly, though clouds were scudding by, he could see stars fading above him.

They'd had the luck to enter the eye of the hurricane. He knew the hurricane was huge and they could not have drifted out of its grasp yet. Only in the eye could the weather have cleared and the waters calmed. He looked down at Brie. She was stirring, her eyes puffy, with dark smudges beneath them. Still, she was incredibly beautiful to him.

Leaning over, he helped her sit up. The three-foot nylon line still held them together and he unsnapped it from his vest. Her waterlogged green Nomex gloves were still on her hands and he watched as she shed them. With fingers white and wrinkled-looking from being in the water so long, she slowly rubbed her swollen eyes. She'd been crying. A lot. His conscience ate at him. How badly he wanted to reach out and touch her, to somehow atone for all the pain he'd caused her over the years.

Taking off his helmet, he let it roll aside on the bottom of the raft. The wind was warm, humid and soft. Breathing easier, Niall saw nothing but gray-green ocean surrounding them no matter what direction he looked in. Turning back to Brie, he saw her ease the helmet off her head. Her copper-colored hair was flattened against her skull, with fine, thin wisps plastered across her forehead. Brows dipping downward, he watched her do something that he'd loved to see her do before, when they were married: slide her long, slender fingers through her thick hair to fluff it up and into place. How much he missed that small gesture, Niall realized. Choking back a sudden lump in his throat, he absorbed Brie's every graceful motion like a man too long starved for touch himself. In that eloquent moment, Niall realized fully just how much he'd missed having Brie in his life.

Trying to balance his predatory hunger for her against what she'd done to him, he found it impossible to reconcile the two very different and divergent feelings within himself. Helplessly, Niall sat there and watched her drag those soft, long bangs across her broad forehead and gently nudge them into place. Despite the bulky flight suit she wore, Brie was feminine in every way. The softness of her lips, now parted, beckoned powerfully to him. Hours ago, after the crash, his lips and hers had been fractions of an inch apart....

Wiping his mouth with the back of his gloved hand, Niall tore his gaze from her. To watch Brie was to open up a wound in his heart that had never fully healed or recovered. Trying to think beyond the personal with her, Niall checked the water bottle in his vest. It was full and had survived the crash intact.

"Are you thirsty?" he asked her.

Brie looked up. In the gray dawn light Niall's narrow face was shadowed and strong looking. His gray eyes were keen and assessing. Feeling his warmth and care—something she'd craved so badly and had rarely found in the last months of their marriage—Brie absorbed his sincere concern now. Ruffling her hair, she lowered her hand and checked the bottle in her vest. "I am, but I want to save it."

Nodding, Niall said, "Yeah...no telling when they'll locate us." Or *if* they would, but he didn't voice his worry. He wasn't out to hurt Brie. Right now, Niall was trying to protect her the best he could.

"They'll be out looking for us." Brie stared at his clean profile, his strong nose and chin. There was so much good in Niall, if only he'd stop running.

Like father, like son. Hurting, Brie absorbed his features, the dark growth of beard making him look even more dangerous and appealing than before. His black hair was plastered to his skull, one rebellious short lock hanging over his furrowed brow. When he turned and their gazes locked, her heart flew open.

"Yes," he answered hesitantly.

"They will," she said stubbornly. "They got our last fix."

"We've been drifting for hours from that location." Niall looked around the raft as the light improved. It was awash with about six inches of water, with strands of seaweed floating on top. He threw it out and began bailing with his cupped hands. There was no sense sitting in water. The weather suits were supposedly waterproof, but some seawater had leaked beneath his collar, and he was chilled.

"Always the optimist," Brie muttered sarcastically. "You haven't changed much." She got on her hands and knees and began to bail with him. There was no room to turn or they would bump into one another. Brie wanted to move away from Niall, but it was impossible.

Stinging from her muttered rebuke, he continued bailing. "Neither have you." *Liar.* Brie looked thinner. And there was a sadness in her eyes. Could he blame her? She was probably still grieving over the loss of their baby. He knew he was. Trying to avoid another argument, he changed tactics.

"You got someone in your life who needs to be contacted?" He hoped not. It was a purely selfish thing to hope, he knew. Niall couldn't stand the thought that Brie might fall in love with someone other than him. Not that he'd been perfect; far from it. But they'd been so close, so wonderfully in love, and had suited one another so well. Holding his breath, he stopped cupping the water to see what effect his question had on her.

Brie froze momentarily. The water she'd scooped up in her palms dribbled back into the raft. The question, so very personal, and so unlike Niall, caught her off guard. Twisting her head in his direction, she raked him with a disgruntled glare. "No. Not that it's any of your business. Do you?" Her tone was scathing. Argumentative.

Shaking his head, he muttered, "No…no one."

"Your mother will be notified by the Coast Guard."

"She died a year ago…." Niall's voice faltered. The soft look that replaced Brie's anger felled him. Her lips parted in shock at the news. In his heart, Niall knew he should have contacted Brie and told her about his adopted mother's death, but he'd still been so angry at her that he hadn't. He saw pain reflected in

Brie's features in that moment. How easily she absorbed his anguish. She always had been sensitive and empathetic toward others. That was one of the many qualities Niall had come to love fiercely about her—Brie's care for others.

"Oh, I'm so sorry, Niall…. I—didn't know." She sat back on her heels, a confused look on her face. "Why didn't you tell me? I wish I'd known…."

Releasing a breath of air, Niall shook his head. He rested his hands on his thighs, the humid breeze caressing him. "Because I was still pissed off as hell at you."

"I was close to your adoptive mother." Brie sat there, feeling once again gutted by his coldness.

"I know…and I'm sorry. Looking back on it now," he muttered, "I should have told you. It would have been the right thing to do." He continued to scoop water because he couldn't stand the anguish in her blue eyes.

"Damn you, Niall." The words came out soft. Broken. Brie sat there, lulled by the slight waves that rocked the raft as gently as a mother would rock her baby. "I just didn't want to believe you were so heartless and immature. I tried to tell myself when I was in that hospital, alone, and in danger of losing our baby, that you'd come to be with me…hold me…help me…."

His mouth contorting, Niall felt every word like drops of fire scorching his naked flesh. Holding her accusing gaze, he snarled, "I'm many things, Brie.

Immature at times? Yeah, no question. But I'm not heartless. I never have been. I was at the hangar when it happened. The petty officer who took the call from the hospital got sidetracked by an incoming SAR, and she forgot to give me the message. It was two hours later before she recalled it and gave it to me. That wasn't my fault.'' His nostrils quivered.

''I often wonder whether, if you had known, you would have come.'' There, it was out, once and for all. The worst problem in their marriage had been their lack of ability to talk to one another. Niall would stalk off anytime her questions got to be too personal, too intimate and searching. He didn't know how to handle intimacy with a woman. How could he? His mother had never been home to teach him that interaction, and he had really no father around to impress him with it, either. Consequently, Brie had known that there was a lot of work to do in this area of their marriage.

Hands balling into fists on his long, powerful thighs, Niall stared at her, stunned by the brazen question. ''Of course I would have! And I did, the instant I got the message. The petty officer found me and told me. She was in tears over the mistake. I told you that, once I got to the hospital, but you were in no mood to hear it. All you could do was cry and accuse me of running away and not being there for you—as usual.''

Brie searched the quiet ocean in desperation. The gentle lapping sounds soothed some of her anger, as well as the soaring pain in her chest as she turned and held his glare. Niall's cheeks were a ruddy color, indicating he was angry. "You were *never* there for me, Niall, when I needed you. And that's the truth. You were a latchkey child. You grew up alone. You never learned how to be a real partner in our marriage."

"I tried," he growled. "Put yourself in my place. Imagine never being wanted by your parents. How would *you* feel?"

"Your adoptive mother loved you, Niall! With all her heart and soul, bless her. She was a single parent, trying her best to make ends meet. You know women get paid a helluva lot less than men. She was working two jobs, scrambling to feed you, clothe you and then pay for your college education. Irene loved you the best she could under the circumstances, so don't throw that old saw at me that you weren't ever loved. That's crap."

Brie sat there, breathing hard. Oh, why was she doing this? Why couldn't she be civil to Niall, as she'd been in their marriage? They'd never come to blows like this. No, it had been a silent union headed for disaster. Neither one had had the courage to speak out. In a way, Brie was glad that she'd had two years without Niall around. She'd grown, become more confident and more outspoken about her needs and setting strong, healthy boundaries for herself. Judging from the stunned look on his face, her changes weren't welcomed by him. Brie didn't care. It was time to come clean, once and for all. Maybe by getting all this anger and poison out of her system, she could finally get on with her life. Maybe.

"And I suppose you're Ms. Perfect? A full set of parents. A mother who spoiled you rotten because you were an only child? A father who loved you even though he wanted you to be a son, not a daughter?" Niall instantly regretted his angry words. Shadows flickered across her narrowing blue eyes. And then he saw anger explode within them.

"I might be Ms. Perfect in your eyes," Brie whispered, "but you're Mr. Abandonment. You say everyone keeps running out on you. I know your father left as soon as he heard your birth mother was pregnant with you, but he was an alcoholic and had serious responsibility problems. From where I'm sitting, you're probably lucky he didn't interfere that much in your life. Growing up with an alcoholic parent is about as dysfunctional as it gets. You don't even know how to count your blessings, Niall. You can't love your adoptive mother for what she's done right for you. You couldn't love me because you were afraid of getting intimate and personal with another human being. You were too scared and you ran. You ran just like your father runs every time things get dicey."

Sucking in a ragged breath of air, he held her challenging glare. "Two years has made you real vocal, hasn't it?"

"Our marriage was doomed from the start, Niall," Brie said, tiredness replacing her earlier emotional outburst. "You never trusted me enough to open up to me. You could never talk to me about day to day things, not to mention anything intimate. You held up

that wall between us real well. You were consistent—
I'll give you that." Her voice dropped. "And when I
miscarried...well, you couldn't handle that, either."

"How could I?" His voice rose. "I got to the hospital and it was all over. You were in a room by yourself, crying." He opened his hands, his voice cracking.
"What could I do? How could I fix it? Fix you? Fix
the situation?"

"Dammit, Niall, I didn't need you to fix anything!"
Fighting back sudden, unwanted tears, Brie held his
glare. She saw the anguish in his eyes and heard the
pain in his tone. "All I wanted...needed...was to be
held. That was all. I was hurting so much. And yes, I
was crying...crying for the loss of our baby. We had
so many hopes and dreams for him. I can remember
the nights we'd lay awake talking about if he'd like
baseball, or hockey...or what school he'd go to for
college...."

Shutting his eyes, Niall felt a sharp stab of grief at
the loss of his son. The pain was so real that he lifted
his hand and pressed it hard against his chest. It hurt
to breathe. It hurt to be alive in this raw moment.
Hanging his head, body bowed forward, he couldn't
say anything. All he could do was grapple with the
old, unresolved grief over his son's death.

Sniffing, Brie angrily wiped her eyes and looked out
at the endless ocean. "You just stood there, helpless,
by the bedside. I had wrapped my arms around myself.
I was in so much pain, physically and emotionally,
that I couldn't speak. And all you could do was stand

there, staring down at me like I was some bug under a microscope. You couldn't even step forward, slide your arms around me and hold me.'' Her voice cracked. ''All I needed from you, Niall, was to be *held*. Was that too much to ask? Don't bother answering. Obviously, it was.''

Lifting his head, he stared at Brie. Tears were rolling down her taut, pale cheeks. She was shivering, her teeth chattering again. She was holding herself just as she had in the hospital bed, her arms wrapped around herself. The devastation in her eyes tore at him as nothing else ever had.

''I wanted to hold you, Brie. But I stood there not knowing how to fix the tragedy, for you...or me. I couldn't believe our son was gone. I mean...it was the sixth month of your pregnancy. And everything was fine. Fine! We'd just seen your doctor, seen the ultrasound that showed us you were carrying our...'' Tears jammed into his eyes. ''Damn...this is so hard to talk about, Brie.''

''Maybe because we never did in the first place,'' she answered bitterly. How cold she was! Brie's teeth kept chattering and there was nothing she could do to stop them. The look on Niall's face stunned her. He was remaining open and accessible to her. The old Niall would have run. Brie reminded herself that he had nowhere to run now—not in the middle of an ocean. No, he was stuck here with her whether he liked it or not.

"You're right," Niall admitted hoarsely, "we never talked after...after it happened."

"After I lost the baby."

"Yes...that..."

"See? Even now you can't touch the subject, Niall. You walk around it. Why can't you say the word *baby* or *my son* or, God forbid, use the name we'd chosen for him—Killian?"

Frozen with anguish, Niall tried to speak. The words came out broken, as if torn directly from his heart. Lifting his head, he stared at Brie. "Because...because it hurts too much, that's why. If I...if I do, I'll cry." His mouth worked as he tried to suppress the barrage of emotions that threatened to overwhelm him. "I've never cried so much in my life as that day. I—I didn't know what sobs were. I didn't know what those gut-wrenching sounds were all about until they came tearing out of me... After I left you I went out in the exit stairwell and sat down. I was reeling. I was crying for the loss...for you, for me...."

In shock, Brie stared at him. Wincing, she could only sit there and hold his wavering gray gaze shot with anguish and grief. "Y-you...cried?" She'd never seen it. "I never saw you cry. Not once after it happened."

"I figured my crying in front of you would be just one more brick on your load, Brie," he said, all the anger going out of him. "You were lying there, devastated. How badly I wanted to reach out to you, run my fingers over your hair and tell you it was going to be all right. But I knew it wasn't. It never would be, from that moment on. I knew how I was feeling about the loss of our…baby…and I couldn't even begin to imagine how you felt. I was shell-shocked, so numb. I kept trying to figure out how to fix things…and I couldn't…."

"Oh, hell," Brie cried softly, and she pressed her hands to her face and leaned forward in a ball of agony.

Niall sat there, dumbfounded. He heard Brie's sobs. Saw her shoulders shaking uncontrollably. What should he do? What *could* he do? There was nothing he could do to fix this, either. The hurtful words they'd thrown at one another like flaming spears had landed directly in their hearts. There was no dodging the serrating truth. His heart told him to reach out, slide his arm around her and hold her. Just hold her. His head said no, that she wouldn't want that from him now— after all this time. Would she?

Chapter 4

Brie couldn't stem the tears. During all these years that had passed since the death of their son, she had thought Niall had never shed one tear. Now, as her own hot tears leaked through her fingers, she realized he wasn't as cold-hearted as she'd imagined him to be. Consumed with new grief, she ached on a level that had never been touched before. He had cared. He had loved their child as much as she had. Why were men so damned uncommunicative? Why hadn't Niall shared his grief with her? Why?

Sniffing, she rubbed her eyes and blinked back the rest of her tears. Around them, the ocean was almost glassy smooth. Brie knew they had to be drifting toward the center of the hurricane's eye for that to occur.

Above, a dulcet blue sky shone in stark contrast to the bank of white-and-gray clouds on the horizon.

As she lifted her lashes, which were beaded with the last of her tears, she saw Niall sitting with his head hung, his hands clasped in a death grip between his thighs. The suffering in his face tore at her. Swallowing hard, Brie asked in a choked tone, "Why didn't you tell me this at the time? Why couldn't you come clean with your feelings? I thought all these years you didn't care what happened."

Feeling wretched, he winced at the rawness in her husky tone. Unable to look at Brie, who had a helluva lot more courage in the emotional department than he ever had, he stared down hard at his clasped hands.

"I...don't know, Brie. When I got to the hospital and saw how devastated you were..." He shook his head mutely.

"I felt so guilty," Brie confided hollowly. "You stood looking at me like it was my fault." Shrugging painfully, she whispered, "Maybe it was. I don't know. I've asked myself that question so many times since then. Was it the stress of my SAR duty? Before the miscarriage, I'd had a week of search and rescues the likes I've never seen before or since." She gave him a sad look. "Maybe it was stress induced?"

"Don't take on that kind of guilt, Brie," he growled. "I did a lot of research after that, and miscarriages usually happen because the baby is malformed. The body knows it. Your body sensed there was something wrong, so it aborted the baby naturally.

That's all there is to this. You didn't do anything 'wrong.'''

Staring at him as the raft bobbed gently from side to side, Brie felt some of her grief assuaged. "You did research?"

"Yeah." Niall sighed. He gave her a quick glance. Her hair was slightly curled from the high humidity, and it softened the angularity of her cheekbones. It was her eyes that Niall found mesmerizing. Even though they were red from crying, they were that incredible turquoise-blue, the pupils huge and black. Brie's eyes were literally a window through which he saw what she was feeling. And right now he didn't quite believe his own eyes. Maybe he was making it up. Her gaze was warm, burning with a sunny, golden hope. Opening his hands, he added huskily, "I was so shocked by what had happened. You know me, Brie— when things are emotionally traumatic, I go into this clipped, cold, hard mental construct so I can think clearly and get things done in an orderly fashion. You were in no shape to think about a funeral. Someone had to think through the hurt, the loss...."

Clearing her throat, she said, "Yes, you did do that before you left..."

"I was there with you at the funeral, too," he reminded her, his tone filled with hurt. "I didn't just run off and leave you after the miscarriage, Brie. I was there for you the best I could be at the time." Opening his hands in a helpless gesture, he said, "I was there for a week—to be with you, to handle the paperwork and legal stuff—before I volunteered for that black ops.''

She sat back and rolled her eyes. ''And from my perspective, you seemed so cold, inaccessible, like a robot on automatic. I wanted to talk to you. I *need* to talk when something bad happens, Niall. When I do, it's like opening an abscess. It cleans me out, allows me to heal.''

''I was so overwhelmed emotionally, I couldn't hear you. Not then,'' he admitted slowly. Niall shifted around so that his back was resting against the rim of the raft, his feet near her right hip. Watching as she wiped her face again, he felt an ache filling him. How badly he wanted Brie. How badly he wanted to simply hold her against him and have her hold him in return. The last two years had made him feel like he was the only human left alive in a desert that had no end. He had no desire to strike up a relationship with another woman. It was as if he were a monk gone into a monastery. Maybe he was still grieving for the loss of Brie, the loss of their marriage, which had been so good before the loss of their baby son.

''We need to start drinking some of our water to stay hydrated,'' Niall told her. He took his bottle from the net closure on the right side of his vest, opened it and took a swig. Wiping his mouth, he capped it. Looking around the raft, he saw there were still some puddles in the bottom.

''You're right....'' Brie took a drink from her own bottle, then twisted the cap back in place and settled it into the net casing on her vest. Inwardly, she felt less angry, less uncomfortable with Niall. They were beginning to talk about things that had never been broached, but should have been a long time ago.

"If we don't get rescued by the time we drift through this eye, we're gonna have to try and collect rainwater from the raft bottom."

"When the waves get high, they're going to splash into the raft and dilute any rainwater with salt, so it won't be drinkable," Brie noted unhappily.

Looking around at the quiet, soothing sea, now a deep marine blue, Niall said, "You're right. But we'll get the rain first before we start hitting high waves. We'll refill our bottles, and keep drinking from the bottom of this thing until that time."

Moving her stiff, cramped legs slowly, Brie murmured, "I'm cold. I can feel the warmth of the breeze, but I'm still freezing." She wrapped her arms around herself and began to rub her body energetically to produce more heat.

"You probably took a lot of water into the neck of your weather suit when we egressed," Niall said worriedly. He saw Brie trying to stop her teeth from chattering.

"How about you? Did you take in a lot of sea-water?"

Shaking his head, he said, "No, I didn't. I'm a little damp in the shoulder and chest, but basically, I'm dry."

"Good," Brie said, relieved. "I'm soaked head to toe."

That wasn't good, but Niall said nothing. Trying to shelve his worry, he said, "You want some help warming up? A long time ago, I was pretty good at massaging you."

Her mouth softened and she held his gaze. His gray eyes were large now, the pupils black and filled with warmth—toward her. Niall was offering to help her. With his touch… Inwardly, Brie groaned. She loved his touch; it was strong and yet incredibly gentle. Always, Brie had looked forward to Niall holding her. Often, after twenty-four hours of SAR duty, she'd come home to their apartment near the Coast Guard base where they were assigned in Port Angeles, Washington, and he would fill a tub full of hot water for her.

After she'd had a long, delicious soak to ease muscles tight from the stressful duty, he'd bring in a soft, thick towel and dry her. The best part for her was when he'd pick her up, carry her to their bed and lay her down, then slather her back and shoulders with fragrant, sensual almond oil. Oh, how Brie looked forward to those massages Niall gave her. Her stress would dissolve beneath the magic of his coaxing, knowing fingers. He knew how to chase away the tautness in her shoulders, tease away the tightness along her spine, and in no time, Brie would fall into a deep, exhausted sleep. Niall would then cover her and allow her to float in that healing darkness.

Mouth dry now, Brie said, "You sure you want to?" She saw his eyes glimmer and instantly recognized that look for what it was: desire—for her. How was that possible? Their marriage had exploded on them. The loss of their baby had torn them apart and they'd split up like two feathers at the mercy of the winds.

Brie longed for Niall's knowing touch more than she dared let herself acknowledge. When she saw his full mouth curve at the corners, a wild, spontaneous heat plunged from her heart to the center of her body. She recognized it for what it was, too, and it stunned her. The coals that glowed within her were those of yearning for Niall—all of him.

"Sure I want to do it," he told her. "You're my copilot. I don't want anything to happen to you that I can help prevent. You're going hypothermic, Brie, and maybe I can help you stop losing body heat."

Her heart plummeted. Oh. That was it. Niall was being a good pilot in command. She was his copilot, and therefore responsible for her. Trying to wrestle with her sudden disappointment, she muttered, "Sure…I can use all the help I can get. We don't know when or if we'll be picked up." And that worried her a lot. The hurricane was gathering force. Before they'd left, there were reports that it could be a level five, the most powerful and devastating type. A storm of that size would make a rescue difficult, maybe even impossible. They could potentially drift for days, maybe a week or more. Or worse, they could be deluged by a monster wave and drowned at sea. No, their lives were not guaranteed, Brie knew.

Moving slowly to his knees, Niall gave her a slight grin. "Don't look so worried, Brie. I'm not going to bite you." He wrapped his hands around her right arm, near the shoulder, and began to gently knead and massage her muscles. Hearing her groan with pleasure, he watched as she leaned back, her head pillowed against the side of the raft, her lashes closed.

"That feels so good..." she murmured gratefully. Brie had no idea how tense she was until Niall applied gentle but firm pressure to her arms, hands and cold, damp fingers.

Concerned, Niall saw that her fingertips were almost bluish in color. That meant she had hypothermia. Quelling his worry, he carefully stroked her long, slender fingers. Just touching Brie was such a pleasure. Looking up, he studied her face—her closed eyes, her lips parted with a soft, beckoning smile. The urge to reach out, to stroke her pale cheek, was nearly his undoing. Frowning, he ordered himself to stick to what was necessary. He'd lied moments before when he'd told her he'd only offered to help because she was his copilot. If Brie really knew how he felt, she'd have rebuffed him for sure.

It was noon by Niall's watch. Worriedly, he watched as Brie continued to sleep. Since he'd massaged her arms and legs, she'd fallen into a deep, healing slumber, rocked by the gentle movements of the raft. Her lips, still possessing that pomegranate-red color even without lipstick, were slightly parted and still calling to him, begging him to caress and then crush them beneath his hungry, exploring mouth. But Niall would never awaken her, no matter how strong his desire. He realized Brie needed this sleep because of the trauma they'd survived last night in that hellish crash.

Rubbing the tense muscles at the back of his neck, he felt the gnawing hunger in his stomach. He was hungry in more ways than one. Right now, he was starving emotionally for Brie, the conciliation of souls that had begun between them. In a million years, Niall would never have thought their coming together again would have produced this...whatever it was. He was careful not to label what was occurring. But with that special warmth growing between them once more, it was almost like old times—before they had lost the baby. He had seen that look she gave him when he'd touched her arm earlier. Yes, there was gratitude in her eyes, but something else lingered there as well— something heated that Niall did not want to name.

Oh, it was a special hell, he admitted as he opened up a side pocket on his flight suit and pulled out a protein bar. Touching Brie earlier was like a dream come true after the nightmare of the past two years. She was just as rounded and soft as he remembered. Maybe more so, now. As he sat there, quietly peeling the wrapper from the bar, he admitted to himself that he'd savored every stroke, every touch of her flesh.

Brie hadn't stiffened or pulled away when he'd touched her. Just the opposite. Niall had seen such relief in her face, such joy deep in her turquoise eyes, that it had made his heart pound with happiness.

As he sat there munching on the bar, and enjoying every morsel of the grains that would feed his growling stomach, Niall had the undiluted pleasure of watching the woman he'd once loved with all his heart and soul, sleep the sleep of angels. In slumber, Brie looked defenseless. She seemed so at peace. The realization that they had both been grieving, suffering terribly after their loss, struck him deeply. Why hadn't he cried in front of Brie? Why hadn't he held her as *she* cried in that hospital bed? What the hell had he been thinking?

Scowling, Niall finished off the tasty protein bar and tucked the wrapper back into the long, large pocket on his left thigh. God knew, he'd wanted to go to Brie and hold her. To this day, he could hear the awful, tearing sounds coming from her contorted lips that day in the hospital. And he'd stood there like an idiot, frozen, feeling utterly helpless with the need to fix something that was unfixable.

With a sigh, Niall snuggled down into the raft, his body nearly touching Brie's. He had to sleep. There was no telling how long conditions would remain calm. The eye of a hurricane was usually around fifty miles in diameter. In the distance, black, thunderous-looking cumulus clouds gathered, warning him they'd probably hit the wall of the storm tonight. And then they'd be back in the same hell they'd known last night. This time, they really might drown. One of those waves might catch and flip them. So many things could happen—all of them potentially bad.

Feeling the urgency of wanting to survive, Niall quietly stretched out in the bottom of the raft, using the inflated portion as a pillow for his head. The gentle rocking motion soon spiraled him into sleep.

"We need to eat," Niall told Brie shortly after she had awakened. Dusk was upon them. That threatening wall of cloud was closer. Though Niall had tried to keep thoughts of the burgeoning danger at bay, he no longer could. Within the next four hours, they would once again be at the whim and mercy of the hurricane's strength and rage.

Brie's eyes were drowsy looking, and he had the urge to reach out, cup her cheek, and kiss that soft mouth of hers. Niall knew he couldn't do any of those things, so he settled for watching her as she pushed her fingers through her red hair and tried to tame it into place.

"I feel so much better," Brie told him. Looking up, she drowned in Niall's dark, stormy-looking gray eyes. He was watching her with an intentness that sent her heart skittering with need. Brie realized the raw hunger in his eyes was for her. Even after all this time and tragedy, he wanted her. That made her heart sing with a special joy. Yet as Brie looked up and studied the approaching wall of dark, massive-looking clouds her fear returned—fear of being at the mercy of the storm once more.

"Better tank up on protein," Niall told her in warning, hooking a thumb toward the darkening sky. "We're going back into hell shortly, and we're going to need our strength to survive it."

Brie nodded. Her stomach felt tight. She knew she must be hungry, but she couldn't feel it. Maybe because Niall was here. Just his presence made her feel safe. That was silly, of course, Brie admitted as she pulled out two protein bars from her vest. Niall couldn't do anything to protect her from the storm that was stalking them.

Fear made the bars tasteless to Brie. She saw the worry banked in Niall's eyes as he looked at the sky. The water was becoming choppy now, the waves two to three feet in height. Finishing off the food, Brie took a long drink of water. Above them, thin filaments of clouds were drifting across the hole of blue, like pale shrouds. Darkness was closing in on them again.

"You slept, too, didn't you?" she asked, tucking the bar wrappers into her vest.

"Yeah. I got about six hours. You've slept about ten. That's good." Scanning her from head to toe, Niall said, "Your teeth aren't chattering, either. Are you warmer?"

She smiled a little. "Yes, thanks to you." Following her heart, Brie reached out and slid her hand into his, which lay along his long, powerful thigh. "I've always loved your touch, Niall. You make me feel safe. Like nothing in the world could ever harm me again." Seeing surprise flare in his eyes, and then hunger, Brie squeezed his large-knuckled fingers. When they curved around hers in return, her heart leaped. "Thanks..." she whispered shakily.

Though he never wanted to let her go, Niall finally released her hand. The unexpected intimacy Brie had shown him sent his heart reeling with giddy hope. Yet his head warned him that she'd abandoned him once before. She'd demanded the divorce shortly after he'd returned from the black ops. Why? Swallowing hard, a frown on his face, Niall studied the approaching storm, then he turned back to Brie.

"You know our chances, don't you?" he said in a low, strained tone. "We could die out here tonight. We'll be strapped to one another with the life line, of course, and I'll hook the raft to my vest in case we get overturned by a wave. But that doesn't mean we'll survive. The dingy could fall on top of us, and we'd get dragged under and drown."

Wincing, Brie tucked her lower lip between her teeth. She clasped her hands in her lap. "Yes, I know that."

"This hurricane's upped the ante," he said, his brows dipping. "It's deepened—probably reaching a five by now. If that's so, no Coast Guard C-130 is going to risk flying through it to try and pick up our radio signals."

"I know...."

"That means our only hope—our only chance of

surviving—is hanging on and hoping like hell we
don't get overturned.'' After glaring at the clouds, he
glanced back at Brie. ''And judging from how dog
ugly this wall is coming up, I don't know that we will
survive it, Brie.''

''I agree.''

Niall stared at her in the dusky light. He saw the
terror deep in her eyes, but he also saw her stubborn-
ness and desire to survive, too. ''I'm scared,'' he
confessed.

''So am I, Niall.''

''More scared than I've ever been, if you want the
truth.'' He opened his hands in a frustrated gesture.
''And there isn't one damn thing more I can do to fix
this situation, either. I feel almost as helpless as I did
when we lost our baby, Brie. There was nothing I
could do then, either.''

Her heart contracted with sadness. They could die.
In fact, they probably would. That knowledge drove
Brie to speak her mind. ''Right now, Niall, I'd rather
be with you in this situation than with anyone else.''
She saw hope burn momentarily in his eyes, saw his
mouth soften as he stared at her in surprise. Brie could
hear the roar of the approaching wall now, could feel
the raft continue to rock and bounce. The waves were
more choppy, with froth on them—a warning of what
they'd face in a couple of hours.

''You're sure about that?'' His voice was deep.
Filled with question. With hope.

Nodding, Brie whispered, ''Very sure. I want you

holding me when we go through that wall. I want to be holding you. If I have to die, Niall, I want it to be in your arms. I'm scared. More scared than I've ever been in my whole life. I—I have an awful feeling we aren't going to make it. I don't want to die...." Brie choked up, pressing her hand against her throat as she stared at him.

Reaching out, Niall took her other hand and simply held it. Her fingers were cold again. "I feel the same, Brie. About everything you've said. I don't think we're going to survive this. The odds are stacked against us. This hurricane is too powerful..." Turning her hand over gently, he lifted it and pressed a soft kiss to her palm. He heard Brie's intake of breath. Lifting his lips from her cool flesh, he gazed deeply into her wide blue eyes.

"We're going to go through hell again in a few hours, sweetheart. I feel like we've been given a second chance to say all the things that we never said when we divorced—the good, the bad of it. I need to say a lot to you, Brie, because if I don't survive this and you do, then I want you to know the truth...."

Choking back a sob, Brie tightened her fingers around his hand. "Yes, let's use this time wisely. Let's not waste a precious minute of it, Niall. I've got a lot to say, too. I've been so afraid, too. At the hospital and after the funeral, you were so detached from what had happened, so far away from me, and I was hurting so much at the time that I wasn't thinking clearly. I needed you, darling. I needed you so much." Brie closed her eyes and gripped his hand hard. "What I'd have given if you had just taken me in your arms and held me. That's what I needed, Niall—just to be held. Held and told it was okay, that it wasn't my fault I'd lost our baby...."

Sadness avalanched through him. Holding her hand gently between his, Niall stroked the back of it. "And you looked so brave and self-assured at that time. I thought you were blaming me for the miscarriage. I didn't think you wanted me around. I hadn't been there for the loss...and I thought you were pissed off about that. You acted like you didn't need anyone, Brie. I guess..." his mouth flattened "...I guess I really misread all your signals, didn't I?"

"Yes," she breathed softly, the pain scalding her heart, "you did. How easy it would have been if you'd just opened up enough to trust me and talk to me about all this, Niall." Brie shook her head. "I've tried to figure out why you're so closed, why you won't communicate. It goes back to you being a latchkey kid, I'm sure. You had no one to go to and ask for help. From the time you were eight years old, you'd come home from school and fix dinner for your mother, do your homework, and be the responsible one, the man of the house. You didn't have anyone to talk with, to tell if you were scared, worried, anxious or happy. I know your mother didn't get home until around 9:00 p.m. on weeknights. And she was tired. That didn't leave much time for her to talk with you or vice versa."

"Yeah, my mother was exhausted when she came home," he admitted quietly. Smoothing his thumb across Brie's cool flesh, Niall added, "I felt bad for her. It was all she could do to sit down at ten o'clock and go over my homework with me. I could see how tired she was. It made me feel bad. I didn't want her to have to work so damned hard. I was angry at my father, who rarely came over. I never saw my stepfather, either. He left her and moved to another state. So I became a clam. I did what I could, but talking wasn't a big thing in my family."

"And I'm just the opposite of you," Brie said quietly as she looked up and studied the approaching wall of the storm. It looked ever more menacing the closer they got. The urgency to talk before they drifted into it made Brie come clean in a way she had never before. This was going to be the confession of her life to Niall. She realized she had never stopped loving him. And now their lives, more than likely, would be taken on this approaching night. A bittersweet feeling filled her. It was now or never. Niall needed to know how she felt about him, no matter what the consequences to herself or her misplaced pride.

Chapter 5

Niall shifted so he sat in the center of the small raft. He hooked his lifeline to Brie's bright red-orange vest. Automatically, as the wind started to sweep chaotically around them, the froth lifting from the peaks of greenish-gray waves, he checked their radio beacons. Both were working, but he held out no hope that a C-130 was flying through that storm to try and track them down. A hurricane could tear a large plane apart. More than one hurricane-hunter aircraft had disintegrated in just such circumstances. The Coast Guard had patterns of search for each rescue mission. Niall knew that to fly this one would be hellish, the chance of failure high. It wasn't worth risking the lives on board to save their two necks. Such was the cold logic of the military. They had talked about the merc and if he was all right. Niall was sure Morgan was worried about all of them. No one had expected their bird to go down.

Brie came and sat next to him, her hip against his as they faced the looming wall of wind and rain, the lightning and thunder that were already beginning to rumble warningly. The first bluish-gray squall was approaching, a curtain of rain so heavy they could barely see through it.

Easing his arm around her, Niall smiled down at her. "Ready for our walk into hell together?"

She smiled bravely and tucked her arm around his waist. "We've already been to hell, Niall. This is nothing in comparison. I felt like I died the day our baby was lost." She searched his dark, hard face as he stared down at her. "I was afraid to see you again. Now my fears seem silly. But the night I learned we'd be flying this mission together, I felt scared. I wasn't sure how you'd react to me."

"I felt shaky, too," he admitted, trying his best to keep communicating with her. Niall was finding that opening up his feelings to Brie wasn't so hard, after all. But then, with hell bearing down on them, he had an added impetus to talk.

The wind slammed against them, strong and powerful. The raft spun drunkenly around. Froth filled the air momentarily, leaving white, foamy splotches all over their weather suits. The squall was approaching.

They'd be pummeled with a deluge of rain within the next few minutes.

"When I got assigned to this station a month ago, I didn't know you were here," Brie admitted, resting her cheek against his shoulder. How good it was to be held by him once again! She felt his strong arm squeeze her gently and continue to hold her close. Sighing, she slid her other arm around his torso and closed her eyes.

"And when you did," he asked, humor in his husky voice, "what did you do? Ask for a transfer?"

She laughed shortly, the sound strained. The wind began tearing at them, riffling her short hair. The first drops splattered across them. In a few minutes, they'd have to put their helmets on once again. "I thought about it. I know the higher-ups in the Coast Guard didn't realize what they'd done. It was no one's fault."

"But you stayed," Niall said, moving his mouth very near her ear. He inhaled Brie's scent. It was always so clean and feminine to him, like a mysterious flower fragrance so evocative it never failed to arouse him. Strands of her copper hair pressed against his lower lip. They were just as silken as he recalled.

"Yes..." His warm breath trailed over her ear and cheek. Brie absorbed the sensation like a starving animal. The intimacy Niall established with her was natural and good. Her heart soared with unexpected joy. They were riding toward their death, and he was holding her.

The rain began in earnest, along with the whipping,

pummeling wind. They put on their helmets. Niall drew Brie fully into his arms and snuggled closer. With their heads pressed together, they lay on the bottom of the raft, feeling the jerky up and down movements as they were sucked into the fearsome wall of the storm.

The wind rose. It howled and then ebbed away. And then it struck again, bringing horizontal chilling rain. Niall lifted his hand and placed it behind Brie's head. He wanted somehow to protect her from the icy, needlelike droplets deluging them. The raft was rising and falling more quickly, bobbing like a cork. Waves were now four to six feet in height, rough and bullying.

"Why did you stay?" Niall placed his lips near her ear. "You could have asked for a transfer. They'd have given it to you under the circumstances, Brie?" His heart pounded as he anticipated her answer. He felt her arms momentarily tighten around his torso. He knew she was scared. So was he.

Shutting her eyes, Brie felt the cold water begin to leak under the collar of her weather suit even though Niall was trying to protect her from the onslaught. Inwardly, she was shaking in fear. Fear of what would come to both of them: a wall of water and maybe their death warrant.

"I...I stayed, Niall, because I hoped...oh, God, I hoped that somehow I could find the courage to come to you and talk. Just talk." There, it was out. Finally. It felt as if a huge weight had just lifted off her quaking shoulders. The wind was howling like a banshee now, the rain so thick she couldn't see anything beyond the bobbing raft.

"When I heard you were at the station, I got scared, too, Brie," Niall confided. Moving his hand, he cupped the collar of her weather suit to try and prevent more water from running down the opening. He didn't want Brie chilled because she couldn't take much more hypothermia. This time, if she got wet and damp inside the suit, he might not be able to warm her up. Ever.

"And then," he admitted, giving a short laugh filled with derision, "as the days went by, and there was no word from you, I figured you were going to ignore me. At first, I felt okay…relieved about that. But then…" His mouth flattened and he bowed his head as the rain slammed into him. Water dripped down his face, off his nose and chin. "I wanted to see you, Brie. You have no idea of the hell I went through daily after finding out you were assigned here. Every morning I woke up thinking about you. My dreams at night…well, they were about the good times, the laughter, the joy we shared before our marriage soured. I'd wake up in the morning aching for you to be at my side. I wanted to roll over and find you sleeping on your left side, like you always did. I wanted to slide my arms around you and pull you near me…and love you. Show you how damn much I still loved you and needed you…."

Brie clung to Niall after hearing his low, emotional words. "Oh, Niall…"

"It's the truth, Brie. I swear to God it is. I was just trying to get up enough courage to go over to your bungalow in Princeville, knock on your door and ask if we could start over. If there was a chance for us again. But I was a coward. I blew it. And now..." He lifted his eyes and saw the squall moving in. Right behind it were black and grey bands of clouds moving quickly in a counterclockwise motion. The clouds resembled skeletal fingers—the hand of death? "Now it's too late.... Damn, I'm sorry, Brie. I ran from you...after losing our baby, because I didn't know what else to do. When that black ops mission from Perseus came up, I volunteered for it. Frankly, I was relieved to get the assignment." He squeezed her hard and pressed a kiss to her damp cheek. "I had to bury myself in something dangerous—something that would take my mind off you, off our loss...."

Choking, Brie looked up. Darkness was falling. She could barely see Niall's glistening, rain-soaked features. His eyes were burning with a fierce love as he looked down at her, however. The taut line of his mouth spoke of his suffering over the loss of her and their baby. Lifting her cold, wet hand, she slid her shaking fingers across his bearded cheek.

"Oh, Niall...I never stopped loving you, either, darling. Not ever. That's why I could never have a relationship with another man. Those two years I felt like a ghost wandering the land...alone and so terribly gutted with grief. I not only lost our baby, but I lost you, too. I wondered what I'd done to deserve all of this.

I thought I'd loved you with all my heart, my soul, but it wasn't enough...."

Catching her hand, he pressed a hot, hungry kiss against her palm. The raft bobbed violently and spun around as the first really turbulent waves struck them. The rain was lessening again, but still stinging and cold against his flesh. Wind shrieked, then ebbed, then howled at them again, as if warning of what was to come.

But at that instant, Niall's heart was centered on the woman in his arms. As he lifted his lips from her wet palm, he clasped her fingers gently. Turning, he gazed deeply into her wide, tear-filled eyes. Brie's lips were parted, pulled down in torment and guilt. He leaned down, his mouth near her cheek.

"Listen to me, Brie. No matter what happens now, you need to know that my leaving had nothing to do with you. It was me. I ran. No matter how I tried to avoid it, I guess I was like my father, after all. He ran when my mother became pregnant with me. He ran from responsibility. He couldn't stay in the heat of the kitchen, the crisis, and take it like a mature, responsible human being." His voice became hoarse. "And I pulled the same thing on you. Only I did it because we *lost* a baby. I had so many hopes pinned on that child, Brie. I wanted to be the father my dad had never been to me. I had all these dreams about how I'd be a great father to our son. I dreamed about it almost every night. I was so happy. But I never shared any of that with you, Brie. None of it, and I'm sorry I didn't. I've learned a huge lesson out of this, but it's too late.''

Niall closed his eyes and held her tighter as the raft began to heave and buck down. The waves were growing steadily worse. Froth slammed into them as the wind whipped it off the top of each crest. Already the bottom of the raft contained inches of water. Niall took in a ragged, painful breath. ''I realized too late that I should have come clean with you, Brie. I should have talked about my hopes, dreams and wishes for us, for our baby and his future. But I didn't. And after we lost him, through no fault of yours, I just fell apart. I was crazy with grief. I couldn't talk. I was afraid to say anything because I was so grief-stricken that I feared I'd burst into tears and start sobbing in front of you. I knew you didn't need your man crying like a wimp at that time.''

''Oh, Niall…no!'' Brie whispered brokenly. ''We could have cried together, darling. We could have held one another and cried over our mutual loss. That would have comforted me. It could have helped you, too.''

''You'd never seen me cry, Brie. Not ever. How could I do it then, at the worst time in our lives, just when you needed me the most?''

''You crazy fool,'' she sobbed, throwing her arms around his neck and holding him tightly, ''you got this all wrong! If you had cried, I wouldn't have thought you weak or a wimp. Just the opposite! A real man can let down and cry, Niall. He can *show* his emotions when he needs to. No woman in her right mind is going to say you're weak for doing that. Oh, I hate what this society has done to men and women! I hate that it has branded you with the idea that you're not allowed to feel. That you can't cry. That it's somehow not manly or brave to show your feelings.'' Sobbing in anger, Brie said, ''Niall, cry with me. Fight with me. Yell with me. Make up with me. Always show your feelings. Don't withhold them from me anymore. I can handle your emotions. What I can't handle is your silence. Your running away without telling me why.''

''I understand now, sweetheart. I do….'' But it was too late and Niall knew it. The raft was wobbling, riding up one wave, tippling for a moment, then sliding down into the next trough. The darkness was nearly complete. Lifting his head, he studied Brie's upturned face, branding the moment of it into his mind, heart and soul, because he feared it was going to be the last view he'd ever have of her. Her eyes were so wide and fraught with pain and love for him. He saw it all and reveled with joy over the unexpected gift that had come out of this tragedy. Stroking his hand awkwardly across her head, feeling her hair wet and thick beneath his shaking fingers, he tried to smile down at her.

''Whatever happens, darlin','' he told her, ''I love you. Just remember that, okay?'' He kept caressing her cheek. Kept smiling down at her because more than anything, Niall wanted Brie to know that she was and always had been the most important person in his life—ever.

Stunned by his huskily spoken words Brie drowned in his warm, stormy gray eyes. That cocky Irish smile of Niall's was her undoing. As his hand moved in trembling strokes across her head, as if to soothe and calm her, she managed a wobbly smile in return.

"I never stopped loving you, Niall." Her voice broke with unshed tears. "Not ever, darling…and when we drown out here tonight, I'll hold you until the last breath of air leaves my body. And when we find ourselves on the other side, we can reach out for one another. We can walk the Rainbow Bridge as one. We'll never be apart again…."

His heart aching with sadness, frustration and need, Niall absorbed every shaking word Brie spoke. How he'd loved her view of life, thanks to her Native American heritage. There was no hell in her belief system; only goodness and hope waited on the other side after one died. Easing his arms from around her, he framed her face, his mouth inches from hers.

With tears flooding his eyes, Niall whispered, "I've loved you with every cell of my being, Brie. I'll always love you, not matter what happens. You're mine, sweetheart. You always were and always will be, whether you knew it or not…." And he leaned down and pressed his mouth hotly against her parted lips.

Brie moaned as his mouth hungrily met hers. This was a kiss of greeting—and a kiss of farewell. It was a kiss to make up for those two painful years of separation. As his mouth rocked against hers, Brie tightened her arms around him and clung as tightly as she could. Her breasts pushed against his chest. Their hearts pounded together in a primal rhythm only lovers could feel and exult in.

Brie's lips were soft, inviting, the kiss haunting, breaking his heart, lifting his soul and plunging him into an abyss of regret over things that would never be. And yet, he reveled in the outrageous joy of finding her once again. The sweetness of her mouth, her punctuated breath against his cheek, the fervent welcome she gave him all lifted Niall's heart on sunlit wings.

As the storm raged around them, lifting the raft and slamming it down in ever deepening troughs, salty froth flew across them, like foam from a rabid dog's mouth. As Niall kissed her, he breathed his breath into her mouth and dragged hers into his body. Their lips were hungry, searching and needy. As he pressed his hand down her long, strong spine to capture her wide, flaring hips against him, the aching need to love her, to claim her once more, surged through Niall like a tidal wave. Truly loving her was impossible under the circumstances, and as he slowly, reluctantly released her soft, wet mouth and looked deeply into her half-closed eyes, which were burning with need for him, he was speechless. No words could express how he felt in this moment out of time. Only the anguish, joy and hope in Brie's eyes told him how she felt about him. He saw the regrets in her gaze. The hope for a future. And the realization that there was no future to hope for. What he saw most clearly, though, was her love for him. Brie loved him. She'd never stopped loving him. The horrible guilt and regrets of two years dissolved as he held her closely in his arms and absorbed her warm, loving gaze.

"If I had one wish," he told her huskily, his voice cracking, "it would be to take you in my arms, love you until you fainted with pleasure, and then know you carried our next child in your body."

Unable to talk, Brie smiled at him sadly. As night descended, Niall's shadowed face became almost invisible. The rain was beginning again. The roar of the wind was stronger, the movements of the raft more violent. "If I had one wish, darling," she whispered against his ear, her hands framing his wet face, "it would be to carry your child again. A child made from pure love. Our love…"

A sob wracked Niall. He didn't try to stop it this time. Whispering her name brokenly, he swept Brie into his arms and held her so tightly that he thought he might crack her ribs. Burying his helmeted head next to hers, his face pressed against that strong shoulder that had carried so many heavy burdens by herself, he cried. The sounds tearing out of him were feral, as if a wild animal had been released from deep within. Brie's womanly arms, warm and strong held him close. Held him with all her strength, caring and love.

There was no shame in crying, he discovered as he clung to her, the sobs coming from his dark, guilty soul over the loss of their baby, the loss of any future with Brie. The primitive animal sounds of his grief were torn from him as the hurricane raged unchecked around them.

The raft was filling with water. The tears streaming down his face mingled with the ocean's salt spray. And through it all, Brie held him, rocked him gently and eased his grief, his pain. And the awful two years of hell finally were given voice, and left him once and for all.

As his sobs lessened, Niall felt a sense of cleanness. He was amazed. There was a new strength, a new resolve, a new hope filling him now. His mind was so much mush, but the brilliant illumination of his heart, the inner glow of his untrammeled emotions, freed for the first time in his life, left him feeling stronger than ever before. As he sat there with Brie holding him, Niall began to understand, finally, that crying wasn't bad. In fact, he'd never felt better—lighter or happier. So this was what women had known all along that men had denied: that crying was an incredible freeing of feelings and pain. It was a natural purging and cleansing of what felt bad within him, and the release gave his heart and soul a new, brilliant life. It also gave Niall a fierce hope he'd never had before.

As he lifted his head, kissed her wet brow, he looked up. Was he seeing things? Light was shining through the storm.

"Brie? Do you see that?" he asked, pointing through the maelstrom. "Am I hallucinating?"

Brie twisted around, her gaze following where Niall was pointing. She saw a light flashing on and off. It came and went, because of the waves lifting them up and dropping them again.

"Oh, my God, Niall! That's a Coast Guard ship!"

Gasping, he stared into the night. When the raft slid down into a trough, the light disappeared. Would it be there when they were lifted upward again? His heart pounded with dread, with hope. He gripped Brie by the shoulders. Breath suspended, he felt her tense beside him. He couldn't be making this up. It *had* to be a Coast Guard cutter!

As the raft surged upward, Niall cried out, "It's them! It's an SAR vessel!" He quickly fumbled with his flashlight, turned it on and waved it frantically above their heads.

Brie sobbed. A cutter! The Coast Guard had sent a cutter into this horrible hurricane to hunt for them. The vessel probably had equipment on board to pick up the radio signals being beamed from their vests.

Sure enough, the light grew stronger. She pulled out her flashlight and began waving it, too. Joy surged through Brie. They were going to be rescued!

"Oh, Niall!" she cried. "We're saved!"

Laughing wildly, he gripped her shoulder as he waved the flashlight. "We are! Sweetheart, we're going to be fine. We're gonna live through this!" He looked at her in wonder. He could barely see Brie's expression in the dim illumination coming from their flashlights. But he could see that the hope was there. Her eyes were filled with joy.

Somehow, the universe had granted them a second chance. As he watched the light from the cutter growing stronger by the minute, he grasped the fact that rescue was coming. The crew had spotted them and had a solid fix on their position. It would be only a matter of time and they'd be safe. Safe!

More than anything, Niall wanted this rescue. When they got home, back to the station, he wanted time alone with Brie. Time to talk without the threat of dying. Time to try and mend the past and talk about a future that would include both of them.

As he knelt in the rubber dingy, one arm around Brie's shoulders, the other waving the flashlight to help the cutter hone in on their location, Niall felt trepidation, joy, anxiety and panic.

Was there a chance for them now? Or had the admissions they'd both made come under the duress of dying? Would Brie feel the same way tomorrow? Niall wasn't certain, but one thing he knew for sure now: he wasn't going to abandon her again. He wasn't going to run away this time. He was going to face Brie honestly, warts and all. She deserved that from him. No, he wasn't his father's son; he was going to prove that to Brie. This was one battle he wasn't running from. Niall was being given a second chance to prove he was a far better man than his father had ever struggled to be.

Chapter 6

"Are you ready to go home?" Niall asked as he came and stood next to Brie, once the doctor had finished examining her. She sat on a gurney, dressed in tan slacks and a colorful short-sleeved blouse. Like him, she'd dressed in civilian clothes she kept in her station locker. As she lifted her head, her blue eyes shimmering with quiet joy, he managed a slight, sheepish grin. His heart bounded with unparalleled happiness.

"Your home or mine?"

Niall waited as the doctor finished filling out her report form and left. The door closed quietly behind her. They were alone. *Finally.* Reaching up, he grazed Brie's pink cheek with his fingers. "Mine." *Where you belong. With me. Like it should have been all along.* Her lips parted softly at his feathery touch. The look he thought he'd never see again, was in her eyes. It was a look of love—for him.

Sliding off the gurney, Brie retrieved her black uniform purse and hung it over her left shoulder. Her heart was beating hard with excitement and anticipation. "I'm ready. Let's go home...."

The words sounded wonderful. As if in a dream, Niall nodded and opened the door for her. They were at the Coast Guard station medical dispensary. After spending two days at sea aboard the Coast Guard cutter that had rescued them, they'd finally made it to shore.

The welcome at the station had been nothing short of overwhelming. Morgan Trayhern had embraced them, tears in his eyes, he was so glad that they were safe. Best of all, his mercenary, Burke Ormand, had contacted him, and his cover was still intact and he was fine. After receiving a lot of handshakes, claps to the back, hugs and tears of relief that they were safe, Brie and Niall had been hustled off to the dispensary for the obligatory medical checkup that any pilots went through after a crash. When they were aboard the cutter, they'd filled out individual reports on the crash, and now administration was looking at their paperwork.

Moving out into the passageway of the highly polished white tile, Brie looked over at Niall as he walked

at her side. As officers of equal rank, they could have
a personal relationship. However, they were on a military base and no hand-holding or any show of affec-
tion was allowed. Brie itched to reach out and slide
her hand into Niall's, but she stopped herself.

Outside, the weather was clearing. Miraculously the
hurricane had suddenly veered away from Kauai, so
the rough ride on the ship had become smoother as
they approached the island. Niall was grateful, because
he'd been seasick from the moment they'd been
picked up out of that cold, black sea. The two days
aboard the cutter they'd spent sleeping, eating and getting themselves together emotionally once more.
There hadn't been a lot of time to speak intimately
with one another. Both had been put into the hospital
dispensary, where they had remained for the voyage
home. With medical technicians always hovering
around, or the doctor, Niall found it impossible to
speak privately with Brie. He had so much to say, so
much he wanted to tell her. Now, they would have a
chance.

Brie entered the small bungalow Niall had. It was
a cozy place filled with bamboo furniture, a red-yel-
low-and-olive-green Oriental rug on the floor, and
photos of bright hibiscus flowers hanging on the beige
walls. Her heart jumped with shock when she spotted
a small bamboo table near one wall that held a number
of photos in silver and gold frames. As Niall closed

the door to his home, she went over and looked at them.

To her surprise she saw that many were photos of their wedding ceremony. Her heart squeezed as she saw a color photo of herself standing in profile, her belly growing big with their baby. She was smiling toward Niall, who had taken that proud photo. Poignantly, Brie remembered that day. She'd been standing outside their home, the wind playing with her hair, which fell to her shoulders. Her eyes were burning with joy, her hands caressed her swelling belly, and a look of love filled her face—love for Niall.

Niall moved quietly to her side and slipped his hand gently across her shoulders as she stared down at the photos. "Good memories," he told her in a husky tone.

His touch was warming. Brie twisted to look up at him. His face was no longer tense with strain. She still saw remnants of the trauma in his features, the darkness beneath his eyes. They'd nearly died. But in a near-death experience, they'd found one another again, too. Her voice was low. "Yes…good memories. The best, Niall."

His fingers closed across her shoulder and he turned her to face him. Brie's hand went around his waist and she rested her head against his shoulder. "We can have them again, Brie," he murmured. "I know we can. We just have to work at it differently this time." Niall's heart squeezed with terror. Would she want to try and get back together again with him? He wasn't sure. Just because she'd said she loved him out there on that storm-tossed ocean didn't mean she wanted to marry him, or live with him, again. He gazed down at her soft profile. When she looked up at him, he saw tears swimming in her turquoise eyes. Her lashes were thick and framed her shimmering eyes. Brie was incredibly beautiful to him, from the freckles that ranged across her nose and cheeks, to her straight red hair, which made her eyes her most prominent feature. She looked like a beauty from an old Renaissance painting to him.

"I meant what I said out there in that raft, Niall."

"That you never stopped loving me?"

Swallowing, Brie nodded. "I tried to stop loving you after I asked for a divorce." Shaking her head, she reached out and touched the last photograph. "But I couldn't. You weren't a bad person. Just...mixed up and confused. I knew the score, and I knew why you were the way you were. I knew it going into our marriage, but I believed that with time, you'd change and grow, and we'd open up those channels between us."

Nodding sadly, Niall whispered, "I was pretty stupid, darling."

"No, just scared and unsure. You had to learn to trust me with yourself, Niall." Brie searched his saddened face. "And you have. Out there in that ocean, after the crash. That's where we learned to trust one another for the first time in our lives."

"Yes," he whispered. "I trust you now as never before. And I'm not going to be afraid to tell you what's on my mind or what's in my heart."

She smiled gently and eased her arms around his broad, capable shoulders. Their hips met and melted against one another. "Here's what's in my heart, sweetheart," she whispered.

Niall cocked his head. Her eyes glimmered with mischief and joy. "Tell me...and it's yours...." he murmured.

"I want you. I want to lie in your arms. Make love with you. Reacquaint myself with you in all ways." Brie slid her hand across his recently shaved face. "What's in *your* heart?"

Smiling unevenly, Niall whispered, "You. I want you so badly I can taste you. I want to love you until you faint with pleasure, Brie. I want to make you happy. I want to see that smile I used to see after we'd made love. I want to kiss your luscious, sweet mouth...."

"Can we bring the past to life again?"

"Yes," he answered, his voice deepening, "we can...."

The queen-size bed with the bamboo head- and footboard was covered with a cream-colored duvet decorated with emerald green bamboo stalks. The window was made of stained glass, the weak rays of sunlight filtering through it casting a rainbow of colors across the bed. There was a bamboo dresser and a bedstand with a pale green lamp on it. The floor was a gleaming teakwood, Brie noted, as she eased off her shoes.

Standing near Niall, she began to slowly undress him, one item of clothing at a time. He was wearing that mysterious smile that had haunted her dreams. The look in his eyes as he slowly unbuttoned her blouse, one button at a time, sent heat flowing from her heart to her lower body. Brie melted beneath his hooded gray gaze as he eased the blouse from her shoulders. She never wore a bra because of her small breasts, only a white silk camisole, which he divested her of.

Sliding his finger provocatively across her waist to the band of her slacks, Niall gently eased it open. The garment fell to the floor around her bare feet.

"You are so beautiful," he whispered, as his hands moved to her silken briefs.

Closing her eyes, Brie felt him run his large, water-roughened hands across her hips to divest her of the last of her lingerie. Unable to think coherently, she managed to loosen his jeans with her trembling fingers. Heart pounding, she closed her eyes, her hands gripping his waist. Niall's fingers moved tantalizingly up across her flared rib cage, then upward to cup and hold her breasts in his hands. Prickles of heat and longing exploded through her. Feeling dizzy, Brie rocked forward, wanting more of his touch. Wanting him.

"It's time," he whispered in a husky tone against her ear. Removing his jeans and briefs, he drew her to the bed and guided her down upon the soft, feathery duvet. As Niall eased next to her, naked, their hips and legs brushing together, he smiled. Brie's eyes were half-closed. He saw the sunlight in their depths, the longing, the need of him as she lay there facing him. Sliding his arm beneath her neck he brought her fully against him. When her breasts brushed tantalizingly against his chest, he groaned. The sensation was so fiercely hot that he felt himself harden instantly. As her trembling fingers slid from his arm to his neck and then on to trace the line of his cheek, he leaned down and captured her tempting, smiling mouth.

A moan of pleasure rippled through Brie as his mouth took hers, with a commanding strength that sent a message straight to her heart: she was his. All his. And he was claiming her; like a man claimed his woman. His breath was ragged and moist against her cheek as he continued his silken assault upon her lips. Hungrily, Brie responded in kind, unable to get enough of Niall, of his taste, his wonderful male fragrance or the rough texture of his skin as he rubbed seductively against her.

When he gripped her hip, pulling her hard against him, letting her know he was more than ready to take her, claim her, she cried out softly.

"Enter me," she whispered raggedly against his mouth. "Take me! I need you so badly, Niall…now…please! Now…" And she thrust her hips against him.

As she looked up into his glittering, silvery eyes—eyes narrowed like those of a predator—she moaned. This was the man she loved. The man she'd waited so long for, and thought she'd lost forever. Now he was hot, sleek and powerful as he moved above her to claim her. Never had Brie thought they'd be in one another's arms again. The moment had sweetness, hope and such a palpable beauty that her heart mushroomed with joy. Her breath hitched in anticipation as his knee moved her thighs even farther apart.

Just as the sunlight broke through the ragged clouds to strike the rainbow colors of the stained glass, Niall entered her aching, tense body. He flowed into her like all the colors of the rainbow. Like sunlight to her heart, she welcomed him, all of him, into herself. Arms closing around his shoulders, tight shoulders, she arched against him with a husky cry of pleasure.

Every movement, every thrust and equally joyful response flowed through Brie until she was breathless, riding on a wave of such pleasure that her world spun out of control. Absorbing his male odor, she reveled in the way their bodies fused and glided together. He fit her so perfectly, melded with her in such a glorious golden cloud of happiness, that all Brie could do was surrender to her wildly beating heart.

Niall was her life. She was a part of him, and he a

part of her. Two halves that made a whole. He made her feel complete, and strong, and beautiful. His breathing was ragged against her ear, his breath hot, his growl deep as he claimed her and made her his. The violent explosion of heat, light and love that occurred deep within her being tore the breath from her. She arched and climaxed, spinning off into a kaleidoscope of rainbow colors.

And when Niall stiffened, his hands gripping her shoulders, fingers digging in, she knew he was gifting her with his life, his love, in that wildly spinning moment torn out of time.

For the next few minutes, all Brie could do was feel the aftershocks riffling through her body, one after another. The pleasure was so intense, she truly did feel faint. All sounds ceased except Niall's breathing near her cheek, his wet kisses against her brow, nose and, finally, her smiling mouth. His hands ranged knowingly along her length, as if reacquainting himself with her in every possible, intimate way. She loved his exploration of her afterward, the gentle touch of his trembling fingers caressing her taut breasts, the way he suckled her and made her moan with want of him all over again.

Time had no meaning to Brie as she languished in Niall's arms, a prisoner of pleasure. How wonderful it was to kiss him in return, to see the joy in his stormy gray eyes, that feral look as he rose above her, that crooked smile of triumph in his handsome face. His dark hair was plastered against his brow, perspiration gleaming on his taut body in the aftermath. Brie watched, mesmerized, as light streamed through the stained glass window, sending color flowing across them.

"The colors of life," she told him, her voice husky, "are flowing across us again."

Niall lay against Brie, propped up on the one elbow, his arm beneath her head. "Yes…" he agreed, watching the gold, crimson and emerald colors move in graceful asymmetry across her hips, torso and breasts. How much he loved her. Looking down at her, he ached to love her again, to show her once more, how much she meant to him. Running his fingers across her damp red hair, he whispered, "You're my life, darlin'. I was a ghost walking the land without you. Now—" he lifted his head and looked at the brilliant, sunlit window "—you've given me back my life. Now I'm not walking in a land of black, white or gray. You complete me. You give my life color, meaning, a reason for being. A reason to wake up in the morning full of hope, of happiness…"

Tears drifted down the sides of Brie's face as she reached up and gently stroked his cheek. "You're no less to me, Niall." She saw his eyes flare with surprise. "It's so wonderful to hear how you feel… I love it. I love hearing how you feel about me…about us."

Capturing her hand against his cheek, he rasped,

"I'm sorry I never shared this part of me with you, Brie. I will now...if you'll give us a second chance?"

How could she say no? Brie smiled and nodded. "Yes, I want that second chance with you, Niall. I'm willing if you are...."

A sigh of relief flowed through him. Placing her hand against his heart, he said brokenly, "When you gave me back the wedding band and engagement ring, I kept them. I never threw them away or sold them. I've kept them in the same red velvet case they were in when I gave them to you the day I asked you to marry me."

Touched, Brie felt hot tears falling across her cheeks, blurring Niall's features. "Oh, Niall...I didn't know...."

Shrugging sheepishly, he wrapped his fingers around her hand. "When you left, I set up that table with those photos. In the drawer are the wedding bands."

"You never quit hoping, did you?" she choked out.

"I guess not. I didn't want our marriage to be over, Brie, but I didn't know what else to do, or how to get you back."

"Because you were in as much pain over the loss as I was." Brie shook her head and slowly sat up. "I was just as blinded and grieving as you were, Niall. I didn't realize all this about you."

"Listen," he whispered, pulling her back into his arms as he lay against the headboard, "we lost our baby. How else could you feel? You were wild with grief. With shock. I understood that later. But not at the time. I was too wrapped up in my past, the abandonment…and I ran just like my father did.'' Mouth turning down, Niall held her in his arms and pressed a kiss against her furrowed brow. "I promise you, Brie, that will *never* happen again. I've learned my lesson. I want this second chance with you. And it doesn't matter if you ever get pregnant again. I'll accept whatever the future has in store for us. As long as we're together…."

Sighing, Brie snuggled deeper into his warm, strong arms, her cheek resting against his darkly haired chest. She could hear his heart pounding. "I want babies, Niall. Even now, I hope that our making love has created one. If it has, I'll be overjoyed. And I'll be scared, too. I'll be afraid of losing this second one as I lost the first."

Hearing the carefully concealed anxiety in her voice, Niall placed his finger beneath Brie's chin and forced her to look up at him. "Listen to me, darlin'. We'll take this one day at a time. If you get pregnant, we won't jump the gun like we did last time. We'll be talking to one another this time, and that will help a helluva lot. In my heart, I don't feel you'll lose the next baby. Things happen for a reason. But we have grown and matured in the last two years, so that this time around it'll be different. Better." And he gave her a devastatingly charming smile.

Niall's dazzling male smile could always coax Brie out of her deepest worry or despondency. That was his priceless Irish legacy—that smile that made rainy days in her life dissolve in the sunlight.

Pressing a kiss to his shoulder, she lifted her head and smiled up at him. "I'm game if you are."

Nodding, Niall sighed. "That's a roger, my beautiful lady."

"I don't want to live with you, Niall."

His heart plunged and he gave her a look of shock. But when he saw her lips curve in a smile, her eyes widen with happiness, he realized what she meant.

"Think we ought to call the station chaplain and tell him what's in our minds and hearts?"

"Yes, and soon," Brie said archly. "And I think you'd better get those rings out, clean them up and get down on your bended knee and ask me to marry you."

Chuckling, Niall ruffled her hair. This was the Brie he loved so much. She was part child, part adult, and someone who loved him unequivocally. Best of all, she'd forgiven him. And now he could forgive himself and move on to a better, happier life with her. Oh, Niall didn't fool himself; he knew they'd have rough times again, unhappy times. But life had taught him many good lessons that he was going to use as positive tools now to make this second chance with Brie a success.

"You know what?" Niall said, his voice an intimate

growl as he cupped her cheek and looked at her, their noses touching. "I'm going to get them right now. And when I ask you this second time to be my life partner, it's going to be forever."

Brie smiled softly through her tears. "Yes…forever, darling. No matter what life throws at us, we'll be there for each other, to protect, support and love one another. I'm not afraid, Niall. Not now. Not with you standing at my side. I love you so much! I always have and I always will…forever…."

* * * * *

Available from Silhouette Intimate Moments:
PROTECTING HIS OWN
by Lindsay McKenna—
a brand-new book in her
MORGAN'S MERCENARIES:
ULTIMATE RESCUE series!

Ring in the season with this quartet of tales that represent the true spirit of giving...*love*.

"The Ice Dancers"
by *New York Times* bestselling author
Rebecca Brandewyne

"Season of Miracles"
by **Ginna Gray**

"Holiday Homecoming"
by **Joan Hohl**

"Santa's Special Miracle"
by **Ann Major**

Look for these titles wherever Silhouette books are sold!

THE
COLTONS

invite you to a thrilling holiday wedding in

A
Colton Family
Christmas

Meet the Oklahoma Coltons—a proud, passionate clan who will risk everything for love and honor. As the two Colton dynasties reunite this Christmas, new romances are sparked by a near-tragic event!

This 3-in-1 holiday collection includes:

"The Diplomat's Daughter" by Judy Christenberry

"Take No Prisoners" by Linda Turner

"Juliet of the Night" by Carolyn Zane

And be sure to watch for **SKY FULL OF PROMISE** by Teresa Southwick this November from Silhouette Romance (#1624), the next installment in the Colton family saga.